THE
WAITER

THE WAITER

AJAY CHOWDHURY

Harvill *Secker*

LONDON

3 5 7 9 10 8 6 4 2

Harvill Secker is part of the Penguin Random House group
of companies whose addresses can be found at
global.penguinrandomhouse.com

 Penguin
Random House
UK

First published by Harvill Secker in 2021

A CIP catalogue record for this book is available from the British Library

penguin.co.uk/vintage

ISBN 9781787301832 (trade paperback)
ISBN 9781787302921 (hardback)

Typeset in 10.75/15.75 pt Scala
by Integra Software Services Pvt. Ltd, Pondicherry

Printed and bound in Great Britain by Clays Ltd, Elcograf S.p.A.

The authorised representative in the EEA is Penguin Random House
Ireland, Morrison Chambers, 32 Nassau Street, Dublin DO2 YH68.

Penguin Random House is committed to a sustainable future for
our business, our readers and our planet. This book is made from
Forest Stewardship Council® certified paper.

To my mother, father and sister – Indira, Mukul and Nandini.
Thank you. For everything.

Neha's voice splintered the dark silence of the car.

'Come back, I need you! He's dead!'

'Who's dead?' shouted Saibal. 'What do ...' but she had hung up. He looked at me in consternation, screeched the Volvo through a U-turn, then gunned it through the lashing rain, making it to Hampstead in record time. Slamming on the brakes, he turned, took one look at his daughter slumped unconscious in the back, then thrust his car keys into Maya's hands. 'Take Anjoli home immediately. Kamil, you stay with me.'

I scrambled out of the car and ran to the shelter of the portico as he hurried his wife into the driver's seat, ignoring her faint protests. He watched her speed off, then walked purposefully towards me and rammed his finger into the doorbell, blinking off the rain that was streaming down his face.

Arjun opened the front door. 'You,' he said, eyes dark, face stony. 'I thought it was the police.'

I noticed his jacket was soaked, but he seemed oblivious to it. Why had *he* been out in the rain?

'What happened?' asked Saibal, pressing past him into the hall.

'Neha found Dad in the pool downstairs. He's ... dead. She insisted on coming up and phoning you. I've called the police; they should be here any minute.'

He led us to the living room where we found Neha, head buried in her arms. As soon as she caught sight of Saibal, she flung herself at him, clinging on as though she were drowning. 'It's okay, Neha, it's all right,' Saibal said, but I could hear the doubt in his voice. 'Just tell me what happened.'

'Rakesh ... a terrible accident ...' Sobs choked her words.

Saibal took control. 'Show me. Tara Tari!'

'I ... can't look at him again. Arjun, please ...' Neha looked beseechingly at her stepson.

He gave a sharp nod and ran us down a flight of tiled stairs till we were enveloped in a sharp, chlorinated humidity. On the floor, at the edge of the swimming pool, was the body of Rakesh Sharma, his clothes and hair sodden.

He might have been asleep if it weren't for the fact that there was a massive hole in the side of his head, blood and brain oozing into the puddle of water under his skull, forming an intricate crimson pattern on the white tiles. His face was peaceful; the rage that had twisted it the last time he had seen me, now vanished.

A parallel image slammed into me. The naked corpse in the hotel. Its skull, too, had been crushed. But there had been more blood. Hell of a lot more. I shivered at the recollection. No, no more of that. Another time, another world. I was a different person. No longer a police officer. I had to deal with the present, with *this* body. The past would have to wait its turn.

My mind flew to the moment we'd heard Rakesh's revelation. The confusion on their faces. The hushed whispers that ceased as I approached with the drinks tray. The clues lay in all I had seen and heard. The cops were on their way, but I had *been* here. Sensed the dynamics; the underlying tensions; the hostility in the air. I knew with an unflinching certainty that Neha was wrong. This wasn't an accident. It was murder.

And it was my calling.

I was the invisible waiter.

The Waiter

Twelve hours earlier.
London. October. Saturday.

The gleaming knife in my hand was polished to within an inch of its life. I laid it parallel to the fork, framing the white dinner plate. As I tried to fold the napkin into the shape of the helmet, which I could never get right, the sight through the window of a woman sauntering along the opposite pavement, a child on either side clutching a hand, lifted my melancholy for a moment. All three dressed in canary yellow with matching umbrellas – floating drops of sunshine on this grey, inhospitable day.

Saibal saw my ineffectual fumblings, put his mobile on speaker, grabbed the napkin from me, deftly created visor, nose and skull and whispered, 'Two months and you still cannot do it, Kamil? What kind of waiter are you? I should fire you!'

He was joking, but it still stung. Even I couldn't have lived down the ignominy of losing two jobs in three months.

'Sorry,' I mouthed back as his phone squawked: ' . . . and you'll definitely send your people at five o'clock?'

I listened absent-mindedly to his call as I laid the tables, trying to catch another glimpse of the golden triangle bobbing up the street. It provided slight relief from the restaurant's oppressive patterned wallpaper, its two dozen cramped booths and the pictures of Saibal with grinning 'celebrity' diners, none of whom I recognised.

Saibal turned his attention back to the phone. 'Yes, Neha. Four waiters, two chefs and some domestics. They will be my best people.'

'Better add an extra waiter. It has to be perfect.'

'One extra waiter, okay. It will be even better than perfect, Neha. It will be perfectly perfect.'

'Okay. Can we go through the menu again?'

I grimaced in sympathy as Saibal raised two fingers to his head and mimed pulling a trigger. He grabbed the fork I'd set down and scratched his back with it before picking up his notebook for the third time.

'Yes, Neha. For starter ...'

'Canapés, Uncle,' she interrupted.

'Yes, for canayp we have aloo tikki chat, poneer pakoda, fish pakoda and chicken boti kabab.'

'I think add the tandoori mutton chops.'

'Okay, I will make note. For main course you will have *all* the TK specials. We have mutton biryani, tandoori chicken, aloo mutter, malai kofta, makhani daal and naan. And raita. And desserts we have shahi tukda, gulab jamun and gajar ka halwa ...'

'Great. I can't have anything go wrong; you know what Rakesh is like. We've got a hundred and seventy-five of our close personal friends coming to celebrate. Duggy J's singing. I got him to compose an exclusive sixtieth birthday song as a surprise.'

'Wonderful! Okay, I will see you later today,' said Saibal, trying to hang up.

'And Maya Aunty and Anjoli are coming?' Neha persisted.

'Yes, we will be there. Dressed up. I got Maya new dress and nice jewellery for the special occasion. Imported from Dubai!' he added, with a hint of pride.

4

'Lovely, can't wait to see it. Thank you, Uncle. What would I do without you?'

'Maya!' Saibal yelled, as soon as Neha had hung up, causing me to drop with a clatter the spoon I'd been polishing.

'Hain? Ki?' His wife shouted back from the kitchen.

'Ei Mrs Sharma'r jonyo ek plate extra mutton chop.'

'Thik achhé.'

There was a pause, then he muttered to himself, 'Aaah keno na … Why not,' before he bellowed, 'Ei, Kamil!'

'Yes?' I asked, groping under the tablecloth to find the errant cutlery.

'I need you at catering party tonight. Not at restaurant. Okay?'

'The Sharma party?'

'Hain. Five o'clock.' He looked around the empty restaurant. 'Quiet today. Take the rest of the day off, it will be a long night. Make sure you change into fresh uniform, okay?' He gestured at my curry stained sleeve and continued, 'You know Rakesh Sharma, no?'

'I don't, but I've heard of him. Basically, I don't hang out with millionaires.'

'Oh, I thought you knew him,' said Saibal, running his fingers through his thick, grey hair. 'I will introduce you tonight, he is an old friend of mine from Kolkata. We were batchmates in college – he, your father, me – we had many enjoyable times. We have been through a lot together.' A shadow came across his face for the briefest of moments before he banished it with his usual warm smile. 'I cannot believe he is sixty – Eh Maa, we are so old now. And Neha is only twenty-eight. Very sweet girl, she is Anjoli's friend and has been like a second daughter to me. It was hard getting used to Rakesh and Neha together. But now I see, they make a lovely couple!'

'Isn't it normal for millionaires to have much younger wives?' I asked wryly.

'Hain, eta satyi. Very true! And she *is* exquisite. Now go!' The bell above the entrance tinkled and Saibal waved me away. He leapt up from the table and welcomed the four customers who had entered, guided them to a booth, put on his 'I am the proprietor of this fine establishment' smile and handed out the laminated menus headed '*Tandoori Knights – Keep Calm and Curry On*'.

In the kitchen, Maya and the three under-chefs were busy with the night's dinner. The smell of fried onions, garlic and ginger filled the air and the sounds of sizzling and percussive tin lids created a hypnotic rhythm as heaps of aromatic spices were tossed into the pots – orange turmeric, yellow heeng, red chilli powder, cumin, coriander, mustard seeds, cinnamon. I loved these aromas. The scent reminded me of home in Kolkata, watching Ma cook my favourite dishes – Ilish masher jhol, hilsa, the bony but wonderfully unctuous fish, with mustard; Shukto, vegetables cooked in milk; fluffy, flaky deep fried luchis to mop up the gravy; luscious Kathi rolls from Nizam's ...

A pang of longing for the life I'd left behind hit, and right on cue, the all-too-familiar bitterness seeped back in, like chronic indigestion. What the hell was I doing working as a waiter in this freezing, grim country at this ludicrously named restaurant? Three months ago, I'd been flying high, a homicide Sub-Inspector in charge of the most high-profile case in India, dealing with senior police officers, meeting Bollywood royalty ... And now? At thirty, when I should have been racing my way up the ranks, I'd traded in my policeman's whites for a waiter's waistcoat and bowtie, and was constantly anxious, always expecting people from the Home Office to be after me. Serving 'canayps' to millionaires was now the highlight of my week. I couldn't imagine a more vertiginous fall. Sometimes I felt I should have just stayed in India, closed my eyes to everything

I'd seen ... But no, I couldn't have kept working with that death on my conscience. And even now, I couldn't go back – it wouldn't be safe. So here I am – stuck between two countries, neither of which want me.

I made a mental note to call Ma and Abba to check on them – we hadn't spoken in ages. Though Abba was still furious with me, Ma always told me how he was. I should call her. And Maliha ... Maliha ...

The smells of the cooking, of my past, became thick and cloying. I felt suffocated. Needed air.

'I'm going out, Maya-di, see you later,' I shrugged on my overcoat as she smiled and nodded from across the kitchen.

I trudged up Brick Lane in the icy drizzle. Pulling my coat closed under my chin, I weaved my way through a sea of parkas, burqas, dashikis, saris and shalwar kameez – I liked this part of London, it reminded me of the chaos and confusion of Kolkata's Free School Street. As I made my way up the narrow road, the surroundings and the throngs changed. I was always caught by surprise at the transformation that occurred when I crossed the invisible boundary near Hanbury Street where the Bengali Cash & Carrys, sweet shops and pawnbrokers reluctantly gave way to a different world – a stylish bubble of camera-clicking tourists and skinny-jeaned teenagers frequenting Jack the Clipper, Amy's Wine House and the Cereal Killer café (*they* could use my detective skills ...). I wandered past the perennial queue at Beigel Bake Brick Lane and decided to plaster over the hollow in my soul with comfort food. I'd never eaten bagels in Kolkata and had become fond of them over the past few weeks, enjoying their savoury cushion-softness and warmth over a cup of strong Assam tea.

As the line shuffled forward, I watched an intrepid busker sheltering in a doorway, failing to hit the top notes of 'Hotel

California'. I liked this about London – there were entertainers everywhere, especially on the tube. In Kolkata, everyone rushed around with no time to think of dark desert highways.

When I'd first arrived three months ago, I used to travel on the underground on my days off to stop myself going crazy, staring at the blank walls of Saibal's spare room while picking over every aspect of the Kolkata murders and missing Maliha with a terrible desperation. I'd go to Bethnal Green underground, close my eyes, pick a destination at random on the map, spend a few hours walking around there, then make my way back. I had seen the wonders of Clapton (Lee Valley, calming marshes but nothing to do with Eric, as I discovered), Silvertown (Thames Barrier, dramatic), Balham (Tooting Common, pleasant), Bushey (bland, was it even in London?) – then it was back to the daily grind of a waiter's life. I hated routine, but that was what I needed now. Structure. To do nothing more consequential than remember the day's specials. With my visa running out in a few months, though, this liminal period would soon end, and I'd be forced to decide on what I wanted to do for the *next* thirty years. My life ahead was not an inviting blank canvas, it was more akin to a locked door for which I couldn't find the key, no matter how hard I looked.

As I walked out of the bakery, provisioned with my soul food, the busker was reaching the crescendo of the song and serendipitously informed me that I needed to find the passage back to the place I was before. 'Easier sung than done,' I said acidly as I tossed a ten-pence piece into his guitar case and returned to the flat above the restaurant. As I fumbled for my key, the door opened. And there she stood, looking surprised to see me. Anjoli. Saibal and Maya's only daughter and, to date, my one friend in London.

* * *

8

We'd first spent quality time together six weeks ago. I'd been lying in bed after another enervating afternoon shift at the restaurant, checking Maliha's Facebook page for updates while listening to Beck tell me that the sun didn't shine even when it was day, when Anjoli burst into my room without knocking.

'Come on, you. I can't stand you walking around looking like a slapped arse, it's doing my head in. We're going to get drunk tonight.'

I tried to protest, but she dragged me to the pub and, much to my surprise, I'd enjoyed myself for the first time in months. Thankfully, she hadn't forced me to talk, happy instead to chatter away about her wild years studying psychology at university; her indignation at being made redundant from her market research job; her on-again, off-again Italian barista boyfriend (I misheard what he did and assumed he was a successful lawyer, until she introduced us in Starbucks a week later). I'd listened, nursing several beers, and eventually she'd got me talking about my life as a detective. Up to the murders, at least. I wasn't ready to divulge that whole drama yet. It was still too raw.

'Baba's always saying you're a brilliant detective. Like Poirot. Or Sherlock Holmes. So, deduce what I'm thinking, Mr Detective?'

'I'm a police officer, not a psychic. Anyway, all that Holmes and his violin, Poirot and his moustache and the other English guy ... the one who drives the big red car and does crosswords ...'

'Morse?'

'Yes, Inspector Morse – that genius stuff is complete rubbish! Nobody in real life solves crimes like that. And it's never a mastermind planning to kill someone by inviting them to a country house and murdering them in an elaborate way in a locked room with no key. Complete nonsense. Real investigative work is boring. You question people. Find out who's lying. Piece things together. Then arrest the culprit. You don't call twelve suspects into a library and show them how clever you are. And it's never the least likely person. It's almost always the *most* likely one who done it! And,' I added, a harsh note creeping into my voice, 'they don't face justice at the end. They just get away with it, leaving idiots like me to pick up the pieces.'

I turned away from her and drained what was left of my beer. She stared at me, taking in the shift in my mood.

'You okay?'

I turned back and forced a smile.

'Yes, sorry. I became a detective because part of me thought I could sit in my room and deduce the identity of a killer using my Poirot "leetle grey cells". It was a bit of a shock when I found out how dull investigating really was.'

She nodded sympathetically. 'What about psychology? I thought you had to understand the psyche of the criminal?'

'Psychology Shmycology. All nonsense. Motives are straight-forward – sex, greed, money ...'

'Okay, Okay, I get it! Maybe you should patent a "new" way of solving crimes and they'll write a book about you – Katching Kriminals with Kamil!' She laughed, then ordered another round of beers.

Yes, that had been an evening where I'd got out of myself and the weight of Kolkata had lifted. Time with Anjoli almost made me more like who I used to be – the 'Pre-Asif Khan Murder' Kamil Rahman. Almost.

* * *

And now here she was, brow wrinkled, wearing jeans and a red cardigan over a T-shirt that said *Coconuts are Hard on the Outside but Sweet on the Inside.* 'How come you're back so early on a

Saturday? Immigration caught up with you working illegally on your visitor's visa? Need to pack your bags?'

'You wish,' I retorted.

I shrugged off my perpetual jumpiness – it wasn't an attractive trait – and squeezed past her into the small hallway, announcing with all the nonchalance I could muster, 'I'm off for the day. Saibal-da asked me to cater the party tonight. How come you're home?'

'Job hunting ...' she said at once. 'Just heading out for some food and a break.'

'Really? Kim Kardashian's Instagram now has job postings?' I awkwardly thrust the plastic bag into her hand as I hung my overcoat on the rack.

'Hilarious. Oooh, bagels and hummus. I'm literally dying for a snack,' she said, peering into the bag.

'*Literally* dying, huh? I'd better call your mother if you're about to shuffle off your mortal coil, I'm sure she'd appreciate a break from the restaurant,' I said, pleased to impress her with the one Shakespearean phrase I knew. Then immediately felt idiotic.

'Oh, shut up Mr Basically,' she countered. '"Basically, I am telling you today's special is quail curry." "Basically, Snapchat is only for kids."'

The sun broke through the clouds and the street below glowed with an autumnal freshness as Anjoli put the kettle on. I watched the small butterfly tattoo on her wrist playing hide and seek behind her silver bangles as they clinked musically up and down her arm. 'Alexa, play The Beatles,' she commanded, and the plangent sitar of 'Norwegian Wood' filled the kitchen.

'Are *you* going to the party?' I asked, tilting back on the wooden kitchen chair.

She grimaced. 'Yeah, I have to. I hate these stupid dos. Fat men and women in tons of gold jewellery with Ma trying to set me up with their "illegible" sons.' She rolled her eyes. 'But it's Neha's anniversary, so I have to.'

'Neha? Now she is … Rakesh's … daughter? Oh no, I mean wife …' I said, knowing it would wind her up.

'Don't be rude! Anyway, it's my fault. I got her the job as Rakesh Uncle's EA after Uni and who could have dreamed that they'd …?'

'And what exactly was it that first attracted her to millionaire businessman Rakesh Sharma who just happens to be double her age?'

'Piss off. She loves him. He can be charming and funny. But,' she gave me a conspiratorial stare and lowered her voice, 'it *is* weird! I mean, I've known Rakesh Uncle since I was born, and Neha since primary school! He was always nice to me – brought me delish sandesh back from Kolkata. We used to hang out at their place in Watford – Pinky Aunty inherited that house after they split. She always served the most delicious fat, flaky, spicy samosas. And then – boom – next thing I knew they were getting divorced – Rakesh Uncle was marrying my best friend and buying her a bloody great ugly mansion in Bishops Avenue as a wedding present. Neha's cool, but her taste is a little … Bollywood meets Iraqi Dictator.'

'Didn't Neha tell you when they started dating?' I bit into my bagel.

'No! I think it embarrassed her. We *both* knew him when we were kids. Guess she thought people would talk about her – rubbish about daddy issues and what not,' the psychology major announced confidently. 'Her parents died when she was young,' she clarified, spotting my confused expression. 'Her aunty raised her. It wasn't easy for Arjun either – watching his dad literally become a cliché, running off with the young secretary, younger than him, even, and leaving his mother behind. Especially when they had to work together every day at PinRak.

12

Neha's petrified because Pinky's coming to the party. She's insisted, because it's Rakesh's sixtieth and no one has had the guts to say no. You may have to mop blood off the floor as part of your waitering-catering.'

Congealed blood on a gold silk carpet in a luxurious hotel suite. I shook the memory off.

'Well, I'll make sure you're constantly supplied with Negronis and aloo tikis,' I said. 'Although I must remember that Neha has instructed us to call them canapés. Apparently, starters are not sophisticated enough for your friend.'

We sat convivially with our tea, bagels and hummus at the kitchen table, the intermittent hum of the dishwasher providing an accompaniment to Lennon as he drank his wine and bided his time.

Anjoli stretched her arms above her head, yawned and stood up.

'Okay, I'd better start tarting myself up. I'm meeting some mates for drinks at The Spaniards before the big shebang. Wanna come? I can introduce them to a handsome Bengali detective-in-waiting. Lol.'

'Handsome?' I raised an eyebrow. She looked me up and down.

'You're right, that is pushing it. But you're not *too* bad. I could *consider* setting you up with one of my single friends. Let's see – tall, good head of hair, athletic, a little paunch coming, though? Too much of Ma's vindaloo?'

I discreetly sucked in my stomach, somewhat hurt she'd noticed. It was true … I had been picking up as many shifts at the restaurant as I could as I liked to keep busy, it kept my mind off things, but there were always irresistible leftovers. Maya was a wonderful cook.

'I mean obviously you'd need better clothes,' she continued, on a roll now. 'Those shiny shirts and fake Levis have to go. And you'd have to shave off that stupid moustache.'

'Your Poirot had a moustache.'

'He was *ancient*, man! And anyway, his didn't look like an emaciated caterpillar had curled up and died in despair on his upper lip.'

I stroked my moustache defensively. 'I can tell you I've seen your friends and basically I am not sure that *they* are good enough for *me*. I'm better off on my own.' I said, turning away.

'Your loss, bro! I think Naila might be perfect for you . . . she's coming. You like her, don't you?'

My head snapped back. Naila was the niece of Salim Mian, TK's head waiter. She'd turn up at the restaurant every now and then to collect him at the end of his shift and would quiz me about being a policeman in her soft Pakistani accent while she waited for her uncle to change into his street clothes. I liked her company and we had something in common – she had come over from Lahore to study nursing and was also adjusting to life in London.

'You *are* interested in her, I knew it!' said Anjoli triumphantly.

'No, I'm not! Anyway, I can't because . . .'

The front-door lock rattled and Saibal strode in, tossing his keys onto the table in the hallway, followed by Maya carrying three full Tupperware boxes, precariously balanced on top of each other.

I was fond of the Chatterjees, not just because they'd generously taken me in at my lowest point and treated me as part of the family without demur, but because they were real Bhadralok – true, well-mannered gentlefolk. Saibal thought he was the boss, but it was Maya who ran the house and the restaurant with an iron fist, never letting things drop. I missed Ma, and Maya had become like a second mother to me.

Anjoli leapt up, gave her mother a kiss and relieved her of the containers. 'Cha, ma?'

'Thank you, sweetie,' she smiled and then turned to me. 'Hello Kamil, having a pleasant time with Anjoli?' Her eyes flitted between us as she joined us at the kitchen table. I'd always wondered if they worried about having a single Muslim guy living with them and fraternising with their single, Hindu daughter. But they'd said nothing. And anyway, after Maliha, my fraternising days were over. Naila or no Naila.

'I came upstairs to change. I'm helping with the Sharma party,' I responded.

'Really?' said Maya, a note of surprise in her voice, as she sat down with a sigh and kicked off her shoes.

'Hain, why not?' said Saibal, plopping next to her, opening the top button of his trousers and stretching out with a happy groan. 'We needed an extra waiter. Cha for me also Anjoli, please.'

'Acchha. You will like their house, Kamil,' said Maya. 'Much bigger than our small home.'

'Your flat is lovely, Maya-di,' I said.

'It's so cramped here, compared to Rakesh's mansion,' she complained.

A thought struck me. Had I outstayed my welcome? Misjudged their liberality? 'I will shift back to India soon,' I mumbled.

'Oh no,' Maya exclaimed. 'I didn't mean that. This is your home, son.' She leaned forwards and gave my face a stroke, the way my mother used to. 'Stay as *long* as you want. We love having you here.' Her head swivelled to face her daughter, 'Anjoli, did you look at any new job postings?'

In-sta-gram, I mouthed as Anjoli giggled, serving them tea and Marie biscuits. 'Yes, Ma. Nothing good yet.'

'You can't waste your life chopping onions. You need to get a wonderful job. Find a good Bangla boy. Forget this love marriage rubbish. Love comes after marriage,' said Maya, smiling at her husband.

'So does suicide,' muttered Anjoli under her breath.

'Leave her alone, Maya,' said Saibal. 'It's good for her to work in the family business.'

'What family business? There's no family business.' Maya threw her hands in the air. 'You and I can run restaurants. Anjoli will be a big advertising executive, Kamil will be a great detective and then I can die happy.'

'Oh Ma, such a drama queen! You're not dying anytime soon,' exclaimed Anjoli over her shoulder as she ran up to her room.

A great detective – I stared out of the window at the pouring rain. Memories washed over me as Paul McCartney entreated me to get back to where I once belonged. If only I could get back and do things differently. It had started promisingly: the call that Monday morning from the Deputy Commissioner – my big chance to show the world what *a great detective* I was. I had been so cocky, so convinced that I knew everything, little anticipating the cesspool of criminality and corruption that I would get myself into. Never dreaming that one week in July would change my life so irrevocably.

The Detective

Three months ago.
Kolkata. July. Monday.

The monsoon raged, its deafening drops machine-gunning my umbrella as I clambered into the dirt-streaked Tata Sumo. While I struggled to close it, a passing scooter splashed my trousers with filthy brown gutter water. I glanced down ruefully – the Deputy Commissioner would think I'd wet myself at his peremptory summons. I didn't understand why an officer three ranks my senior wanted to see me, a mere Sub-Inspector working homicide. I had done nothing wrong. As far as I knew.

'Lalbazar, driver, tara tari!'

My driver started the SUV and it lurched forward through the flooded streets, the choking midday traffic doing its best to impede the progress of the tens of thousands of us going about our daily business. I liked Kolkata in the monsoons – the buildings looked cleaner, the air fresher. The rains had been late this year, the sky fierce, the air oppressively hot and dusty while the entire, irritable city held its breath, waiting for the heat to break and the rains to provide desperately needed relief.

When the first fat drops finally arrived and the scent of petrichor filled the city, the tension lifted as children and adults alike ran outside to soak themselves in the deluge. But the joy soon turned to frustration as the antiquated drainage systems as usual failed to cope, dust turned to mud and the streets instantly flooded. Kolkatans stoically persevered as we had for centuries, lifting trousers, skirts, lungis to avoid the deepest puddles, cursing as the water sloshed over shoes, chappals, stilettos.

Struggling through the water, the car crawled past a line of schoolchildren dressed identically in white shirts and blue pinafores, huddling under umbrellas and waiting to enter the strange Anglo-Bengali-Muslim white marble meringue of Victoria Memorial, now glowing eerily against a background of dark, dangerous, roiling clouds. As a child I'd called it 'Toria Moria' when Abba had brought me here to introduce me to the wonders of the British Empire. *You are like this building Kamil, English educated* and *Bengali* and *Muslim, remember that ...* my father, the retired Commissioner of Police trying to inculcate his Anglophile rectitude in me to make sure that I made it through 'honest hard work' as opposed to the typical Kolkata-cop route of sloth, indifference and bribes. Unfortunately, that meant I'd had to start at the very bottom and work my way up the never-ending ladder of the Kolkata Police.

I remembered the diamond-bright optimism I'd felt the day I graduated from the Kolkata Police Training School. They had asked Abba to give the exiting speech to the fresh recruits and the pride I'd felt in his words was overwhelming.

What you have all chosen is a calling, not a job. When you put on your uniforms, you are the guardians of the public. Never forget that they are looking to you for protection and justice. That, and only that, is the reason for your existence. You must ensure that those who do evil, those who cause pain and suffering in the innocent, are punished for their crimes and their victims get the justice they deserve. Only then can society function. You are the thin line between order and anarchy. Never forget.

I had left the School with a burning fire to help those that needed me ... then spent the next three years as a constable on traffic duty. I wasn't sure how dealing with rickshawallahs running red lights in Sealdah had helped bring more justice into the world. I'd hinted that Abba might put in a word to fast-track me, but he'd insisted I pay my dues. So I'd laboriously worked my way up through Assistant Sub-Inspector to my current post in the homicide squad of the detective department, where at least I could make a difference.

We snaked our way past hoardings proclaiming in twenty-foot-high letters

KOLKATA METRO: BUILDING THE WORLDS MOST ADVANCED TRANSPORT SYSTEM. ANOTHER PROUD PROJECT FROM PINRAK INDUSTRY'S

I loved those transgressing apostrophes. Posters for the upcoming elections peppered the billboards, creating a noisy patchwork of capital letters and Party symbols:

CHOOSE YOUR FRIEND, NOT YOUR ENEMY – VOTE RANJIT SANYAL, UNITED PARTY

STOP THE MUSLIM REFUGEES – VOTE KARTHIK SEN, PEOPLE'S PARTY.

Hopefully this year's polls would be more peaceful than the last when we had to charge rival bands of supporters while dodging stones and bottles. I had not impressed Maliha when I'd showed her my various cuts and bruises. *Stop trying to be a bloody hero and get a proper desk job, I don't want a dead fiancé* she had said as she applied Mercurochrome and band aids, ignoring my theatrical winces.

When we arrived at Lalbazar Police Headquarters, Detective Department, a peon came along and told me the DC would see me at once. This was unexpected – I knew my place and had been prepared for a long wait.

He escorted me into a massive office, cold as a freezer with what appeared to be four air conditioners running simultaneously. I shivered, rain-soaked shirt icy against my skin. At the end of the room, the Deputy Commissioner looked tiny, ensconced in a high-backed swivel chair behind an enormous, sparse desk decorated with a nameplate saying *DC-DD Shri Amitav Ghosh IPS,* an Ashoka Pillar, a photo of his smiling family and a worn, brown, open cardboard folder.

I approached the desk and snapped a stiff salute, breath tight, trying to hide my nerves, which increased exponentially when I noticed my photograph staring back at me from the file on his desk. I'd never been in the DC's presence one-on-one. And now here I was, standing in front of him as he studied me up and down through tortoise-shell glasses, thinning hair Brylcreem'd back, wearing a spotless khaki uniform, the three stars on his epaulette gleaming his exalted rank. He angled his head from side to side as though he was looking for reasons to demand a discount on a carpet in New Market. His gaze settled on my drenched trousers. 50 per cent off. At least.

Then, like the sun emerging from clouds, his face broke into a wide smile. 'Rahman! Here you are, my boy. Coffee? Sit,' he shook my hand vigorously, grabbed my personnel folder, and guided me to the sofa in the far corner of his vast office.

I exhaled in silent relief. 'Thank you, sir. No, nothing, sir. I am fine, sir.' I sat at attention on the edge of the sofa.

'So, *you* are the bright young Sub-Inspector I have been hearing so much about,' he said, taking off his spectacles, shrewd eyes piercing through me.

'Sir?'

He put his glasses back on and looked at the file. 'You did an excellent job on the murder of that shopkeeper in

Gariahat last month, your inspector recommended you for a commendation.'

'I was lucky, sir,' I said, trying to sound as humble as possible.

'Luck is only talent plus timing,' he said in what was obviously a well-worn aphorism as I nodded appreciatively at his wisdom.

He flicked the folder shut and leaned forward conspiratorially. 'Rahman, I have a case. Ultra-sensitive. Hi-pro. It will need the utmost discretion. I want you to handle it personally. Tell me, can I rely on you?'

What was I supposed to say? The DC wasn't someone you ever said No to. Or even someone you asked what you were saying Yes to.

'Absolutely, sir. Basically, I will do all I can to help.'

'Excellent!' He leaned back and folded his arms behind his head. 'Do you know who Asif Khan is?'

'The Bollywood star, sir?'

'Exactly. The actor. A terrible thing, but someone murdered him last night in his suite in the Grand Hotel. I want you,' he leaned forward and jabbed a finger at me, 'to lead the investigation. This is top priority and you need to make sure it is handled well and wrapped up quickly. Drop everything else.'

Asif Khan dead! And I was to be handling his homicide! My heart felt like it was trying to drill through my ribcage and escape, but I tried to maintain my professional demeanour. 'Thank you, sir,' I managed to reply.

'You will report directly to me on it. Understood? Get your notebook out and listen.'

He filled me in on the details of the case, my hand shaking with excitement as I scribbled – this was my chance to prove myself. Now I could be a 'real' cop and a proper seeker after justice and not just a bag man. He told me that the hotel manager had called Control Room two hours ago and they then informed New Market Thana, who had to inform the DC on all hi-pro cases. I rushed to write everything down. I couldn't afford to miss a thing.

'Go to the hotel now, Rahman. Good luck.'

Dismissed, I stood and saluted as the DC walked back to his desk. I turned to leave, hesitated, and said, 'Sir, may I ask one question, please?'

'Ask.' He looked up.

'Why me, sir?'

He paused, then tapped my file. 'Are you not the right person for this, Rahman? Should I find someone else?'

'Yes sir, I mean oh no, sir ...' I was burbling.

He grinned. 'Relax, young man! I have been observing you for a while. As I said, you did well on your last case and your inspector thought you were ready for a bigger challenge.'

'Thank you, sir. I won't let you down.' I saluted again.

And just as I walked out the door, I heard him say, 'Say hello to your father for me.'

And there it was. I'd thought I'd done this on my own merit, but it seemed my father's influence had earned it for me. I shrugged it off. It was about time. And I had a date with a dead superstar.

The Waiter

London. October. Saturday.

As we headed to the party, I tried to stem my overactive mind, pushing back the memories that wouldn't stay hidden. The flames of excitement in the DC's office that day ... how could it all have turned to ashes so quickly? No matter – a lifetime had passed since that rainy Kolkata afternoon. My detective days were behind me and I was gradually rebuilding my shattered life.

So, here I was, squeezed in the back of the restaurant's delivery van with five other waiters, two 'domestics', two chefs plus all the food, plates, pots and pans more appropriate for a five-day wedding than a birthday party. I cursed myself for bothering to waste half an hour steam-ironing my uniform. We trundled down the A1 in a vehicle teetering at the edge of its MOT and turned into The Bishops Avenue.

I had wandered around here during my explorations of London, curious to see the famous 'Billionaires Row'. A wide, leafy street leading to Hampstead Heath, Saibal had told me it was *the* location of choice for Russian oligarchs, Arab sheikhs and Indian business magnates. Each tycoon would pay tens of millions of pounds to buy a twelve-bedroom high-spec from some other mogul, only to tear it down and build an even larger one in its place. And so, the cycle continued, each new mansion shinier and more opulent with even more technology and marble than its predecessor. Instead of this futuristic nirvana, I found a deserted, shabby road with half the houses in total disrepair, hidden behind forbidding black hoardings and padlocked iron gates. It looked as though the billionaires had fled the country en masse after a people's revolution. And *this* was where Rakesh Sharma had built a mansion for his new wife? I guess glitz always covers garbage.

I slid my finger under my bowtie, trying to loosen my collar. I hated being in this uniform. I hadn't been crazy about my Sub-Inspector's whites, but at least those conveyed authority. This penguin suit was just a constant reminder of my drastic diminution in status, a nagging toothache that just wouldn't go away.

'Stupid outfit, no?' said Salim Mian, looking at me sideways. 'I try to tell Saibal to move with the times but ...'

'Old is gold,' chorused the other staff. We burst into laughter, bobbing in the back of the van.

I liked Salim Mian. Diabetic and overweight, he'd wander around the restaurant, an abstracted expression on his face as though he had momentous matters on his mind, while we did the heavy lifting. He'd been with Saibal and Maya from the beginning and behaved like the patriarch of the Tandoori Knights family, taking me under his wing without demur and teaching me the basics of being a waiter. Which in many ways was more complicated than being a cop.

It was 4.55 p.m. and we hadn't yet found the house. Saibal had described the Sharma coat of arms as featuring a tiger and an elephant on their hind legs and, just as we were about to give up and phone him, that hideous vision arose before us, glinting in the late afternoon sun from between two forbidding metal gates. They screeched open and we trundled up the driveway.

The Sharma mansion was a large, double-fronted Georgian house, in the centre of which an overexcited architect had plonked a portico. At the entrance sprung four tall white columns topped by a triangular pediment displaying sculptures of Hindu gods and goddesses disporting themselves in various states of undress. Underneath was a large plaque engraved with the words 'Sharma Manor'. It was a unique Anglo-Greco-Bollyweirdo style of architecture.

The driver parked at the rear of the mansion and we spilled out of the van, carrying the pots and pans to the vast kitchen that, ultra-sleek and modern, looked as if it had never been used. Mr Sharma's butler, dressed in an old-fashioned tailcoat, oversaw our entry, making sure everything was 'shipshape' and made me feel as though I was visiting Blandings Castle. Spotless sinks, six hobs on an island in the middle of the room, various shiny ovens, fridges, wine fridges, microwaves and other technology I couldn't fathom filled the room.

'We need a computer scientist! How are we going to use this stuff?' I exclaimed, throwing my overcoat into a pile with the others in the corner.

'No tension,' grinned Chef. He pulled out four ancient primus stoves and dumped them onto the shiny granite counters. He lit them, put the huge pans onto the fire and ladled the food in to heat.

The kitchen door opened and a tall woman wafted in on six-inch heels making her tower over us, a cloud of expensive perfume trailing behind her. Exquisite, in a long sheath of silver sequins, light brown hair twisted on her head, fingernails painted a deep red, she looked as though she'd wandered off the set of a Bollywood extravaganza. I guessed this was Neha, Rakesh Sharma's current wife and ex-executive assistant – and of course, Anjoli's old school pal. I could not, for the life of me, picture them together.

'Ah good, you are here,' she said, unperturbed by the stoves belching black smoke into her gleaming kitchen. 'Where's Saibal Sahib?'

'He coming, madam,' said Chef.

'Okay, make sure everything's ready for the guests' arrival. You three, come with me,' she imperiously beckoned to me and two of Saibal's other waiters.

We followed her in a line into the vast living room. Which was … extraordinary. The size of Saibal's entire flat, its walls were cushioned in red velvet studded with tiny crystals, giving the impression of a vast and opulent padded cell. Massive purple sofas were scattered around the room and plush rugs lay underfoot, my feet having to fight to walk through them. As my eyes scanned sideways to avoid the blazing chandelier light reflecting off the many diamonds around Neha's neck, in her ears and on her fingers, my gaze settled upon paintings by famous Indian artists whose styles I recognised – Husains, Shaikhs, Razas.

'Nice, no? I designed it myself,' said Neha.

'Lovely, madam,' I said, suppressing a smile that came close to a grimace.

'You like the Bikash?' She spotted me staring at a painting of a young woman whose eyes were imploring me to help her escape this Pasha's nightmare of a room. 'Cost a hundred and fifty grand. Rakesh bought it for me as a birthday present,' she continued, before leading us to a sweeping bar in the far corner.

'You get the drinks ready here. Serve the Black Label, not the Blue Label, that's for my husband. Bar ON!' she announced, and LED lights shimmered behind myriad bottles of luridly coloured liqueurs. It was a visual representation of a migraine.

My head spun. I wanted to tear off my ridiculous bow-tied uniform and run as far away from these mad, rich people as possible, back to Kolkata, to my flat, my bed and my fiancée. Who wasn't my fiancée anymore. But that wasn't an option. So, instead, I straightened my jacket sleeves with a quick tug on each and began polishing glasses and sorting out mixers, passing the occasional trenchant comment to the other waiters about the decor.

* * *

By the time the doorbell chimed at around six-thirty, I was bored and jobless. Neha had insisted on five waiters when there was only work for three. Eager to see what types of guests frequented this type of do, I surreptitiously followed the coattails of the butler as he glided to the front hall.

He opened the door and I caught sight of Saibal in a smart suit, his grey hair combed for a change, and Maya, resplendent in a pink salwar kameez under a red coat, her new gold butterfly necklace from Dubai glinting in the light of another oversized chandelier.

'Hello, son,' said Maya smiling as she spotted me, her dyed-black hair offsetting the round red bindi in the centre of her forehead.

'Maya-di,' I replied, stepping forward. 'You look very nice. Where's Anjoli?' I scanned the driveway behind her.

'What a flatterer you are. But is Anjoli not here yet? She said she would meet us.'

'Everything okay?' asked Saibal, eyes darting around as he took off his overcoat and handed it to the butler.

'Yes boss. Chef has everything under control,' I responded.

'Here you are, at last! I was wondering where you had got to,' Neha tottered over and gave them affectionate hugs. 'Why are you here, waiter?' she snapped at me. 'Go back inside to serve the drinks. There is so much to do.'

'Oh Neha,' Saibal interjected. 'You have not met Kamil, na? He is the son of my great friend, Police Commissioner Adil Rahman and is staying with us in London. I asked him to help tonight.'

Neha looked at me as a human for the first time as Saibal continued, 'He used to be a famous detective in Kolkata and solved plenty plenty cases – murders and dacoity and thefts. He will make sure none of your guests run off with your jewellery tonight, ha ha.'

'But my guests are our close personal friends, Uncle,' said Neha, parroting her phrase of the day. 'They have their own jewellery and I don't expect any untoward goings-on tonight. We don't need a security guard, thank you very much. Anyway, welcome to our home, Mr Detective, Anj told me about you. But please bring our drinks now. Rakesh will be here soon, when he has finished work.'

I almost saluted but before I could follow her orders, the bell rang again. It was Anjoli, looking stunning in a blue cocktail dress, pashmina over her shoulders and a simple gold chain with a stylised 'A' nestled between her collarbones.

'Sorry I'm late.' She was a few drinks in, I could tell. She entered and squealed at Neha who squealed back as they fell into each other's arms. She finally extricated herself and winked at me. 'I'll have a Negroni please, *waiter*, I'm literally dying for a drink. Scotch for Baba and white wine for Ma.'

'At your service Madam, I shall *literally* save your life.'

The bell rang again, and before I ran to get the drinks, I watched the new arrivals: a well-upholstered older woman in a pink chiffon sari, her hennaed hair sparkling with diamonds; and a younger man, tall, handsome, in his late thirties, with a trimmed beard, wearing an elegant suit and tie.

'Welcome. Welcome to my house,' said Neha, face hardening.

'Aunty Pinky, Arjun!' shrieked Anjoli, rushing to hug them.

'Hello Anjoli, you look *so* pretty,' said Pinky embracing her and ignoring Neha. 'How are you, my darling? Any handsome husband on the horizon yet?'

'This girl does what she wants,' griped Maya, kissing Pinky and Arjun. 'I've had to ask my sister in Kolkata to find someone from India because she won't bother herself.'

Anjoli rolled her eyes at Neha as Pinky released her from her substantial grasp and sailed further into the house. 'So, the famous Sharma Castle! It is very ... modern.'

'Sharma Manor,' muttered Neha, looking helplessly at Anjoli.

'Oh, I recognise that table,' Pinky continued, bustling into the living room, pulling Saibal and Maya along with her. 'It was in the kitchen of our old house.'

Arjun wandered in languidly, paying no attention to the seething tensions around him, eyes trained on his mobile.

'Velvet walls. How ... *nice*. You can bounce on them. Wow! Embedded diamonds! Oh no, just Swarovski,' disappointment dripped from her voice. 'What a *beautiful* living room, Neha. Did you design it yourself?'

'Yes,' muttered Neha.

'You are so talented! You must give me a tour of the entire house when Rakesh is here. Is he still working late? That fellow is never on time. I hope you've checked he is not with his secretary. Who knows what he gets up to, he is such a rogue. Enjoy all this – while you have it. It may not be for long.' She threw her head back and laughed.

Arjun glanced up from his phone and spat out, 'Ma!' with an annoyed look, but Pinky ignored him. I was enjoying the show from the sidelines, until Pinky spotted me and I remembered I was a waiter, not a guest.

'Waiter, champagne. Dom Prig-non, not the rubbish stuff,' she commanded.

'Scotch, Blue Label,' said Arjun, throwing himself onto a sofa.

As I served the drinks, I spotted Neha nudge Anjoli and they headed into the kitchen. I followed close behind, leaving the Chatterjees and Sharmas exchanging news.

The kitchen was buzzing; Chef adding finishing touches to the food, waiters polishing glasses and laying out fresh bottles of whisky on the granite islands, ready for serving.

'What a bitch!' Neha burst out as soon as we walked in. '"I hope you checked he is not with his secretary". Can you believe her? *And* Arjun is being horrible again. I thought he'd finally accepted me!'

'Don't worry, Neha,' consoled Anjoli. I picked up a glass and started polishing it, making sure I was still within eavesdropping distance. 'Aunty Pinky is just … Aunty Pinky. And Arjun is a twat. You won't have to deal with them that much.'

'I don't know, Anj,' said Neha, sighing. 'Rakesh has been so distant over the last two months, I have no idea what's going on. I try to be patient and understanding but …' her face twisted and she looked as if she might burst into tears.

'Have you met Kamil?' asked Anjoli, raising her voice, trying to change the subject. 'He's staying with us.' My head snapped up and I tried to look as if I hadn't just heard everything they'd said.

Neha looked at me. 'Yes, your dad told me,' she said, regaining her composure. 'Are you really a detective or was Uncle joking? I don't always understand his humour.'

'Yes, it's true, madam. Or rather, I was one. Seven years in the police.'

'So why are you a waiter now?' I hated this question and deflected it as usual.

'It's a long story. Can I get you a drink? That's what I'm here for today,' I smiled, hoping she wouldn't push it. She didn't.

'Champagne,' she replied, before turning back to Anjoli.

30

'I'm sorry we've seen so little of each other over the last few months, Anj. You and Saibal Uncle and Maya Aunty are the only actual friends I have, and I've neglected you.'

When I returned with Neha's drink, a large man waddled into the kitchen ahead of me. Bald, in a well-cut suit, sausage fingers protruding from the sleeves, he resembled a walrus wearing Savile Row. 'Neha!' he bellowed.

'Rakesh! Finally!' said Neha, taking the champagne glass from my tray, with a subtle nod in thanks before skittering towards him in her heels.

'Hello, Anjoli dear,' said Rakesh. 'And there you are, my darling wife. Why are you hiding? Our guests are arriving.' He stretched upwards and Neha swooped down in a smooth, practised move as he kissed her on the cheek.

So, *here's* the famous millionaire, I thought, watching them. Absolute proof that money can buy you love.

He pulled away from his wife as Neha said, 'Rakesh, this is a friend of Saibal Uncle's. He was a famous detective but is helping as a waiter tonight. His name is Kamil Rahman.'

I stuck on a smile and held out my hand to shake. Rakesh whipped his head around, eyes drilling through me, benevolent beam twisting into poorly concealed fury. After a moment he controlled himself and hissed, 'Ah, the police wallah. Yes, Saibal told me you were lodging with him. I didn't know he would bring you here. Scotch. Blue Label.'

Rattled, I withdrew my unshaken hand as Neha said, 'I'll do it . . .' She tore the foil off a fresh bottle of Johnnie Walker Ghost and Rare and opened it. As she poured the whisky, she said, in a little girl voice, 'Rakesh darling. Pinky's being horrible to me. Why did you have to invite her?'

Rakesh tore his eyes away from me and said, 'It *is* my sixtieth birthday, my love. Arjun wanted her here. Don't worry about her. She is a nobody. Tonight is all about you.' He grabbed the

bottle and glass from her hand and splashed himself a generous measure.

'But it's *our* anniversary Rakesh,' pouted Neha, walking out
after him.

Their voices faded as he said, 'It is my darling, but wait till
you find out the surprise I have for you ...'

'Wow!' said Anjoli, watching them leave. 'What did you do to
him, Kamil? He looked like he hated you! I thought you said you
didn't know him?'

'I don't,' I said. 'Bizarre. I guess he didn't like me being near
his wife. Lowly waiter that I am.'

'Weird, he's always been nice to me,' she exclaimed, straightening her hair. 'Okay, time to go on show! See you later, lowly waiter.'

I tried to put Rakesh Sharma's strange behaviour out of my
mind and get on with the job at hand, but his incandescent stare
haunted me.

Several hours later, the party was in full swing. I avoided Rakesh
Sharma and rushed around serving drinks and setting up the
food stations while Saibal and Maya chatted with old friends.
Pinky and Neha paraded around as if they were both chatelaines
of Sharma Manor and Rakesh waddled from guest to guest,
exuding charm and expensive eau de cologne, shaking hands
('Minister, how is Layla? Politics at Durham I hear? Takes after
her father!'), embracing ('Mukesh! Thank you so much for coming! Did you and Tia get the Diwali sweets we sent?') and
air-kissing ('Eva, you look so glamorous, as always! How do you
keep that gorgeous figure of yours?').

Meanwhile, Anjoli had already had one too many Negronis
and was pointing out various low-rent celebrities to me: two disgraced politicians ('Greedy, corrupt bastards'); presenters from
Asian radio stations ('He's well known for sending flowers to
himself'); and some of the cast of an Asian reality show ('They

cancelled it after one season'). Rakesh Sharma's hundred and seventy-five close personal friends provided ample fodder for gossip. Everywhere I looked were diamonds, gold spangly dresses and glossy manicures shoving empty glasses at me.

Duggy J had set up his band on one side of the vast ballroom. A couple of dozen guests were working off their dinner, shimmying with their arms out. To Anjoli's excruciating embarrassment, Saibal gallantly escorted Maya to the dance floor and attempted to whirl her around, laughing as they collided with other dancers. Then I spotted someone who looked familiar. A dazzling woman dancing with Rakesh, her black dress made of oversized sequins connected by metal rings, which slashed shards of light across the other dancers, reflecting the mirror ball. As I tried to place her, two worlds collided. With a stomach-sinking fall I was plummeted back to Lalbazar, Sergeant Hazra whispering in my ear: *That Taania Raazia is mirchi hot, sir*. I froze and the Asif Khan case, the film party, the light and the dark all came tumbling back.

'Waiter, waiter …' impatient fingers waggled an empty champagne flute in front of my face and jerked me back to the present. There was no reason that Bollywood star Taania Raazia shouldn't be in London hanging out with the other jet-setters, but it unsettled me.

At eleven-thirty I saw Duggy J look down, take a breath and exhale as if he was getting into some sort of zone. The music changed, and he announced, 'And now a special song for a special man – MR RAKESH SHARMA!!!'

Silence. The keyboardist played a chord and nodded his head to the two waiters in the doorway who had commandeered a gilded drinks trolley to transport the five-tier birthday cake. As they wheeled the trolley in, fire-spitting sparklers lighting up the bemused faces of the party guests and making their clothes glitter, Duggy J began a bhangrafied rendition of Happy Birthday. The guests sang along, tunelessly. This was presumably the song he had 'specially' written for Rakesh. The scene was reminiscent of the worst part of my job, trooping behind three of my colleagues in the restaurant, singing discordantly while carrying a carrot halwa with a candle in it for a drunken diner. The trolley ended its journey on the final 'YOU' with a stylish swerve in front of Rakesh, beaming and red-eyed as a professional photographer captured the unfolding ceremony.

'Wait! Wait! It's the wrong way around!' Neha gestured to the waiters to swivel the trolley so the snapper could get the front of the cake emblazoned with the words 'Happy Birthday My Darling Rakesh' with a stylised '60' below it. He got a last shot before the sparklers died.

Rakesh, microphone in one hand, a tumbler of whisky in the other, faced the crowd. 'My friends, my very, very good friends,' he bayed, slurring his words as he tried to deepen and re-shape his voice, clearly hoping to channel the distinguished accent of Amitabh Bachchan in a futile attempt to sound more sober. 'Welcome and thank you for this wonderful reception. I am now sixty years young!' He raised his glass in a sweeping movement and the whisky swilled and splashed out to the rug below, as he paused for the requisite cheer from the crowd. 'And I can't believe a boy who grew up in the Basanti slum in Kolkata is now standing in this magnificent house on Bishops Avenue with his delightful wife and his accomplished son.'

He slung his thick arm around Neha's waist and pulled her to him. His weight momentarily destabilised her, but she recovered rapidly to enjoy her delight and validation in front of their close, personal friends. 'Come up, son, come up here.'

Arjun, tight-lipped smile painted on, wound his way through the guests to stand next to his father. 'Neha and Arjun,' continued Rakesh, 'You are my rocks. I owe this to you.'

The guests raised their glasses and Arjun slipped away, leaving Neha and Rakesh together, hands entwined.

Anjoli shook her head in disgust and tiptoed to whisper in my ear, 'Pinky Aunty is the one who dragged him out of the slum. Didn't even mention her! And poor Neha, having to endure this shit. Look!'

I followed Anjoli's gaze to settle on Pinky who was to the right of the watching crowd, shooting poisoned darts at her ex-husband and his ex-secretary. 'Let's get out of here and explore the house!' Anjoli whispered.

'I can't go wandering, I have to do waitering,' I whispered back, pointing to the empty tray I had clutched under my arm. 'I've been standing here talking with you for ages. Your dad will notice in a minute.'

'Oh, don't be a bore. No one will miss you. You've only been in England five minutes, you're not integral to the team.'

She grabbed my arm and tried to drag me away as Rakesh said, 'But I have a special announcement to make. Now I am sixty I have decided to move to the next stage of my life – to live a simpler existence.' I saw Neha's face droop as he continued. 'To step back. To spend more time with my beeeyoootiful wife.' He kissed her. 'So, I am going to sell PinRak Industries and all my associated businesses.'

I heard a few faint gasps. Pinky and Arjun were expressionless. Saibal stood stock still, Maya looked puzzled. Neha frowned in confusion but tried hard to keep the smile on her face. A little to the side, I saw Taania Raazia staring at Rakesh, glowing with admiration.

'Yes,' Rakesh continued. 'I will sell these businesses. It is our first anniversary today, so, as a special present to my wife, I am going to set up a charitable foundation in the name of Neha Sharma. We will spend the next thirty years – God willing – giving away my money and doing good. I will start in Basanti in

35

Kolkata. I will make sure ten, twenty, fifty more Rakesh Sharmas come from the slum to make their way in the world.'

The room broke into loud applause as Rakesh embraced
Neha, who now looked stunned. He walked to the trolley,
covered her hand with a hairy fist, cut into the cake, picked
up a big slice with his fingers and stuffed it into Neha's
mouth.

'Neha was hoping for a Birkin!' laughed Anjoli. 'I didn't see
that coming. Charitable work? Rakesh Uncle? I don't believe it.
He literally lives to make money. Poor Neha, she thought he'd
be at work all the time when she married him – now she'll have
him hanging around, cramping her style.'

'Looks like no one else saw this coming either,' I said medita-
tively. 'What's a Birking?'

'Birkin, not Birking. Never mind, forget it. Come ON, let's
explore. I've never seen the entire house, only the bits she
wanted me to see.'

Yet we stuck around for a while longer, as I could see Saibal's
eyes on me, checking I was doing my job. When everything died
down and there was less work for me to do (or pretend to do), we
snuck out of the ballroom and back to the foyer where we
ascended one side of the spectacular double staircase, each step
backlit with LED lighting.

As we reached the landing, she whispered, 'Let's go this way'
and we found ourselves outside an intricately carved teak door
inlaid with mother-of-pearl with a brass sculpted handle. Anjoli
pushed the door, to reveal a room with large windows overlooking the expansive lawn, a massive circular bed against one wall
– once again covered in red velvet – and a chandelier hanging
from the ceiling.

'Ooh, this must be the master bedroom! Whoah. All this gold
is making my eyes go funny. Right, I'm going to raid Neha's
clothes!'

She wandered into a walk-in closet, lined with clothes and a dressing table at one end covered in cosmetics and jewellery boxes. I stayed in the bedroom, feeling out of place, while Anjoli rummaged around and shouted random words at me.

'Louboutins! Stella McCartney!

'This,' she announced triumphantly as she emerged stroking something bright red and shiny, 'is a Birkin! Of *course*, she's got one!' she giggled, before disappearing back inside the closet.

I had no idea what Louboutins were, couldn't be bothered to ask, so I walked around, inspecting and prodding the assorted gadgetry dotted around the room. The opulence of the house, the chatter of the party and my having to keep a fake smile plastered on my face as I served the guests was weighing down on me and I opened a window to get some fresh air. As I breathed in the damp night, two voices wafted upwards. I leaned out and, silhouetted in the amber light of an exterior wall lamp, saw Saibal and Rakesh.

'Enough,' shouted Rakesh, waving a bottle of whisky. 'You do this to me in my house and expect me to be grateful? You expect me to show compassion? This is *all* your fault.'

Saibal murmured something, but I couldn't make out his words.

'No, we are NOT brothers, Saibal! Look, I have said no, and I mean no and if you cared for our friendship, you would not have put me in this position. I cannot believe what you dared to do. At my birthday party! This is *your* problem and you will have to sort it out. I will do what *I* have to do. Now I am going back to my party to enjoy myself.'

He strode back into the house. Saibal lingered, took a deep, thoughtful drag on his cigarette, the glowing tip lighting up his face, then chucked it to the ground and stubbed it out underfoot.

I shut the window as quietly as I could; I didn't want Saibal to know what I had overheard. Anjoli emerged from the walk-in closet wearing red heels that were too big and a bright pink dress that was too long on her.

'Whoah!' I said. 'That's fatafati, Anjoli! Basically amazing! You look great.'

She twirled, floating the dress around her. 'There are certainly benefits to being married to a millionaire. Shall I see if one of Rakesh Uncle's close personal friends wants to be my close personal millionaire?'

'How about the boyfriend?'

'Oh,' she flicked her hair. 'I can have him on the side. Millionaire on Mondays, Wednesdays and Fridays; Italian barista on weekends.'

'And on Tuesdays and Thursdays?'

'A girl's got to have time for herself,' she said, stroking the fabric of her dress. 'God, this stuff is gorgeous. Neha literally has terrible taste in interiors, but she's always dressed well. She's gone from Primark to Prada in twelve months!'

'Come on, let's go,' I urged. I didn't tell Anjoli what I'd overheard – I wasn't sure what it was about, and I figured that Saibal wouldn't want to talk about it. 'I'd better get back to my job.'

'Okay, okay, Mr Boring. Push off while I change back into my exclusive Reiss sample-sale garb.'

It was 1 a.m. The party had wound down; the Tandoori Knights staff and butler had all been dismissed. I was the last 'domestic' left standing, dead on my feet and desperate to go to bed. As I cleared the last of the glasses from the living room, I tried to catch Anjoli's eye, but she was chatting animatedly with Neha, who didn't appear to be listening but was scowling at Rakesh having an intimate tête-à-tête with Taania Raazia, knees touching. Saibal and Maya, conversing in a desultory fashion with Pinky and Arjun opposite, ignored me as well.

I wandered back to the kitchen and finished the last of the washing up, as Anjoli swayed in, carrying a plate of dessert. 'Where's my drink? I need something to wash down Chef's delicious shahi tukda. Come on waiter, get me my champagne.'

I poured a glass of Dom Perignon for her and whisky for myself. She sat in silence, enjoying her milky fried sweet, as I packed the dishes away, stopping every so often for a sip that cost more than I earned in tips in a day. Finally, she gave a satisfied sigh, washed her plate, dried it and handed it to me. She watched me for a second then asked, 'So, how was your first taste of the London high life?'

'Quite a show. Neha's certainly landed on her feet. And you're drunk and falling off your feet,' I gave her a mock-castigatory glare.

'Yes, she did, didn't she? Not that this is my type of place, but it's impressive, I'll give her that.' She took a gulp of her champagne.

'Your barista doesn't have a mansion, then? Starbucks doesn't pay enough?' I said, half thinking of myself and my new status as a waiter.

'Yeah, right. Even if he had one, I'm not sure I'd ever be able to introduce him to Ma and Baba.' She took another morose sip of her drink, leaning against the sink. 'Fuck my life. This isn't how I imagined it would be. A skivvy in a restaurant, sneaking around to see my boyfriend, while my best friend has all this,' she made an extravagant gesture around the kitchen, creating a semi-circle of champagne on the marbled floor. 'I've literally become the cliché of the second-generation Indian girl. I have a bloody Master's. Had a brilliant job, till the bastards made me redundant. Why am I wasting my time with Ma guilt-tripping me to get married? I swear, if I have to meet one more *illegible* suitor, I'll literally throw up.'

'That's Indian mothers, Anjoli. Mine's the same,' I said, experiencing a bout of maudlin self-pity brought on by the whisky, as I remembered how much Ma had loved Maliha. 'Tell me, how many Indian mothers does it take to change a lightbulb?'

'How many?'

'"Don't worry about me, I'll just sit in the dark!"' I said, waggling my head.

She burst into raucous laughter, over-egged by the champagne. 'You *are* funny,' she said. 'It's nice you're staying with us and I have someone I can talk to. Even if you don't talk to me back!'

'What do you mean?'

'Well, it's weird, isn't it? Something obviously happened for you to give up your job, your fiancée, your parents and come from Kolkata to work in Baba's restaurant of all places. But you never talk about it. Not properly, anyway.'

My stomach knotted. 'Yes ... well ... another time. When you're not drunk.'

'See? You're doing it again. Tell me one thing you did in Kolkata. Go on! I dare you!'

'It's in the past now,' I said and thankfully, before she could push any further, the kitchen door opened and Saibal strode in, overcoat over his arm, followed by Maya.

'Anjoli, Kamil. Let's go, the party is finished. It is late and we have work tomorrow,' he said.

Anjoli tore her gaze away from mine then muttered, 'I'll say bye to Rakesh Uncle and Neha.'

'Eh Maa, look at the state of you,' Saibal remonstrated. 'Kamil help her to the car and Anjoli, don't vomit on the way out.'

'You okay, Ma?' asked Anjoli, swaying on the spot.

'I'm exhausted, Anjoli. Come, let's go,' Maya replied.

We followed her parents out of the kitchen, into the living room. Neha was now sitting with Arjun and Pinky, hands clenched, face pale – Pinky had obviously had another go at her. We said our goodbyes, but Neha barely acknowledged us.

'You okay, Neha?' asked Anjoli, concerned, glancing at Pinky and picking her shawl up from where she'd left it on the sofa.

Neha started to say something. But a sharp look and slight shake of the head from Arjun dissuaded her and she replied tonelessly, 'Yes, I am fine. Thanks for coming, Anj. Saibal Uncle, Maya Aunty, I'll see you soon.'

Arjun's phone pinged. He glanced at it, tapped a quick reply, looked at his mother and said, 'Dad.'

'Where's Rakesh Uncle,' asked Anjoli, swaying dangerously now. 'I should say bye to him.'

'I'm not sure,' said Neha, distracted. 'Probably crashed out, asleep.'

Arjun waggled his phone at her and shook his head, but she continued, 'It's okay Anj, you go home to bed, you look like you need it. I'll tell him you said bye. I'll call you tomorrow.'

'Ami Aaschi,' murmured Saibal-da and we left.

'Ami Aaschi' was one of my favourite Bengali phrases. The Bangla equivalent of 'goodbye', it literally meant its opposite – 'I am coming'. We Bengalis said it when we left somewhere, implying we would soon be back. They were the last words Maliha had said to me, though I was fully aware now that *she* was never returning.

It was freezing and bucketing down outside, so we dashed, coats tight around us, to Saibal's old Volvo, which was looking completely out of place next to a shiny Daimler with the number plate R41ESH.

'Ooh, everything is spinning,' mumbled Anjoli.

'Maya, you sit in the back with Anjoli in case she vomits,' said Saibal as he unlocked the car. 'There are carrier bags in the seat pocket.'

I opened the door and pushed aside the detritus on the back seat so that Saibal could bundle Anjoli into the car next to her mother. I got a strong whiff of whisky as I closed the rear door and slid into the front passenger seat.

'Are you okay to drive, Saibal-da? I can drive if you want?' I said, glancing at him, not convinced that I was in a fit state either.

'I am fine. I did not have much to drink. Put on Waze,' he handed me his phone and started the Volvo.

I launched the app as Anjoli's snores filled the car. 'Thik achhé Maya?' asked Saibal, looking in the rear-view mirror as we turned from the drive onto the street. Maya nodded her okay, stroking Anjoli's hair.

'Kamil, how is this girl going to find a husband? You tell me this. Drunk at parties ...' Saibal grumbled.

'Oh, I don't know,' I replied. 'She's pretty special.'

Saibal's phone pinged, amplified through the car speakers.

'What is that? Check, Kamil please?'

I scrolled to his WhatsApp messages. 'It's from Rakesh Sharma.'

'Oh? What is he saying?' asked Saibal.

'Erm ... "I'm sorry. Things shouldn't have come to this my friend. I have made many poor decisions in my life and maybe this is another one. But I don't know what else to do. I don't think anybody can help."' I thought of their conversation in the garden. What was this about?

'He's drunk. Stupid fool.'

'Do you want to talk to him? Shall I call him back?' I asked.

He thought for a second, then shook his head and said, 'It's late, leave it, I can't talk to him when he is drunk. Text that I will call him tomorrow.'

I sent the text as Maya said, 'How much longer, Saibal? Anjoli is not well.'

42

'Half an hour. Look after her,' said Saibal, speeding up through the rain.

The rhythmic slap of the wipers and exhaustion caused me to doze off till the ring of Saibal's phone jerked me awake twenty minutes later. I opened my eyes and saw 'NehaMobile' on his screen. Saibal-da grimaced and muttered, 'Now what?' as he hit 'Accept'.

'Hello?' he bellowed.

Neha's voice splintered the dark silence of the car.

'Come back, I need you! He's dead!'

My mind flew back to a car filled with policemen in Kolkata racing to the murder that had killed my career.

The Detective

Kolkata. July. Monday.

M y team and I tumbled out of the Tata Sumo and ran, sweating, into the cool foyer of the Grand Hotel.

'Where is he?' I barked, believing I would let the side down if I didn't uphold the clichés about rude Kolkata cops.

'Finally, you have come! Abhijit Mitra is my good name, sir,' the man said, ignoring my brusqueness and pointing to the metal name badge on the lapel of his dark blue suit. 'I am the manager. That this could happen at the Grand. The housekeeper who found him is in shock. Anything you need, please ask. You will help keep it discreet, no?'

India's biggest star had just been found dead – I wasn't going to promise anything. 'I'm Rahman. Inspector Rahman,' I said, intentionally dropping the 'Sub'. I needed to be taken seriously today. 'Take me to the room.'

'Of course, sir. Asif is ... *was* in our Presidential Suite. He always stays here when he is filming in Kolkata. Follow me, please.'

Mitra unlocked the door to the suite and waited outside as my forensic and finger-and-footprint squad filled the room, slipping on their bibs and rubber gloves. I followed them, walking past an abandoned housekeeping cart just inside the door, next to a mahogany console table displaying a heavy vase of pink lilies. Picture windows flooded the living room with watery afternoon sunshine giving it an eerily cinematic look, while outside, Kolkata, fresh and green, spread out like an Impressionist painting. A Kashmiri silk carpet, dappled red and gold, covered the polished parquet floor and, right in the centre of the rug, almost as if deliberately positioned for optimum lighting, lay a man's naked corpse, face up.

Bile rose in my throat. This was my first time in sole charge of a homicide and I had to show nothing but complete professionalism. Throwing up at the sight and smell of the body would not be a good start. I pulled myself together and walked over to what was left of Asif Khan.

He was six feet tall, athletic, with a properly defined six pack. His dead eyes stared unseeing at the filigreed wooden fan rotating lazily above. The head was an oily mess, half of his skull crushed, congealed blood clotted into the thick, wavy black hair. I tried to keep calm, to stay focused, even though my heart vibrated inside my chest.

He'd been pushed into a coffee table and shattered glass surrounded him, with great gouts of blood spattering a cream velvet sofa. Two crystal tumblers lay on the floor, along with an empty bottle of Chivas Regal, the whisky spilled out in a golden pool on the parquet. As I got closer to the body, a confusion of smells – acrid alcohol, perfumed lilies and the sour, iron stench of blood assaulted my nostrils. I raised my sleeve to cover my nose and stopped myself retching.

'Bo-ka-cho-da! But this is Asif Khan!' swore Sergeant Hazra, eyes wide with shock as the forensics and FFPS team stared at the corpse. A technician snapped a quick photo on his mobile.

'Hey you, stop that!' I said, glaring at him. 'This is a VIP case and DC Sahib has put me in sole charge. We have to be extra careful, extra fast and extra vigilant. This is confidential! Nothing must leak.'

Hazra gave him an extra glare to show he was backing me up, paan-stained teeth gleaming red, white police uniform threatening to burst open over his ample belly. While Hazra looked the part of the usual lazy, time-serving Kolkata cop, never without a greasy snack in his hand, he was experienced, sharp and loyal. A good man to have on the team.

I leaned over the body gingerly, breathing through my mouth and trying to avoid stepping on the shards of glass. There was a surreal quality to the scene – a huge star like Asif Khan, whom I'd seen punching out villains a few weeks ago, literally larger than life on the immense PVR screen, now lying in front of me, no longer the hero of his own story.

A gold Patek Philippe watch glinted on his wrist. The second hand was still ticking. If only it had smashed at the time of murder and become our first clue – but nothing worked as it did in Agatha Christie novels. Real life was blood, brains and bits of skull in front of a detective focused on keeping his breakfast down.

'Any sign of the murder weapon?' I demanded, trying to avoid the staring eyes and crushed skull.

'Did not see it yet, sir. They hit him many times. Very hard,' said Hazra helpfully.

'Great detective work, Hazra, I'd never have guessed,' I responded to my sergeant. 'Look at that expensive watch. It wasn't a robbery, that would have been the first to go. Ask Mitra if anything is missing from the room.' I walked away from the body to examine the suite, relieved not to have to look at it anymore.

A minute later, Hazra returned with Mitra, who told me, 'There should be a statue of Kali, on the table next to the sofa.' He scanned the room, pointedly avoiding the body in the middle.

'Heavy?' I asked.

'Very,' he responded.

Killed by Kali, I thought. Destroyed by the Goddess of Destruction. Appropriate, in a macabre way.

'Let's assume that was the weapon and the killer took it,' I hazarded. 'The table smashing would have made one hell of a noise. Hazra, when you finish here, interview the guests in the adjoining rooms to see if they saw or heard anything.'

Mitra protested, 'This will cause a scandal, Inspector Sahib. Our guests are very private people!'

'This is a murder investigation. They will have to cope. Do you have CCTV?'

'In the public areas, yes. I will get you the files.'

'Thank you, as fast as possible. Is anyone else from the film staying in the hotel?'

'Only Mr Khan. There was a big party last night. Lots of filmy people. Mrs Khan was here.'

'Sabina Khan?' I asked, immediately interested. The first rule of a murder investigation was always suspect the spouse. The marriage of the King and Queen of Bollywood had been all over the papers a few years ago – *Heartthrob Asif Khan Finally Settles Down*. 'Was she staying with him in this room?'

'No, just him.'

'Where was she staying then?'

'The production company gave a Lake Gardens address for him on his registration. Perhaps she stays there?' said Mitra, trying to be helpful.

Why would Asif Khan have stayed in the hotel, when he had a flat in Kolkata?

'Thank you. I need to interview the housekeeper who found the body. Could you bring her to me please?' He scuttled off as I walked into the master bedroom to find a four-poster bed with gauzy drapes and rumpled sheets. My forensics team were photographing Calvin Klein boxers, socks and shoes strewn on the carpet; an open suitcase shoved to one side of an ottoman near

47

the bed, clothes falling out of it. Something shiny caught my eye – two torn condom wrappers – Kohinoor Xtra time ... Asif Khan didn't have any Xtra time now.

'Twice in one night, sir! Asif Khan was a real stud!' Hazra winked as he bagged them.

'Hazra, be serious,' I snapped. 'So that's why he wasn't staying at home, he was here with someone else.' I shone my torch under the bed, the dust-moted beam catching something that looked like a slim paperback. I pulled it out with a gloved hand to see Gandhi grinning up at me from a pristine brick of a hundred two-thousand-rupee notes.

I whistled, riffling through the bundle. 'Two lakhs! I assume the culprit missed it. Follow the sex and the money, Hazra – that's the first rule of police work. Have this checked for prints. And when everyone is done here, send the body for the post-mortem – I want experienced doctors for this one.' I'd been shocked by my visit to a post-mortem hospital during the last murder case I'd worked on. Bodies lying everywhere in the refrigerated room, some stacked on top of each other, sometimes more than one on a stretcher. Some looked as if they hadn't been touched in months. When I'd joined the homicide division, Abba had drummed into me, 'First rule of police work, get a good PM doctor. The bad ones miss things all the time and you will be on a monkey chase.'

There was a knock on the door and Mitra entered with a young woman who looked Nepali. 'Inspector, this is the maid who found him.'

She stood in the vestibule, hands clasped in front of her, eyes fixed on her feet. 'Her mother is my sister,' he added, as if this explained everything. 'You speak to the Inspector, tell him what you saw. Don't be scared.'

'Yes, Uncle,' she whispered.

I walked her and Mitra to the corridor outside the room – not only was it obvious the scene was making her nervous, I also didn't want to contaminate the evidence any further. 'Tell me how you discovered the body.'

'I did housekeeping at eleven o'clock, Sir. There was no DND on the handle, so I knocked. No answer, so I entered and … and …' she shivered, nails digging into the palms of her hands.

'It's okay, just tell me.'

'He was lying there, Sir. With no clothes. Eyes open. And the blood … so much blood … Has someone closed his eyes?'

I knew what she meant. His stare was haunting me too. Her breathing quickened as she relived the trauma.

'Don't worry about that. What did you do next?' I asked.

'I screamed and ran out, told Uncle and he told me to wait and …' she subsided.

'And then you came to the room?' I asked Mitra.

'Yes,' he replied. 'I touched nothing. Such a terrible sight. I phoned one-zero-zero and they told me someone would be here at once. But that was hours ago. You took so long!' He looked accusingly at me, but I had rushed to the hotel as quickly as the Kolkata traffic had allowed me.

'What time did you call?'

'Around eleven.' I checked my watch. 2.13 p.m. He was right. It had been *much* too long, especially for a hi-pro case.

'Did you tell the Control Room it was Asif Khan who was dead?' I asked.

'No, just that someone had murdered one of our guests.'

Another oddity. A murder at the Grand would have had New Market cops all over it like flies on raw meat. Lalbazar handled hi-pro crimes, but how were New Market aware that it was hi-pro if Mitra hadn't mentioned Asif Khan? Were all murders at a place like the Grand now automatically considered hi-pro?

Tears started to leak from the maid's eyes. Mitra gave her his handkerchief and said, 'Can she go now, Inspector?' I nodded and texted the DC an update: *Making progress sir. Checking CCTV and going to interview wife of deceased.*

I needed to see Sabina Khan – India's sweetheart, Asif Khan's celebrity wife and … murderer?

* * *

'Madam, I am very sorry to report that Shri Asif Khan is dead.'

'Madam Sabina, I am sorry to say someone has murdered your husband.'

'Madam, I am sad to say your husband had his head bashed in with a Kali statue while having sex in his hotel room.'

Maybe not that last one, I thought wryly, as I rehearsed in the car how to tell Sabina that her husband had been killed, never having had to break this type of news. If she was his murderer, it wouldn't be news to her, of course. It was possible she had found Asif with someone after the party and, in a fit of rage, killed him. I needed to tread carefully and make sure I picked up any false notes.

Just as we arrived at Sabina Khan's apartment, I received a text message from Abba. My message to him had been short – discreet, but meaningful. *They have put me on a hi-pro case. Top secret for now. DC Ghosh asked for me specifically!*

Abba's message was similarly brief: *Congratulations, son!*

That single word meant the world to me, for Abba was parsimonious with his praise. Then, as always, I chastised myself – a thirty-year-old shouldn't care so much what his father thought of him.

Yet the smile remained on my face as the security guard escorted me up to Asif Khan's flat and I had to make a conscious effort to shake it off. When the guard rang the bell, to my surprise Sabina Khan herself opened the penthouse door – the luminous actress who had melted hundreds of millions of hearts (including mine) across India for years. She stood there, elegant with her short black hair, dressed in a blue churidar-kurta. I opened my mouth to speak, but words escaped me and I gawped like a star-struck teenager.

Used to having this reaction on people, she raised a shaped eyebrow. 'Yes?'

I pulled myself together as best as I could, fumbled my ID out of my pocket and cleared my throat. 'Um … Mrs Khan? I am Sub-Inspector Kamil Rahman. I am sorry to disturb you at home, but can I come in? I need to speak with you on a sensitive matter. Would you like a friend or a female policewoman present?'

'It's fine. What's this about?' she asked, examining my ID and handing it back.

'Perhaps we could sit?'

She looked at me for a moment, decided that I was no threat, then stepped aside to let me in.

The interior was a curated combination of heritage pieces from the East and understated luxury from the West. Lush Persian carpets, Bikaneri chests and Hyderabadi wooden screens lay side by side with luxurious Italian sofas and Swedish tables.

Sabina led me to a living room overlooking the lake. I needed to compose myself before breaking the news so walked over to the window to look through the sheets of rain now coming down. Rabindra Sarovar lay underneath us, green-grey water undulating as storm clouds lowered overhead, the watery lights of cars crawling down the road far below and tiny black umbrellas bobbing and weaving on the pavements.

She cleared her throat and I reluctantly tore my eyes away from Kolkata at its most stunning. My next words would change her life forever. After this moment, it would always be 'before

Asif died' and 'after'; the responsibility was too much to bear. She gestured for me to sit and sipped at a cup of tea.

I took a deep breath and dove in.

'I'm afraid I have terrible news, Sabina Madam.'

'What?' she said, warily.

I wanted to shut my eyes as I told her so that I wouldn't see the pain my words would inflict. But I had to see her reaction. I gazed at her levelly. 'I'm sorry to say that your husband, Mr Asif Khan, has been found dead.'

Her eyes widened in shock. She put the cup down, rattling the saucer.

'What ... what did you say?' she whispered.

'A maid found his body at the Grand. We believe he died last night.'

She raised a hand to her mouth. 'Died! Last night? But it can't be. I *saw* him last night.'

'I'm very sorry, Madam. My deepest condolences for your loss.' My words were inadequate. Her pain appeared real and I doubted she was a suspect – but then again, she was an actress. An excellent one at that.

She stood and turned away, blinking back tears. I handed her a napkin and she took it, twisting it in her hand, staring blindly out of her window.

'What happened? Heart attack?' she asked in a muffled voice, not looking at me.

I couldn't bring myself to tell her the details. 'Not a heart attack, Sabina Madam.'

She nodded. My heart reached out to her and I hated myself for causing such grief. 'Then what?' she asked. She turned to look at me, eyes red.

'Evidence suggests he was murdered.'

And there it was. The word hung in the air, almost visible in the rain-darkened room.

'Murdered?' she whispered. She was quiet for a few seconds then gave a single shake of her head and sat, mute, hands folded in her lap, wedding ring glinting.

'We're doing everything we can to find out what happened to your husband. And I'm sorry to have to ask this at such a hard time, but would you mind answering a few questions?'

She nodded.

'Thank you,' I said. 'When did your husband check into the hotel?'

She looked like she might let out a sob but swallowed it. 'Asif and I arrived from Mumbai yesterday. He was shooting here for his next movie.'

'Are you in the film too?' I said, attempting to find a neutral topic to begin my interrogation.

'No.' She paused, looked blankly at the cup in her hand, then took a sip of tea. 'I don't act anymore,' she continued. 'I used to, that's how I met Asif. We made *Saavdhan*, fell in love on set and got married. After marriage, I gave up acting at his request.'

The entire country knew this, but I nodded encouragingly, glad she was talking, hoping she would continue. 'I saw *Saavdhan*, you were superb.'

'Thank you.' She downed the dregs of her tea and poured another cup, hand shaking.

'And how long have you been married?'

'Two years.' I scribbled in my notepad.

'And how was your relationship?'

Silence. I looked up. 'I'm sorry, Sabina Madam, these are intimate questions, but I need answers to everything.'

She let out a sigh. 'Our relationship was … normal. We had difficulties like everyone.'

I thought of the condoms in the hotel room and the story they told. This was the opening I needed.

'Sabina Madam, I believe that there was a party at the Grand for the film. May I ask why he was staying at the hotel instead of here at home?'

Another pause. She looked away. 'Asif liked his privacy when he was shooting. His hours were erratic. He didn't like to keep me up at night,' she said, finally.

'And did you visit his room in the hotel?'

'No.'

'I see. Would it be all right to take your fingerprints for elimination purposes? I can send my sergeant to your home.'

She half shrugged, half nodded.

'And what were your movements last night, Sabina Madam?'

She stood up, placing her cup of tea down as she did so. She walked around the room, straightening pens and paper on a writing desk by the window. Was she giving herself time to come up with an answer? I couldn't imagine this graceful and poised woman raising a heavy metal statue and smashing her husband's head in. But my lack of imagination didn't mean she was innocent.

'I was at the party, but I must have gone home at,' her eyes darted to her left, which Abba always told me meant the person was telling the truth … I would wait to see. '… midnight,' she responded after a moment. 'I was tired and couldn't stay longer, but Asif was the star, so he had to.'

'And how was he when you left?'

'He was drinking a lot. I asked him to slow down, but … you can't … could not … ever tell Asif anything.'

'Was he spending time with anyone in particular at the party?'

'Not that I saw.'

'And he was still there when you went home?'

'I think so. I'm not certain when he left. Or with whom. There was a videographer there. The producers can get you the video.'

'Was there anyone he might have invited back to his room? We believe he was … not alone.'

She betrayed no emotion, appearing not to care. 'I don't know.'

It was time to press harder. 'I'm sorry to say this Sabina Madam, but there *was* someone with him in his room. Was he having an affair?'

Now it was out there, I couldn't take it back. She said nothing, looking down at her lap. The silence lengthened. I needed to be even more explicit.

'We found empty condom wrappers at the crime scene.'

Still no discernible reaction. She looked away and said tonelessly, 'What Asif does or doesn't do is none of my business. As I said, I let him have his privacy.'

I wasn't getting anywhere with this line of questioning so changed tack. 'We found a sizeable amount of money in his room. Was he in the habit of carrying a lot of cash?'

Her head swung around. 'How much?' she asked.

'I'm afraid I can't give you specifics, but it was substantial,' I said.

It was clear that it was this revelation about money, as opposed to Asif having an affair, that interested her. 'I don't know where that could have come from,' she said. 'After demonetisation we have not kept much cash at all. What has happened to the money?'

'It's being held in evidence,' I replied. 'It'll be released to you once we conclude the case.'

She nodded abruptly. 'I don't think I can answer any more questions. Please … leave.'

And then the dam broke. She turned away from me, shoulders heaving as she tried to stop herself from crying in front of me. I wanted to put my arms around her, comfort her, tell her it would be all right but the detective in me held me back. And … she was Sabina Khan.

I quietly said that I'd be in touch, then let myself out, silently closing the door behind me. As I took the lift down, I mulled over what I'd learned. She had been genuinely distressed about Asif's death, but something felt off. Her lack of reaction to her husband sleeping around, the interest in the money. Did she know more than she was letting on? What next? Get hold of the CCTV to confirm that she had indeed left the party at midnight. And to make sure that she hadn't come back.

The Waiter

London. October. Sunday.

The air around the swimming pool was stifling after the icy rain outside and I took a breath sharp with chlorine to regain my composure. Saibal approached his friend's body with trepidation and stood over it, eyes wide in distress. He was breathing hard, muttering something, hands shaking. I placed a hand on his shoulder both to comfort him and steady myself, but he shook it off and mumbled, 'He cannot be dead. Not Rakesh.' He bent over the damp body, feeling for a heartbeat under Rakesh's jacket.

Squatting, he closed his eyes and whispered a prayer, tears squeezing past his eyelids. He wiped them with a sleeve, leaned over, put a palm on Rakesh's cheek and closed his unseeing eyes. He stood, calmer. 'He is no more. How did this happen?'

I entered cop mode and crouched by the body, peering at the lacerated skull with the leaking blood and noticing another smear of blood on the tiles at the corner of the pool above the water.

'It looks like he was standing here, then fell, smashing his head on the pool edge. Who pulled him out?'

'I did,' Arjun said, shivering as he rubbed at the blood on his soggy sleeve. 'Neha found him and screamed the house down. He was lying face up in the water. I dragged him out, tried to do

CPR. His head ... blood everywhere.' He looked away from the body.

That explained Arjun's wet jacket. He appeared fit, but it would have been an effort to pull his father's dead body, both of them in water-logged clothes, out of the water. In the pool, tiny rivulets of blood dripped from the curved lip of the pool edge into the blue water, creating swirls of mauve, which, like everything else in this godawful garish house, was backlit by underwater LEDs. Then I spotted something at the bottom of the pool.

It was a high-heeled shoe and next to it, a broken whisky bottle, dark against the sky-blue tiles. I leaned back and heard a crunch under my heel – fragments of glass. I berated myself – I was contaminating the crime scene, if it was, as I suspected, a homicide. The pair of the shoe in the water, bright red sole gleaming under the lights, lay at the side of the pool surrounded by broken glass.

I remembered the shards of the table that had haloed Asif Khan's body. What did the glass here mean?

'The bottle,' Saibal said, following my gaze. 'The bloody fool was drunk. That's why he slipped. What was he doing here? He only messaged me a little while ago.'

'When?' Arjun asked.

'Thirty-forty minutes ago? Just after we left.'

'What did it say? He WhatsApp'd me too just before you left.'

I remembered Arjun getting the message as we were saying our goodbyes to Neha.

Saibal read the message out to Arjun. 'Could it have been suicide? Eh Maa! After what happened?' he whispered.

'I doubt it,' I said, circumnavigating the pool. 'No one commits suicide by throwing themselves into a swimming pool. It's unlikely to kill you.'

Arjun turned to me, still in my waiter's uniform, and scrutinised me from top to bottom.

'Who *are* you?' he asked, abruptly.

'I'm a friend of Saibal-da's.'

'You're a waiter, right? How have you suddenly become a CSI expert?'

'I am – was – a detective. In the Kolkata Police. Homicide squad,' I said, calmly removing my bowtie and stuffing it into my pocket.

He gave me a hard stare, then turned back to Saibal.

'He must have died just after he sent the messages,' he said.

'What did his WhatsApp to you say?' asked Saibal.

'Similar to yours. He was sorry. I wasn't sure what he meant and now I can't … ask him.'

His voice broke.

'Has anyone seen his phone?' I asked.

Arjun shook his head.

'Any other exits from this basement?' I continued, as the doorbell rang.

'I'm not answering any more of your questions. That will be the *real* police.'

Arjun and Saibal left to answer it. I started to follow them up the stairs then stopped. Was this my chance? To use the skills I had been trained for and not just be a useless waiter? I knew these people, had been at the party. Maybe I'd seen or heard something that could help crack the case. I'd have to hurry before the 'real police' sealed the scene. I wouldn't get another chance as they were unlikely to share any of their findings with me.

Yes, I could redeem myself after what I had done in Kolkata. Get justice for Rakesh. This was exactly what was necessary to pull me out of the desolation that had sucked me in for the previous three months.

Decision made, I took my phone and photographed the broken whisky bottle in the water, the shoes, the shards of glass on the edge and the blood around the pool. Rumpled towels covered a deckchair and I saw something obscured under one of them. I lifted the cloth with my phone to reveal a paper-thin shiny black metal disc, an inch across, with a hole at one end. I didn't know what it was but photographed it, then turned back to Rakesh's corpse.

I shone my phone's torch at the wound on his head and saw glints of glass. My instincts had been right. This wasn't an accident: someone had hit him with the bottle. His right fist was clenched. If this were a detective story, there would be a clue in his grasp, I thought, smiling inwardly. I glanced at the entrance to the pool to see if anyone was coming, then prised open the fingers, trying to control my abhorrence at having to touch him. Luckily, rigor mortis hadn't set in yet. And, to my surprise, in the palm of his hand was a gold ring with a sparkling blue stone. Sometimes real life *was* akin to a detective story. I took a quick snap with my phone and closed his fingers back over the ring. It looked as it had before, so hopefully I wouldn't have sent the SOCO people haring off in the wrong direction.

I wrapped a small towel around my hand and patted the body down. There was something hard in the inside pocket of his suit. I delicately pulled out the iPhone I had been looking for, holding it by the edges so as not to contaminate the evidence. I stared at the damp, black screen for a second as I remembered the strange messages Rakesh had sent Saibal and Arjun. Had he called or texted anyone else? This phone might well hold the secret of the murder. Should I check? I knew I shouldn't touch it but … screw it! I had to finish my investigation of the crime scene before the cops arrived. They would share no forensics and I wanted, *needed*, a shot at solving this murder.

I recklessly threw the towel off my hand and pressed the home button, which took me to a lock screen with a picture of Neha. I typed in the previous day's date on to the wet screen on the off-chance Rakesh had used his birthday as a passcode ... no luck. That would have been too easy. I thought for a second, subtracted sixty from the current year and entered the year of Rakesh's birth. Bingo! It opened and took me straight to Whats-App, showing the last message sent had been to Saibal's phone at 02.12 with my reply a minute later, with two blue ticks showing it had been received and read. Ten minutes earlier was the message to Arjun, a terse *Sorry for this mess* with a single thumbs-up emoji from Arjun, also received and read. As I heard voices approaching, I regretted my rashness – my fingerprints were now on the phone and I'd have to inform the police. Just three months had passed since I'd left the force and I was losing the training that had been ingrained into me. As I put the phone back where I'd found it, my arm brushed the back of Rakesh's head, blood staining my waiter's uniform. Great. I was going from impetuous to inept. My fingerprints on the phone, blood on my sleeve and glass under my shoe – I'd be the ideal suspect. Lucky I hadn't been here when he died.

Two police officers, led by Arjun, walked into the pool area and stopped when they saw me standing next to the body.

'What the bloody hell are you still doing here?' shouted Arjun.

'All right, sir, we'll handle this. And you are ...?' said the policewoman in charge.

'Kamil Rahman,' I said, shaking her hand. I could tell she had noticed the blood on my sleeve. 'I used to be a police officer,' I said. 'I was just checking out the crime scene.'

'I see,' she said. 'I'm DI Campbell and this is PC Harris from Kentish Town nick. Which force were you in?'

'Oh, I was with the Kolkata Police. I'm here on holiday,' I said feeling inadequate and not wanting to mention I was now a waiter. Especially one working without a visa.

She hesitated for a second then nodded. 'Thank you, sir, please stay clear of the area.'

I watched as Harris put on surgical rubber gloves, checked for a pulse, then tried CPR, compressing Rakesh's chest and breathing into his mouth as Arjun looked away, blinking back tears. Harris gave Campbell a quick shake of his head. Must be standard procedure to check for signs of life, I thought, Rakesh was clearly dead.

He murmured into his radio 'IC-4 male, sixties, no signs of life, 0316 hours. Please inform LAS, SOCO and on duty CID. Sharma Manor, Bishops Avenue. Please inform Duty Officer, Inspector Campbell.'

'Yeah control,' said Campbell into her radio, 'Duty Officer on scene and informed.'

My interest quickened. I wasn't sure why Harris had asked his control centre to inform Campbell when Campbell was standing right there. I assumed that they were trying to ensure a clean record of which policemen were at the scene. Not something we bothered with in Kolkata.

We moved to the living room, where it seemed their interviews would begin.

Arjun paced up and down in front of his mother, who was sitting on the edge of an armchair, nervously wringing the end of her sari. Neha was slumped on the sofa, sniffling into a handkerchief, legs tucked under her, leaning on Saibal. There was a large Elastoplast on the heel of her left foot, but I noted there were no shoes lying around. Inspector Campbell broke the silence. 'We appreciate this is a difficult time for you.'

Harris walked in and said to Campbell, 'Area secured.'

'I always told him those tiles were dangerous,' said Arjun. 'There's no grip anywhere and he was wearing his black leather shoes, which would have made it worse. But Neha wanted the Italian look and ...'

'Yes,' A horrified realisation came over Neha. 'It's true. It's my fault! I wanted a pool.'

'Excuse me officer, but can we go? I don't live here. My son and I were just here for the party,' Pinky butted in.

'I'm afraid not. We must question everyone present.'

'Okay, well. *This* is what you need to know,' fumed Pinky. 'I am certain this was not accident. You mark my words. This was no accident. Giving his money away. Suddenly he has become a bhakt? All holy. Holier than you. Charity in *her* name. Most charitable thing he ever did was marrying her. She was just a secretary, officer. A rubbish secretary also. Got his appointments wrong. He told me. Bending over him in her low-cut dress every day as she gave him his papers, so he almost became blind. Then he die-vorces me. And gives her this horrible house. Have you ever seen anything more ugly, officer? Why else would she marry him but for his money?'

Campbell had pulled her notebook out just in time and had been frantically making notes throughout this irate speech. She now tried to interrupt, saying, 'Please stay calm, Ma'am, we will take a formal statement later,' but Pinky was in full flow, not caring who was listening. I felt genuinely sorry for Neha, sitting mortified in the corner with Saibal, having to listen to this ugly tirade.

'Her father was a shopkeeper. You think she knows what to do with a house like this? Sits in the pool in her bikini all day long.' She took a breath and continued. 'But Rakesh was a wonderful man, officer. She led him astray. He loved his son. And me. He would have become tired of her and realised proper family is what matters. And left her with nothing. We named PinRak for me and Rakesh – not her!'

She lowered her voice a couple of decibels to what she believed was a whisper but was barely a couple of decibels quieter. 'You check what she did. She found him. When he made his speech, she knew it was all over. So, she pushed him in the pool. And she just admitted it was her fault! You check, Inspector. Check carefully. Now I am going home!'

She marched out of the room, followed by Arjun as Harris ran after them saying, 'Wait, Madam. We have to take your son's statement as well . . .'

Neha let out a loud sob as I considered what Pinky had just said. Yes, Neha might have a motive, but did Pinky and Arjun have one too? Rakesh marrying Neha must have dented their fortunes and if Rakesh was going to sell PinRak and put his money in the name of Neha's charity, what did that mean for what Arjun might inherit? Had he taken pre-emptive action to ensure that this wouldn't happen?

The inspector interrupted my line of thinking as she turned to me and Saibal. 'Excuse me, were you here at the time of death?'

'No, we had left. Neha called me, so we came back,' Saibal said. 'It may be best to go home. Please leave your details with my colleague, and we'll be in touch to interview you soon.'

I couldn't delay this any longer, I had to tell the Inspector what I had found.

'May I speak with you, Inspector?' I asked and she nodded.

'As I said, I used to be a detective and I'm afraid I entered auto-pilot mode when I got here. I saw glass in his wound and there was a strange, shiny object on a deckchair. I also noted a ring in his hand and his phone in his pocket. I'm afraid I touched the phone and am happy to provide my prints for elimination. I don't believe this was an accident. He was there with someone.'

'Taania Raazia . . .' an involuntary whisper came from Neha on the sofa. I looked back at her, my eyes narrowing, wondering if she had let something slip. A motive? As the thought struck me, I could see the realisation cross Neha's own face and she turned away. I continued, 'It was his sixtieth birthday party. There were lots of guests. I am happy to help in any way I can.'

The inspector looked at me severely, making me uncomfortable about my waiter's uniform. 'If you were in the force, you should have known not to interfere with the crime scene, sir. You have done enough damage and need to be careful we don't bring charges against you. You can leave now.'

She was right. I had behaved like a Mickey Mouse cop, just out of training. The body was barely cold, and I had already messed up the investigation. Not only that, if Campbell followed through and did bring some kind of charge against me for obstructing justice, I was toast. I'd be thrown out of the country and that would be that. I felt like throwing up at my recklessness. And for what? To prove myself to whom? What had I been thinking?

I barely heard as the inspector turned to Neha. 'Now, Mrs Sharma, is your home equipped with security cameras?'

And I was back in the Grand, interrogating Mitra about the missing CCTV footage.

The Detective

Kolkata. July. Monday.

'Mitra, obstructing the police is a grave crime. I can have you arrested,' I said, pouncing on the manager who had refused to show Hazra the CCTV footage of the night of the party. 'Now produce the video at once!'

'Sir, sir,' squealed Mitra, eyes darting as he smiled weakly at the guests milling around the hotel lobby, staring over at us. 'I'm sorry but it is out of my hands. We have only just now found out about this fault.'

'Show me,' I said, shoving him to show I meant business.

I didn't believe in coincidences. In Kolkata crime, coincidences were invariably the result of a hidden hand tipping the scales and the 'mysterious' disappearance of the hotel's CCTV footage was no exception. Mitra led me, Hazra in tow, from the opulent lobby to a small office behind the reception desk. He pushed a stack of folders out of his way, logged onto a PC and scrolled through a lengthy list of files.

'See, sir. The system records continuously and saves to the Network Video Recorder.' He clicked at random on a file. 'This is Saturday, July eighth, one p.m. Camera Three in the lift, sir.' A silent overhead video of a man gazing blankly forward, picking his nose played. 'But the recordings stop on Sunday night. Ninth July. Look, sir.'

I leaned across and peered at the screen, then grabbed the mouse and clicked on the last file on the list – two guests sitting in the lobby having a drink.

'Did something happen to your system?' I asked, suspicion and disbelief dripping from my voice. He looked away from me.

'It stopped recording at midnight. The disc must have got full or something. I am not a computer expert. But sometimes it happens.'

I didn't believe a word of it. A squirrelly fellow who couldn't even meet my eyes had replaced the extremely capable and helpful manager from the morning. He was hiding something.

'Are you telling me the truth?'

He nodded his head frantically.

'Mitra, if I discover you're behind this, you will be in the lockup in five seconds. Lying to a detective is a very serious crime. Who else has access to this computer?'

'Anybody sir. It just sits here. We don't have a full-time guard watching.'

I slapped the table in frustration. 'Right. I'm impounding your NVR drive. Hazra, unplug it and sort out the forms.'

'Oh, but Inspector Sahib, I can't do that,' protested Mitra. 'It is not allowed. I will call the technician to fix it, but we need our security.'

'What security, Mitra?' I jabbed my finger at him. 'Someone murders a superstar in your Presidential Suite and your CCTV malfunctions at the same time. I am taking this drive for testing. Give me the password. If you want to protest further, you can do it at the station. Is that clear?'

He appeared to be about to demur, then bowed his head, muttered 'CCTVpassword' and walked out.

With Mitra out of earshot, Hazra unplugged the drive and turned to me. 'Very preliminary post-mortem result is that Asif Khan died of heart failure,' he announced.

'Heart failure?' I asked, surprised.

'*Everybody* dies because their heart stops,' he cackled as I groaned – how had I fallen for that stale gag? 'But actual cause of death was battery with a metal object before heart failure, they are doing more detailed analysis. I got it fast-tracked,' he said hurriedly as I shook my head at his inappropriate joking. 'We have the evidence analysis. Lots of chance prints in the room, but that was expected in a hotel. None on the whisky glasses or bottle, someone wiped them. But two sets of prints on the two-lakh bundle – one Asif's and one unknown. And the same unknown prints on the condom wrappers. A prostitute? We found no used condoms. Probably flushed.' He could barely contain his excitement. 'And sir, they found cocaine on the broken table. *And* I got the video from the party.' He reached into his shoulder bag and triumphantly pulled out a USB stick, handing it to me with a proud smile.

Unknown fingerprints, that was something. For the umpteenth time I bemoaned the fact India had no National DNA database, so testing was pointless. The number of DNA samples Kolkata Police had on hand was pitiful.

'Ok, get elimination prints from Sabina Khan and Mitra.' I could see Hazra perk up at the mention of Sabina Khan. I'd better make sure there was a female constable present, if only to stop Hazra embarrassing himself. 'Anything from the interviews?' I continued.

'Yes, sir. The hotel guest next to the Presidential suite heard shouting and a crashing noise at around quarter to two in the morning. He thought of calling reception but then fell back to sleep. Must have been the table breaking. Nobody else heard or saw anything – the night manager did not notice anyone leave. Search of premises did not produce the Kali statue.' He stood grinning like a dog expecting a treat. I clapped him on the back. He had done well.

'Excellent work, Hazra. Was it a man or woman he heard?'

'He couldn't tell, sir,' said Hazra, mournfully. 'It was muffled, he said.'

That would have been way too easy. Someone from the party had gone back to Asif's room. But who? Sabina said it wasn't her and didn't appear to be bothered at the thought of Asif cheating. Was it because she knew already and had sorted out the problem by killing him, or that she didn't want to implicate herself by showing anger? I touched the USB stick in my pocket – this might offer a clue.

Back at Lalbazar, we made our way to the Cyber Crime Cell where Ashutosh, our Cyber Crime analyst, oblivious to the world in oversized headphones, was tapping away furiously at his laptop, wearing the usual Metallica T-shirt that barely covered his belly. He started as Hazra banged the CCTV drive on his desk.

'Hi Ash,' I said cheerily. 'Air conditioning gone again?'

'Load-shedding. Generator can't cope. Crap for my equipment,' he murmured, hanging his headphones around his sweaty neck, not looking up from his laptop. 'What can I do for you, my man?'

Ashutosh was one of the few buddies I had in the force. We had become friends after meeting on a training course two years ago, bonding over beers and a shared love of U2 and Kanye. We sealed our friendship one drunken karaoke night at Veronica's Bar & Kitchen (never to be spoken of again) bawling out 'Where the Streets Have No Name'. It was lucky that I needed his technical ability, not his inability to carry a tune.

I perched on the edge of his desk under the antiseptic, buzzing tube light and fanned myself with a well-thumbed copy of *Raga to Rock*, as Hazra collapsed in a chair, wiping the sweat from his forehead with a grubby handkerchief. 'I need a couple of urgent favours from you, Ash.' I leaned forward. 'The DC's asked me to run the investigation into the Asif Khan murder.'

Saying those words still felt good. 'This NVR drive has CCTV footage of the night but the hotel manager tells me there was a malfunction. It stopped recording just before the killing. Which seems convenient for them. Can you take a look at it, please, to see if it has been corrupted or if someone wiped it?' I waved the USB stick at him, 'And I must examine the footage on here.'

Ashutosh snatched his precious magazine from me, handed me a laptop and fiddled with the CCTV drive. I plugged the stick in and sat back to watch the video with Hazra. The USB footage hadn't been edited and comprised long clips of the party at different times and locations. There were several hours of it, the videographer had been busy.

'Fast forward to find Asif,' I told Hazra, who was surprisingly adept at using the laptop, given he looked like someone to whom a calculator might be alien technology. He sped through the video, and we soon clocked Asif, dressed in a plaid shirt and jeans, dancing.

'Stop,' I said. Hazra paused the film to a still of Asif, mid-gyration.

'Did we find those clothes he's wearing – that shirt and jeans?' I asked.

Hazra scanned the inventory he had made in his notebook. 'No, sir, nothing like that.'

'Odd. They should have been in his hotel room. The killer must have taken them. Probably to conceal incriminating evidence,' I ruminated. 'Okay, keep going.'

We spotted a clip of Sabina Khan in a pink dress, champagne in hand. 'When you see Mrs Khan, ask to see that dress. If she is our killer, it may have traces from the crime scene.'

We continued inspecting the video, Hazra more focused on star-spotting than looking for suspicious behaviour ('That Taania Raazia is mirchi hot, Sir').

Then I spotted something. 'Wait,' I said. 'Play that one again.'

As the camera panned the dance floor, it caught ten seconds of Asif in profile at a table towards the back, deep in conversation with a man, one hand on Asif's arm, the other jabbing a finger at his face. The man was in the shadows, but looked familiar, though I couldn't place him. I paused the video. 'Who is that?'

'I don't know, sir.'

'Doesn't look too friendly. They look like they're arguing. Try to get sound and ... '

Ashutosh interrupted. 'The NVR is functioning fine, Kamil. No sign of any corruption. Someone erased the footage.'

Now we were getting somewhere.

'Can you restore it?'

'I think so, but it will take time.'

'For a computer genius like you, Ash? I thought you were supposed to be good at this stuff!'

'Yeah, yeah, go back to your traffic duty,' he said, fingers flying over the keyboard.

The CCTV must have captured the murderer – why else would someone erase it? This was excellent – I had something I could tell the DC, only a few hours after he had given me the case.

'It's urgent, Ash. Asif Khan's killer may be on that CCTV footage. Please restore it and tell me when you do. Hazra, you log the clips in the party video, identify everyone dancing with Asif. We need to question whoever he was in contact with. Find out who was the last person to see him. I'm off to report to the boss.'

The DC looked tired as I saluted. 'Ah, Rahman, good, you are here. What news?'

I updated him on everything we had found – my speculation about the motives and the missing CCTV footage, which I hoped were only moments away from being magically restored by Ash.

He nodded. 'Outstanding work. Any suspects?'

'Our next aim is to find out who accompanied Asif Khan to his room. The hotel manager has raised doubts in my mind – I believe he may have erased the footage himself, but I can't yet work out his motive. The killer stole nothing from the room, and I don't see any prior connection between Mitra and Asif Khan. Also ...' I hesitated, trying to find the right words, 'there are slight oddities about the behaviour of Mr Khan's wife.'

'Remember, she is grieving,' he responded. 'Don't overthink it. But well done. We need a fast result, Rahman. There is intense pressure from my seniors to wrap this up before the media get hold of it and starts making all manner of speculations. Tell me whatever you need, and I will facilitate it – people, equipment ...'

As he dismissed me, I yawned and looked at my watch. It had been a long day and I was late for dinner with Maliha. I texted Hazra to tell him to update me if anything else came in, then headed off to see my fiancée. I couldn't wait to tell her how my career had been jump-started and was now racing towards the summit.

The Waiter

London. October. Sunday.

My mind was in overdrive. I remembered the early excitement of the Asif Khan case, the thrill of those first clues, piecing the scene together like a jigsaw ... before each piece smashed into a thousand fragments. But the Rakesh Sharma killing was different to any case I'd worked on before. I wasn't a police officer anymore, just a waiter. I had no official standing to question anyone and, even if someone were prepared to speak to me, it was unlikely Saibal would give me the time off I needed to investigate this murder.

I did have a few clues to get started. The tension between Neha and Pinky, Neha and Arjun. Saibal and Rakesh. Neha's shoe in the pool, her cut foot. The ring in Rakesh's hand. The shards of glass in the wound ... surely, I could put them together? But ... Campbell had told me not to interfere and I couldn't afford to get on the wrong side of the authorities.

Well, she couldn't stop me speculating. I presumed there had been an argument – Rakesh had pulled the ring off the killer's finger and fallen into the pool after being hit. So, the murderer was a woman. The evening's revelations had given both Neha or Pinky a motive. But there was only a ten-minute window between Rakesh's WhatsApp to Saibal and Neha finding the body so whoever murdered him had either been very lucky or very skilled.

And where was Taania Raazia when Rakesh died? Something about her niggled. Was it just a coincidence that she was at Rakesh's birthday do, when the last time I'd seen her she had been dancing with Asif Khan on the video footage of his party? I didn't like coincidences. Rich, powerful men seemed to drop dead like mosquitoes when she was around. What could her motive be? And why did Neha let slip that Taania was at the swimming pool with Rakesh? And Rakesh's decision to give his money away … what was behind that? Money. It always came down to money. And sex. The first rule of policing. How did it fit here? Who would have inherited Rakesh's fortune before he gave it to charity? Arjun? Neha? Was that why he was killed?

Nervous exhaustion allowed me a few hours of restless sleep before I woke at nine with a raging thirst, the events of the previous night still racing around like rats in my skull. I heaved myself out of bed and made my way to the kitchen where Anjoli was propped up on the table, head in hands, moaning to herself. Her crumpled T-shirt proclaimed *I Know I'm Worth It* and Alexa was playing something soothing.

'How's the head?' I asked, trying to sound as upbeat as possible, despite the tumult in my mind.

'Mmmngh,' she mumbled.

'That good, eh? Well, that'll teach you. Where's your mother?'

'Dunno,' she said with some effort.

'Have you seen your dad?'

She shook her head and groaned. It was obvious she hadn't heard the news; it might be down to me to tell her – we couldn't keep her in the dark. But how could I shock her with Rakesh's murder while she was in this state? He had been family to her, she'd known him forever.

'I know what you need. Here, drink this.' I handed her a glass of water and two Nurofens and took one myself to clear my head.

'Coffee,' she groaned.

'Okay. One coffee and my special hangover cure coming up.'

I made her coffee (drop of milk, one sugar, just the way she liked it) and busied myself with breakfast.

I beat four eggs ('Quieter, please!' moaned Anjoli) in a bowl, added salt and pepper, then into a frying pan went onions, ginger, green chillies, ground coriander and tomatoes. I fried the vegetables in butter with turmeric and cumin and, when they were soft, added the eggs. A quick stir and I plated two servings, one of which I plonked in front of her with a fat slice of buttered white bread. It was a recipe my mother used to make whenever I was unwell. The smells always reminded me of her. Of a home that was now lost.

'Here you go! Ekoori. Parsi dish. Fatafati!' I said, throwing enthusiasm and cheer I didn't feel into my voice. I needed to tell her what I knew.

'Eww. Take it away,' she pushed away the plate.

'Eat only, sweetie,' I imitated her mother, pushing the plate back and putting a fork in her hand. 'Better than your greasy fry-up things. Have a bit. Money back if not satisfied.'

She looked up, grimaced, and took a small forkful. Then another, larger one. 'Hmm, not bad. The chillies go well with coffee,' she said, cautiously.

I winked at her. 'You'll be your usual lovely sarcastic self before you know it.'

After breakfast, we sat in silence as she nursed her hangover. Enya sailed to the Orinoco Flow as I decided how to break the news of Rakesh's grim end.

'Anjoli, I have terrible news, I'm—'

'Alexa, quieter ...' Anjoli groaned. 'Can't be any worse than this hangover.'

'No, this is serious.' Her head rose with effort and she looked blearily at me. For a moment, I saw Sabina Khan in her

75

penthouse, teacup in hand, equally unsuspecting of the bomb about to change her future. The difference was that I knew Anjoli well, cared for her. And I didn't like to cause pain to the important people in my life.

'After the party last night, Neha called your dad to tell us that Rakesh ...' I paused, no idea how to say it. 'Rakesh is ... no more.'

I waited for the sobs, the wails. Instead, she just looked at me blankly.

'No more what? What does that mean?'

I would have to be more direct.

'I'm sorry Anjoli but last night, after we left, Neha found him ... deceased. In the swimming pool.' I heard a sharp intake of breath and her eyes widened.

'He had hit his head,' I added, hoping it might help to have more detail. It didn't. Her hand flew to her horror-stricken face, covering her mouth.

'Oh God, poor Neha! And Pinky Aunty and Arjun. How's Neha taking it? Is anyone with her? I must see her.'

'Not good,' I said. 'It wasn't pleasant.' She needed the truth, so I added, 'And, well ... I don't think it was accidental.'

Confusion replaced the horror on her face.

'Someone hit him on the head. With a whisky bottle,' I added.

'No! You think Uncle Rakesh was ... murdered?' she whispered.

I nodded soberly and told her what I suspected. I tiptoed around Neha's involvement, not knowing how deep her loyalty to her friend ran.

'I can't believe it. You really think it was a woman?'

I shrugged. 'I do, given that ring.'

She considered this then shook her head and said, 'No, I can't see Neha or Pinky Aunty killing anyone. They don't have it in them. It must be that Taania woman.' She massaged her temples, rising from the table. 'I have to go see Neha.'

She stood up quicker than she should have, swayed and held her head. There was a pounding on the staircase and Saibal flew through the kitchen door.

'Kamil!' He said, in the voice he used when I had done something wrong in the restaurant. 'Kamil. I need you. The police have taken Neha in for questioning – I believe she is their chief suspect. You need to prove them wrong.'

Anjoli and Saibal's eyes were on me, desperate, afraid for their friend. My heart raced with excitement, mixed with trepidation. I couldn't mess this up.

I had needed no persuasion from Saibal to work the case. He was convinced it was an accident and couldn't understand why the police were taking it so seriously, so wanted me to collect evidence that would help Neha. I agreed but was careful not to say it was with the expectation of getting Neha off. To be frank, I saw it as the police did: the spouse was often the murderer.

The thought of using my skills again was exhilarating. Given my visa situation, I would have to operate under the radar. I was acutely aware that the police wouldn't appreciate my trampling over their case as I had done on the crime scene. Anjoli, somewhat recovered from the double blow of Rakesh's death and the police interest in Neha, appointed herself as my sidekick – Neha, Arjun and Pinky, three of the people I had to interview, would be more likely to open up to her than to me. So, we hatched a plan. We'd use the restaurant – neutral ground – as our base, and Anjoli and I would probe them for answers. For all my excitement, however, a small voice questioned me. Was I up to it, after everything I had allowed to happen in Kolkata? I needed to centre myself, so I left the house to clear my head.

Making my way through Shoreditch in the metallic sunshine, I passed the wondrously named 'Museum of Happiness' – a building I'd always liked to imagine being full of euphoric memories, preserved in time. You'd put on a neural headset and instantly be transported to the most joyous moment of your life. When was mine? I knew instantly. Maliha in the Kolkata Botanical Garden. She was lying under the famous banyan tree, eyes closed, head on my lap as I looked down at her, stroking her hair. Then, without intending to, I blurted out 'I love you'. Silence. I wished I could take it back. Then a slow smile spread across her face, her eyes drifted open and she said, 'I love you too.' I'd leaned over and kissed her as the warmth of the summer evening enveloped us.

A stiletto twisted in my heart. That was the problem with your sunniest memories. Night inevitably fell and then they tormented you. Maybe the Museum of Happiness needed a sister gallery called the Museum of *Un*happiness, displaying *exactly* the same exhibits.

Could I make Maliha proud of me now? If I got justice this time and sent a killer to jail?

I fell out of my reverie and noticed a woman on the pavement in an adorned lehnga – light glinting off the metal beads and sequins.

A piece clicked into place. Taania's dress at the party! That metal object I'd found on the deckchair had been part of Taania's outfit! I pulled up the photo I'd taken at the pool, trying to remember what Taania had been wearing when I'd seen her dancing with Rakesh – a black, spangly number. Yes, this sequin was definitely from there! So, if Taania *had* been on a deckchair with Rakesh as Neha had suspected … that opened up several possibilities and possibly presented a prime suspect. I would have to speak to her. And I should tell the police.

Galvanised, I walked on; past art galleries, colourful murals and artisanal coffee bars where I spotted a man who Anjoli described as a 'hipster' wearing braces, white shirt and a bowtie, with a full bushy beard tied at the bottom. He was serving a young Muslim man in an ankle-length white thobe and a beard the same length as the hipster barista's – brothers from different mothers.

A voice came into my head, 'We are not brothers, Saibal!' Rakesh and Saibal arguing the night of the party. What had that been about? And Rakesh's look of hatred in the kitchen. Was that why he had glared at me – because he was angry with Saibal and I was Saibal's guest? Another mystery to be solved.

I walked to where trendy Great Eastern Street turned into grungy Commercial Street, then the flea market and Brick Lane, with the street names in English and Bengali, people speaking Bangla everywhere and the sweet shops that stocked the Kolkata delicacies I craved. The CCTV above Modhubon Sweets caught my eye, its unblinking eye constantly scanning the passersby. I texted Anjoli, my new Hazra. *Do you think you could get the CCTV from Neha's? We need to create a timeline.*

When I arrived back at the restaurant, Anjoli was nowhere to be seen, so I got to work. Chef was putting away dishes from the party; as I joined in to help, he asked, 'Rakesh thik achhé? Shunechi or kichu ekta hoyechilo?'

'Very sad news. Mr Rakesh passed away last night,' I mumbled.

'Ya Allah! Ki holo?'

'The police are investigating.'

'I think you poisoned him with your fish pokoda, hain Chef? They will take you to jail and we will stop killing our customers,' laughed Salim Mian from the opposite end of the kitchen as he gathered the leftover food from the party to give to the homeless shelter, something Saibal insisted on us doing once a week.

'You shot op. Saibal aaj asché?' snapped Chef.

'I don't know when he is coming in so we should get lunch ready,' I replied, before adding, 'Did you see anything weird last night? Rakesh behaving funny?'

'He is always behaving funny, that man,' said Salim Mian. 'Whenever he is in the restaurant, he is always acting like he is here on a secret mission. Just comes in and fights with Saibal. He thinks he is very, very important but when it comes to tips … nothing!'

Fights? What was behind this animosity between Rakesh and Saibal? Saibal had said they were friends.

I spent a few minutes questioning my colleagues who had been at the party to ensure they had all left together and they confirmed they had all gone back in the van after the butler shooed them out as he himself left. None of them had noticed anything out of the ordinary, so that didn't get me anywhere. Well, good investigation was about closing out possibilities as well as uncovering fresh ones.

I started making up the tables for the lunch crowd – Sundays in Brick Lane could be busy with people coming from all over London for the curries, waiters standing outside the restaurants (all of which were 'award-winning') trying to entice them in. The competition was intense, and I'd often heard enterprising waiters from the Jolly Rajah next door whispering to potential diners we had rats in the kitchen and that they'd be taking their lives in their hands by even dreaming of eating at Tandoori Knights.

Just inside the entrance to the restaurant, next to the incongruous suit of armour that Saibal thought symbolised the restaurant's name, was a photograph of an Indian man with a dandyish handkerchief in his left hand, wearing Regency dress comprising a black formal coat and a stiff roll neck collar covering his entire neck. Under the picture stood a bottle of Head & Shoulders shampoo. I had asked Saibal why on earth there was a bottle of shampoo on display at the entrance to a restaurant, and he'd replied, proudly, 'Ah my boy. This is Sheikh Din Mohammed, a Bangla Muslim like you. He opened the first Indian restaurant in this country in eighteen hundred or seventeen hundred … He was the first Tandoori Knight! He *also* introduced shampoo to the English *and* was the first Indian to write a book in English. Before him, these Angrez were cursed with dirty hair, bland food and boring books. We invented all the splendid things – shampoo and soap and zero and chess and …'

As the restaurant filled with the predictable hubbub of assorted Sunday lunchers, we assumed our well-practised roles. Most of the food elements were pre-prepared and had only to be combined depending on what guests ordered, unless someone wanted the less popular dishes on the menu, which then had to be prepared from scratch: Maya's mouth-watering rezala, lamb neck cooked in milk and prawn malaikiri, fat prawns in coconut. The kitchen buzzed with activity as everyone performed their allotted tasks; we had a camaraderie I had not experienced in the police force. I ran between table and kitchen smiling and serving and taking orders and smiling and serving and taking orders, occasionally stopping to pretend to recognise a regular who claimed to know me. It wasn't my fault, but these white people, with their nose rings and tattoos, all looked the same to me. Back and forth I dashed, as the patch of carpet between kitchen and restaurant wore undetectably thinner.

I groaned with relief as the last of the daytime rush trickled out to spend their afternoon dodging the rain in vintage shops, trying on dead people's clothes and examining ancient records. I needed peace after the lunchtime clamour and the gentle clinking of cutlery being washed in the back sounded like wind chimes in my tired head. I hadn't had much sleep and considered sneaking upstairs for a brief nap. But then the door opened and in came Anjoli (*The First Brexit was in 1947* emblazoned on her T-shirt) with Neha, Maya and Saibal. The nap would have to wait. The investigation was underway.

Anjoli looked edgy. She sat Neha down at one of our best booths, before taking me aside and whispering, 'Listen, Kamil. We just brought Neha home from the police station. She's literally freaked out, terrified. She said they were really aggressive. She's sure they will arrest her if they find any more evidence. They've done over the house, taken the CCTV and everything. But Neha's given me access to the files in the cloud, as you asked.'

I nodded. 'Do you think she'll speak to me now if she's already been interrogated today?'

'Yes, she wants your help. But she hasn't slept all night, so go easy . . .'

I looked around. The restaurant was almost empty – it could serve as our interview room for now. Back at the red upholstered booth I squeezed in next to Saibal and Maya, Anjoli sitting opposite us with Neha; I'd never had this many extra people in an interrogation before. Neha looked exhausted and wholly different from the chic hostess I had met the previous night.

'Can you help me, Kamil?' she asked in an indistinct voice.

'Of course, he will help you,' interrupted Saibal, before I could respond. 'Kamil is an outstanding detective. You are totally innocent. Who knows what the police are thinking.' Maya vehemently nodded her agreement.

'Tell me what happened,' I said. 'What did the police say?'

'They were there all night,' Neha rubbed her eyes. 'Asking all of us questions, wanting to know every little detail. They wouldn't stop asking why I was at the pool, how did I find him, what was I doing before . . . And they made me try on a ring.'

'Did it fit?' I asked.

'Yes, it fit, but it wasn't mine, I swear! Must have been Pinky's, it was the type of rubbish she wears – a cheap sapphire thing. Then they took me to the station this morning for more questions. I have had no sleep …' she trailed off as Saibal and Maya looked at each other.

'What were the questions?' I asked.

'They found out …'

'Tell him, Neha,' said Saibal gently.

'Pinky told me last night the charity was a sham. Rakesh has lost all his money. We are bankrupt. There's nothing left!' Neha burst out. 'Arjun told the police as well and now I'm a suspect! They think I killed him because there was no money left.'

Rakesh Sharma bankrupt? This was beyond belief. I'd figured that money might be one reason for Rakesh's death but *this*? Rakesh Sharma, one of the most well-known industrialists in India, was broke? How could that have happened?

I had to ask. 'But how could he suddenly lose everything? It doesn't make sense?'

'I knew that he had problems,' said Saibal, sombre. 'I was not aware that it was this bad.'

'I don't know,' said Neha. 'It was a complete shock to me. Arjun wouldn't tell me what happened.'

Salim Mian came to take our order. Anjoli shooed him away with a wave of her hand but Neha said, 'I'm parched after talking to the police, Anjoli. I'd *kill* for a cup of tea and a samosa.'

There was utter silence after we realised what she had said, then Saibal let out a guffaw, breaking the tension.

Neha smiled weakly and continued. 'Pinky told me after everyone had left. You and I were sitting in the living room talking, remember, Anjoli? Then you wandered off to the kitchen to get a drink and I joined you guys,' she pointed at Saibal and Maya, 'when you were talking to Arjun and Pinky. Rakesh was showing Taania out. He had been dancing and whispering with her

83

all evening, making me feel terrible. That's why I thought he was at the pool with her. After,' she said hastily, 'I only thought that after.'

Salim Mian brought Neha her tea, samosas and onion bhajis. She sipped her tea and nibbled on a samosa as she continued. 'Pinky told me I would have to give everything up, the house, everything I had, because Rakesh was bankrupt and the creditors would take everything. I'm sure they deliberately waited for my party so they could ruin it.' A bitter note entered her voice. 'I didn't believe her at first, I thought she was just being horrible, but she kept rubbing it in. Arjun confirmed it was true – the company had deep financial problems and couldn't survive. Rakesh gave the party as some kind of last ego trip, he said. Pinky was so smug. The money *she* got in the divorce, it's safe. I have nothing. But it's not the money, I don't care about the money. It's ... it's that my Rakesh is dead and I'm a ... widow at twenty-eight ...' Her face twisted in anguish, and she buried herself into her arms as we looked on, not sure how to help her in her desolation. I remembered her white face when we said goodbye after the party and the tension between her, Pinky and Arjun. This would explain it.

'*That's* why Pinky came to the party,' Anjoli breathed, nodding to herself as she stroked Neha's hair. I moved Neha's tea out of her way so she wouldn't spill it, then addressed Saibal and Maya. 'You heard Arjun say this, too?'

'No,' said Saibal. 'We came to get you two from the kitchen. Remember? He told her then. But Rakesh had told me before that things were not good.'

I debated whether to ask him about his argument with Rakesh, then decided the time wasn't right. I nodded and turned back to Neha.

'What happened after that?' I asked. 'How did you find Rakesh?'

'I don't think I can go through this again,' Neha moaned, lifting her head and looking to Anjoli for help. Anjoli put an arm around her friend's shoulders, and we were silent for a while as Neha composed herself.

She told us that after the three of us had left she had rushed to look for Rakesh to ask him whether the news about PinRak was true. She'd searched all over the house before going to the pool, where she'd found his body. She screamed for help and Arjun and Pinky had come running down. Arjun struggled to get the body out of the water ... Neha's voice faltered, unable to bring herself to picture her husband's corpse.

Saibal whispered to me, as Neha dried her tears on a red serviette, 'I was sure he'd had an accident, or ... taken his own life. But the police are thinking differently.'

'They kept asking me *when* I had gone to the pool and how long I had been there,' said Neha, exhausted now. 'I kept telling them it was only a few minutes, but they didn't believe me. Pinky said I was gone for ages. But I was in shock. I couldn't believe what I was seeing.'

'How did you cut your foot, Neha?' I asked.

She stared at me, then said defiantly, 'After I saw Rakesh's body and screamed and before the others came down, I thought *I* should try to pull him out. I kicked off my shoes and knelt beside the pool and one of my heels must have fallen into the water. Then Arjun came and I stood up and something sharp jabbed my foot. I shouted that I had been cut but everyone ignored me. Arjun pulled the body out. The police took my other shoe away because there was broken glass in the sole. I don't know where the glass came from. That's what cut me. And they were my favourite Louboutins.'

'Was there anyone else in the house?' I asked.

'I didn't see anyone,' said Neha. 'Other than the four of you, the last guest to leave was Taania.'

85

'Did you see her leave?' I asked.

'No, Rakesh saw her out.'

'When?'

'I don't know. Forty, fifty minutes before you left? I didn't see him after that.' She broke into tears, realising that that had been the last time she had seen her husband alive.

'And did Pinky or Arjun leave the living room when you were there with them?' I asked.

Anjoli's look of hope turned to a grimace of disappointment when Neha whispered, 'No, they were having too much fun telling me I was a pauper.'

I tried to figure out the sequence. We'd left at just after 2 a.m., so Rakesh would have shown Taania out at 1.20 or so, soon after I'd seen them together in the living room. Or said he was showing her out. Because she hadn't left then. Rakesh had taken her down to the pool. Possibly things got out of hand, she'd smashed his head with the bottle and made her escape. I needed to check when the CCTV showed Taania leaving.

'It wasn't an accident, Neha,' I said. 'It was murder. He was hit by a bottle, probably wielded by a woman, given the ring. If you didn't do it—'

'—I didn't!' '—She didn't!' Neha and Anjoli exclaimed simultaneously.

'If you didn't do it,' I continued, 'then it was Pinky or Taania. We need to speak to them. And ... I think you were right. Taania *was* at the pool with him. I found a sequin from her dress there.'

Neha looked at me in shock. 'So, he took her to the pool! Why?'

I shrugged, not wanting to state the obvious.

Anjoli put an arm around Neha. 'Don't worry Neha, of course we believe you. We *will* sort everything out. I promise.'

'Please take me home now, Saibal Uncle. No, not home, I can't go back there. To Aunty's in Southall,' said Neha tearfully.

86

Neha sitting there, tears rolling down her cheeks, caused my heart to constrict. I remembered Sabina, another woman left alone by a brutal murder. She had taken the news of Asif's death better, but the pain she experienced must have been as intense. I had no words for a time like this. Anything I might say – 'He ... now', 'It will pass', 'You will find happiness again' – were just platitudes. The depression and hurt I felt after Kolkata didn't compare to the raw grief I was seeing and my self-indulgent misery over the previous few weeks felt shameful.

We watched Saibal show her out and I had to get back to my restaurant job.

On Saturdays and Sundays, we stayed open all day and didn't get a break between lunch and dinner as there was a regular trickle of diners from the tourists wandering around Brick Lane. So, as guests left, I wiped surfaces, covered them with the starched, white tablecloths and took the dirty coverings and soiled cutlery to the back for washing. As I laid the plates for the next lot of diners, Anjoli beckoned me over to where she was sitting with her laptop open, logged into Neha's CCTV account. I sat and we watched it, heads close over the laptop, making notes. We saw the van leave with my colleagues from the restaurant at 0046, followed by a smaller car, presumably the butler's, and then Saibal's car leaving with us in it at 0208. Nine minutes later another car pulled up and collected someone obscured under an umbrella.

'Who is that?' asked Anjoli, a note of excitement entering her voice.

'I don't know,' I said. 'I thought we were the last to leave. Weird.'

'There's no sign on the CCTV of anyone leaving when Taania was supposed to have left, so it must be her! She did it!' said Anjoli.

'Hold your fire, Captain Hastings,' I grinned. 'There may be a better explanation. Let me finish work, then we can do a full timeline.'

I walked into the kitchen to get the cutlery as Maya beckoned me over to tell me the specials based on what she'd bought from Bangla Town Cash & Carry ('One Place For All Your Grocerys') that morning. Her wan face told me she was handling her shock by throwing herself into her cooking. My stomach rumbled as she informed me that she had found some excellent goat meat so was making Paya, the curry made with goat's trotters, and Haleem, the minced goat and lentil dish cooked for hours over a slow flame. I squeezed her shoulder and said I hoped that not too many people ordered those dishes – they were two of my favourites and I was holding out for leftovers. She smiled and said she would save me some. After finishing the tables, I grabbed two samosas to appease my grumbling belly and left with Anjoli.

We found a bench outside Brick Lane Mosque, deserted except for a few stragglers at this time of the late afternoon. There was a homeless chap perched on the other end, so I handed him a samosa and Anjoli and I squished in closer to each other. Anjoli seemed unfazed by our proximity, but I could feel her thigh against mine and, despite the chilly day, it made me sweat. I offered her the remaining samosa and was glad when she refused, gobbling it up myself in two big mouthfuls. I started scribbling in my notebook, telling Anjoli what I had seen. She leaned in and read my scrawl out loud:

> 5 p.m.: Kamil arrives at Sharma Manor
> 5.15: Kamil sees Neha
> 6.30: Chatterjees arrive
> 6.35: Pinky and Arjun arrive

88

7.00: Rakesh meets me (why did he look pissed off?)
11.30: Rakesh gives speech
11.50: Kamil hears Saibal and Rakesh arguing

'What argument?' Anjoli said, brushing a stray samosa flake off my coat. I realised I hadn't mentioned it to her, so gave her the gist of what I had heard. Uncharacteristically, she said nothing, and we continued:

0.46: TK staff and butler leave.
00–1.00: Living room. Anjoli and Neha. Saibal and Maya with Pinky and Arjun. Rakesh with Taania.
01.15: A goes to kitchen to see K.
01.20: Rakesh leaves living room with Taania to show her out (or not).
(When did Taania leave? Sequin found at pool). Neha, Pinky, Arjun, S & M in living room.
02.00: S & M come and pick us up from kitchen.
02.05: Neha in living room with Pinky & Arjun. Has learned about PinRak collapse. Chatterjees and K say bye. Arjun gets message from Rakesh.

'Must say, I don't remember leaving, I must have been out of it!'
'Well, you were really drunk. Your parents weren't pleased!'

02.08: Neha shows us out and goes looking for Rakesh.
02.12: S gets WhatsApp from Rakesh.
02.17: Someone leaves by car (Taania? Cab?).
02.25: Neha finds body. Cuts foot, drops shoe in pool.
02.35: Neha calls S. Arjun calls police. Has blood on wet sleeve.
02.50: We arrive back at Sharma Manor.
03.10: Police arrive.

I showed her the photos I had taken of the crime scene. Her face tightened when she saw Rakesh's body, but she said nothing. 'Let's do this systematically,' I said, gazing at the picture of the blood at the pool, hoping for an answer to leap out at me. 'We have four suspects – Neha, Arjun, Pinky and Taania. Everyone else had left. Unfortunately, Neha is the most obvious. The ring fitted her finger,' I swiped to the photo of the ring in Rakesh's dead hand and continued, 'And she had the means – the whisky bottle; the motive – PinRak's collapse, Rakesh's behaviour with Taania; and the opportunity – she found him at the pool. It was clearly not premeditated – the killer used Rakesh's whisky bottle. So, it's possible she was looking for him, found him cleaning up after his dalliance with Taania and, enraged, hit him with his bottle. He grabs her ring, falls back and smashes his head against the pool's edge.'

Anjoli went silent for a moment, then said adamantly, 'Neha had nothing to do with his death, Kamil. I know her. She's no more capable of murder than I am.'

I sympathised; I had also been inclined to believe Neha in the restaurant. Even with the circumstantial evidence against her, this violent crime didn't fit the character of the scared young woman I had interviewed. But evidence was evidence.

'Then we have Pin—' I continued, just as Anjoli exclaimed, 'I have an idea,' waking our neighbouring snoozer. He turned to glare at her, before settling back. She lowered her voice to a whisper and said, 'Taania had means, motive and opportunity too. How about this? Rakesh Uncle came on to Taania in the sitting room, we saw that – and he says he is showing her out but takes her to the swimming pool where they won't be disturbed. He tries it on with her, she hits him with the bottle to get him off her. He grabs her ring, drowns and she runs off and lets herself out of the house! And Neha finds the body later.'

Her face was flushed with excitement. I pondered this, then asked, 'But if he was assaulting her and she hit him, when did he send the messages? That makes no sense. I mean she *was* there with him, we know that because of the sequin, but more likely he would message after she left. I reckon she left the pool before 2 a.m. and then, in a fit of remorse, he sent the messages. She was probably the one taking the cab at 2.17. I'm not sure why she would hang around the house for another seventeen minutes if she went upstairs from the pool earlier, though. And *we* never saw her when we left. But we need to interview her. You're right, there are questions that need answering.'

'How are we going to get to her?' asked Anjoli.

'I don't know, I'll figure it out,' I replied. 'Let's move on to Pinky. Neha goes looking for Rakesh after showing us out and Pinky rushes to the pool, kills him and comes back up. The window of opportunity for Rakesh's murder is slim – he died between 2.12 and 2.25. That's thirteen minutes. It might just be possible, but it would have to be totally premeditated. That isn't enough time to find him, argue, kill him and then come back up as if nothing had happened. We have to see if the ring fits Pinky's finger. And she tried hard to put the blame on Neha to the police. Was that because she was guilty, or was she just being vindictive? Also, what would her motive be?'

'Pinky Aunty has always been vicious about Neha. She hated Rakesh for the divorce – there's a motive right there. What about Arjun?' asked Anjoli. 'He must have been pissed off about the charity business and PinRak losing everything? Maybe *he* went to the pool while Neha was looking around, argued with his dad and smashed his head in? You said he had blood on his sleeve; it's possible that came from earlier and not when he pulled the body out.'

'Remember the ring, though,' I said, waving my phone at her. 'Arjun wouldn't have been wearing that ring.'

'Unless he put it in Rakesh's hand to deflect attention?'

'That seems pretty far-fetched – why would he have a ring on him? And same issue as Pinky, he would have to have planned it in advance. There wasn't enough time for it to be a crime of passion.'

We fell into a despondent silence with an accompaniment of light snoring from our neighbour. 'Okay, listen,' I said decisively. 'The evidence against Neha looks bad, but I'm with you. I'm not convinced it's her either. Let's do this systematically. We need to speak to Arjun and Pinky and Taania.'

'Excellent idea,' she said, looking at me expectantly. 'Where do we start?'

'You sort out Pinky and Arjun. I'll try to see if I can get Taania to meet with us.'

'No problem. But Kamil, where was the butler during this? We have to interview him too, the police must have.' Anjoli continued to stare at the timeline, furrowing her brow.

'I saw him leave with the other staff, Anjoli. This isn't Cluedo!'

'Seems like it is ... Rakesh, in the pool, with the whisky bottle ...'

She stared moodily at the mosque opposite, then shivered, 'I'm getting chilly. Come on, let's get back to the restaurant. We'd better help with the evening shift.'

'Here, take my coat,' I said, shrugging it off.

'No, it's fine, I don't need ... okay, thanks.'

I held back a few paces, looking at her striding down Brick Lane like a flag of justice, flying resplendent and unabashed. A smile twitched my lips as I took her in from top to toe – tight jeans, white T-shirt, blue oversized cardigan, bright red woollen scarf draped around her neck with my coat hanging loose around her shoulders. She was quite something, my indomitable assistant.

* * *

We got back to the restaurant as the first evening customers trickled in. I enjoyed serving these early birds, they appreciated the food and were invariably polite and good tippers. I disliked my job after the pubs closed. That's when the drunks rolled in, ordered five lagers and the hottest vindaloos, called the waiters 'Abdul' or 'Hey You' and spent their time trying to see how much louder they could be compared to the table next to them.

As the restaurant got busier that evening, Anjoli helped with the service as Saibal had given two waiters the night off for serving at the party. She smiled at me as we passed each other in the kitchen, balancing dirty plates en route to the industrial-sized sink.

As I served the couple who came for dinner every Sunday, never saying a word to each other, just staring stony faced anywhere except at each other, the restaurant door opened and two people I recognised walked in.

'Kamil Rahman?' It was the police officer from the other night and her sidekick. 'We'd like to get your statements about the events of yesterday evening. And are …' she consulted a small black notebook, 'Mr, Mrs and Miss Chatterjee here as well? We would like to speak to them too.'

My antennae twitched. Was I a suspect? Had my incompetence – the phone, the crime scene – put me on their radar? I suspected they wouldn't go easy on me. And I knew from my experience in Kolkata that I didn't do well under interrogation from senior police officers when I had screwed up badly and compromised evidence.

The Detective

Kolkata. July. Monday.

I was meeting Maliha for dinner in Tangra Chinatown, the largest in India and home to 2,000 Hakka Chinese, who had lived there for 200 years. I loved this part of Kolkata, resplendent with bright orange and yellow lanterns; exotic birds in cages cawing and screeching at me as I passed; corner stores piled high with unrecognisable groceries, the Chinese owners incongruously speaking fluent Bengali; Buddhists praying side by side with Hindus at the Kali Mondir; and, of course, the Hakka food, so different from the ubiquitous Cantonese and Szechuan cuisines. I threaded my way through the crowds and went into Kim Ling, sitting proudly next to the wonderfully named Relax Foreign Liquor Shop.

As I entered the restaurant, the noise of chat, laughter and clinking dishes and the sweet and spicy aromas tickling my nostrils immediately unwound the stress of the day. My stomach rumbled as I looked around and spotted Maliha at the window table, glossy black bob bent over her phone, which cast a moonlit glow on her pale skin. I approached and leaned over to kiss her on the cheek.

'Another attack on Muslims in Punjab,' is how she greeted me. 'Two murdered by Hindu extremists for running a completely legal abbattoir. And the police are doing nothing. When a guy being beaten by one of these fanatics implored a watching policeman for help, he was told, "We have no orders to protect you." Can you believe that?' She threw her phone on the table in disgust.

'Yes, nice to see you, my Jaan,' I beamed.

'This stuff is getting worse and worse. It makes me so angry!'

She got up and stretched her arms around my neck. I hugged her, breathing in the familiar perfume as her hair tickled my nose. 'Stop this tweeting and repeating, Jaan. It upsets you too much.'

'Of course it upsets me. Doesn't it upset you?' she shot back and slapped my backside.

I smiled and sat. 'Are we going there again, sweetie? Of course, it's important but what can we do about it?'

'There's so much we can do! We can protest! I'm a lawyer … you're an inspector. We should be able to make a difference! We can …'

I nodded in agreement – her passion always invigorated me. I admired her immense care for others, for strangers, for injustices in the world. 'Other than that, how was your day?' I pulled the menu towards me.

'Oof, don't ask! The usual, I was in court.' She put on her spectacles to read the specials.

'In jeans and a horsehair wig? How very modern for Kolkata High Court! Anything exciting?'

'I went home and changed, idiot. It's becoming so stale yaar! Another boring property case. Tenants refuse to leave. Landlord tries to make their lives a misery by switching off the water. Tenants stop paying rent … usual ding dong. I'm getting really bored with this. How was yours?'

'Let's order first. I'm starving. The usual?'

She nodded, put away her menu and flicked her glasses to the top of her head.

I beckoned the waiter over, 'One Manchurian fish, one hot garlic button mushrooms, one tofu Sichuan and a … chilli garlic fried rice. Oh, and two beers.' I couldn't wait to share my news with my fiancée – strictly speaking I should have kept it confidential but … it was Maliha. I turned to her and whispered, 'I got a new case. High profile.'

'Oh wow. What?'

'It's not public yet and I'm not supposed to tell anyone, but Asif Khan has been murdered.'

Her eyes widened and she whispered back, 'Shit! Really? We just saw him in *Jango*! What happened?'

'Someone bashed his head in his hotel room. The DIG asked for me specially and … I'm running the case!'

'Kamil.' She took my hand. 'That's fantastic. I'm so proud of you.'

I paused as the waiter handed us two cold beers in frosted glasses.

I didn't have to put up a front for her. 'To be honest Maliha, I'm basically terrified,' I confessed. 'This is my first big case. I've no idea what I'm doing. Yet, I'm the boss. Imagine if I screw it up? What an embarrassment. And I'll never hear the end of it from Abba.'

'No, no, that's just imposter syndrome, Jaan – everyone gets it, even me, when I'm in court. I have full faith in you, darling. You're the smartest person I know – almost as smart as me,' she grinned. 'Just walk the walk, talk the talk. You have great instincts; you will know what to do.'

She was exactly what I needed – always there to build me up, always there for me. We dug into the spicy food, Sichuan peppers making our mouths go numb, leavened by the chilled, hoppy beer. I could put my racing mind into neutral as Maliha discussed plans for our wedding in October and we toasted each other with a few too many drinks ('I'm so proud of you Kamil',

'No, I'm proud of *you*, darling!'). We ended the evening sharing a plate of dragon's beard, then trickled reluctantly back to our separate homes.

I woke the next morning confident and energised after a good night's sleep. With luck and vital information from the CCTV, I might find the killer today. I loved the intellectual stimulation of investigative work. It brought to mind the 'connect the dots' pictures I used to do with Ma as a child. Even Abba would sometimes join in, although he was keener on my learning to box, not something I ever became good at. No, what I enjoyed most was linking the series of numbers scattered seemingly randomly on the page and by magic producing the image that had been hiding in plain sight.

And that's what I had to do for everything to fall into place, take stock of my dots: Mitra, Sabina, the women at the party, the CCTV footage, the man in the party video, the fingerprints on the money, the condoms – I just needed a few more to see the picture in its full glory and then arrest the perpetrator.

I lay in bed looking at the stripes formed by the sun shining through the barred windows onto my 'New York – Gateway to the United States' poster – Lady Liberty in a jail cell. A double bed dominated my Spartan police quarters together with a simple sideboard and steel almirah. Maliha had tried to brighten the room with colourful travel posters – 'It's always a delightful time to visit London' and 'Paris – la Ville des Lumières' – but it still resembled my student hostel room.

Having grown up as a child in large flats and houses provided by the police service to Abba, there wasn't a day where waking up in this broom cupboard didn't cast a shadow. One day I'd move out of here and buy a charming two-bed flat in Alipore in which Maliha and I would raise our own kids … perhaps sooner than I had expected if things went well today.

I checked my phone; the story had broken and was front page news on every website, massive headlines and photos of Asif and Sabina dominating. One of the sites had even managed to get a picture of the body – that tech who had taken the photograph at the crime scene would feel the end of my boot. Maliha had sent me a link to a tweet in the *Telegraph* 'Sub-Inspector Kamil Rahman, son of Retired Commissioner of Police Adil Rahman, is leading the Asif Khan murder enquiry'. As I Googled myself, enjoying my five minutes of fame and sipping the freshly made coffee, my phone rang.

'Rahman,' I said. 'Hain, Ash. What's up?'

'Kamil, I've got bad news,' Ashutosh said, his voice placid as always. 'They have confiscated the NVR drive.'

My mood went from warm sunshine to freezing rain.

'Shit! I'll be right there.'

I downed the rest of my coffee, added the dirty dishes to the three-day pile in the sink, and ran out.

As soon as I reached the Cyber Crime Cell, Ashutosh ambushed me. 'I was close to recovering the footage but got back to my desk this morning and the drive was gone. My boss said we didn't have the right paperwork.'

'Take me to your boss,' I said, agitated.

'In there.' He gestured to a cabin in the corner. I thumped on the windowed door whose sign read 'Assistant Commissioner, Cyber Crime Cell', didn't wait for a reply and walked in. I'd seen it done on TV and it seemed to get results. The young bald man with a handlebar moustache behind the desk didn't look up from his laptop as I stormed in.

'Good morning, sir, I am SI Kamil Rahman,' I said, in a rush. 'I believe you confiscated the drive we impounded from the Asif Khan case that DC Ghosh Sahib assigned to me? This is top priority – we need it back for urgent analysis—'

The AC held up his hand, stopping me in mid-flow, and carried on tapping on his computer, the desk lamp reflecting off his polished head. I waited in frustration. Finally, he pushed away the laptop, took a packet of cigarettes and a silver lighter from his jacket pocket, tapped a cigarette out, lit it with great precision, put the packet and lighter back, took a long drag and exhaled a cloud of smoke in my direction.

'And you are?'

I repeated what I had just said, as patiently as I could manage, repressing the urge to pull the cigarette out of his mouth and stamp on it.

'I see,' he said ruminatively. 'You think you can come in and get my staff to drop everything to do your kaaj? With no paperwork? No forms? No RFI?'

'Sir, I will do the paperwork needed, but this is ultra-high importance. It is direct from DC Ghosh Sahib, sir!' I said, frustration filling my every pore.

'Sorry *Sub*-Inspector Rahman. I run a tight ship in *my* department. Unlike you maverick detective wallahs. You can inform DC Ghosh of that if you like. No Request for Information form, no results.' He opened a drawer and took out a photocopied sheet. More smoke blew into my face as he spoke. 'Fill this out and I will release your drive forthwith.'

I scrawled out the form as fast as I could and handed it back to him. I hated this police-bureau lunacy – nothing could be done unless we had requested it in triplicate, checked it, stamped and filed it – all in the interests of officers covering their backsides. The AC read it through as I itched with impatience. He nodded, rubber stamped a chit and gave it to me. 'It's in the malkhana,' he said, waving me away.

I rushed deep underground to the dismal malkhana where we stored captured arms and other evidence and presented the chit to a bored subedar reading *Filmfare* at the desk. In response, he sighed, put down his magazine, smoothed the pages and disappeared into the malkhana cage.

I peered at the paan stains and damp patches on the bare concrete walls of the malkhana. It was sweltering here, the slowly rotating fan above doing little more than distribute the humidity around the room. The police headquarters became grungier and more dilapidated the further down you came; the executive offices at the top, pristine, wood panelled and air conditioned; the holding cells at the very bottom in the sub-sub-basement suffocating, filthy, stinking and damp.

When the subedar returned, he sat back and picked up his magazine. 'Don't have,' was all he said.

'What don't have?' I snapped back.

'Computer don't have.'

As he turned the page of the magazine, I reached across and prised it from his grasp. 'AC told me they brought it here last night.'

'Don't have now.'

'Show me the logbook,' I said through gritted teeth. I was panicking. I needed that drive. 'Someone must have signed it in and out.'

The subedar grudgingly handed over a dirty, battered logbook. I looked through the previous night's entries. Of course, it was just my luck, there was no mention of the drive being logged in or out of the malkhana. I slammed the book onto the desk and stomped back upstairs to see the Cyber Crime AC. I felt like a stroppy teenager but fought back a rising sense of apprehension.

Back in the smoke-filled office. 'Sir, the drive is not in the malkhana,' I said, my voice tight.

'What?' He looked up from his laptop.

'Sir, *there is no record of it being logged in or out.*'

The AC rubbed his shiny head, lit another cigarette and waved a hand at me.

'What can I say, Rahman? I sent it there. These subedars never bother with proper paperwork.'

I was losing the little patience I had left.

'Who took it there, sir?'

'My peon.' He shouted at an old man in a brown uniform sitting outside his cabin.

Snapped out of his reverie, the peon slid off his stool and ran in. 'Sir, sir, yes sir?'

'What did you do with that computer I gave you for evidence yesterday?' the AC asked, exhaling smoke.

'Sir, I took it to malkhana, sir,' the peon replied virtuously.

'*He* says it is not there now.' The AC pointed at me.

'I took it there only, sir.' The peon, now sincerely offended, was staring at me accusingly. The AC heaved a sigh.

'Go with the SI and enquire.'

The peon and I traipsed back to the malkhana where he and the subedar had an enjoyably heated argument, the peon insisting he had dropped off the drive, the subedar insisting he had not. I watched them for a minute, becoming increasingly irritated. I didn't have time for this nonsense. I needed to wrap up the case for DC Ghosh without delay and this was getting me nowhere. If the drive was gone . . .

'Enough,' I roared, banging the desk, causing them to stop in surprise and look at me as if I was a real inspector for the first time that morning. 'Let me in there, I will look for it myself!'

'No, no, you cannot go in, you are not allowed!' protested the subedar.

I shut my eyes for a second to contain my rage at this jobsworth. 'Listen,' I hissed. 'I am working directly for DC-DD Sahib. Now, you either let me in or look for another job.'

Muttering under his breath, the subedar stepped aside and let me into the dusty cage. Every shelf was filled with boxes; I had no idea where to begin. I rummaged around for the next twenty minutes but there was no sign of the NVR drive. The one con-crete bit of evidence I'd found – the most important connecting dot – had been erased. Where had it gone? What could I do? Where did this leave me?

I stood in the dim, dank room, suffocating in the malodorous air, claustrophobic shelves closing in on me. If only I'd followed procedure and filled in that stupid form before asking Ashutosh for help. If only I'd stayed with the drive at night instead of going to dinner with Maliha. If only ... but these 'if onlys' didn't help now, they just made it worse. A sense of utter failure replaced my immense pride of last night. I couldn't go to DC Ghosh now; my incompetence would appal him and he would replace me without a second thought. And I would be on a fast-track to nowhere. End of my career.

What could I do? There had to have been a reason for Mitra to wipe the disc. Could he have stolen the drive back? The idea was fanciful – he was a hotel manager, not a supervillain who could sneak into a police station, steal a drive and then vanish. But I was certain he had something to hide. His niece had found the body, and it was he who had reported the crime and had access to the NVR drive and been nervous when I'd taken it away ... he was the only bet I had. After all, we had nothing on Sabina Khan, nor any idea who the man with Asif Khan in the party video was ...

I needed to return to the first dot. To listen to the 100 call Mitra had made to report Asif's death. It had to tell me something.

The Waiter

London. October. Monday.

The police questioning had rattled me – not just because it was strange to be on the receiving end of an interrogation (although that *was* weird) but because I had to lie judiciously. Having been on the opposite side of the table, I knew *they* knew I was lying. They'd asked me why I was there in the house, and because I couldn't be honest about working illegally as a waiter, I told them I was helping Saibal, my family friend. I told them of my past in Kolkata, my detective work (but not my disgrace in the Asif Khan case – I didn't know how far my past had followed me – or whether it would mean anything to them). I didn't tell them about the argument I'd heard between Saibal and Rakesh – that was his secret to reveal. Or not. The good news was that I didn't appear to be a suspect.

They had questioned the Chatterjees as well but learned nothing new. Before she left, Campbell produced the ring I had seen in Rakesh's dead hand and asked Anjoli and Maya to try it on. 'Pretty, but too tight' said Anjoli, as she tried and failed to slip it over her finger. She handed it to her mother who had the opposite problem, finding it a little too loose for her slim fingers. Disappointed, Campbell pocketed it, said, 'I'll be in touch,' and left the restaurant with her colleague, the bell tinkling as she shut the door behind her.

That night, my sleep was fitful. I had a terrifying nightmare. I was watching the sacrifice of a white kid goat, the animal bleating helplessly as blood gushed in rivers from a slit in its throat. What was even stranger was that the animal was hanging from a ceiling fan in the middle of a room as the butcher sawed at its neck, the goat's cries unaccountably getting louder and louder as the blood flowed. I was standing underneath it, looking up, unable to move. The goat's blood covered my face, entered my eyes, my nostrils, my mouth till I suffocated.

I woke, blankets thrown off me, sweating. 8 a.m. My heart was still pounding as a voice entered my consciousness and Anjoli burst into my room. 'Wake up, Kamil! Neha's been arrested! They've got something on her. We need to do something! You can help, right?' she gabbled, barely stopping for breath. She looked panicked, worried for her friend. The anxiety in her eyes turned to concern when she saw me, drawn and sweating on the bed. 'Are you okay? You look awful!'

I pulled myself upright, 'I guess your mum's paya didn't agree with me. Can you get me a coffee, please,' I said, my voice croaky. I couldn't concentrate – I needed to wake myself up, get the memory of the dream out of my consciousness. Did it mean anything or was it just the rich, gluey goat curry I had wolfed down?

'How on earth can you eat those animal feet, Inspector Morose? It serves you right!' Anjoli said, as I joined her at the kitchen table ten minutes later, clocking her *Keep Talking, I'm Diagnosing You* T-shirt. Then her tone changed, and she became more serious. 'Listen, Neha's being held by the police. They found something – I've no idea what – but apparently it connects her to Rakesh's murder. I don't believe it for a second. I know her, she couldn't have done it.'

My brain went into overdrive. I had been expecting this. The shoe, her cut feet, the ring. What else did they have?

'We know she's the obvious suspect,' I said, gratefully sipping the coffee she had made.

'I don't think they have concrete evidence. How can they? And what about Taania leaving later?'

'They don't need concrete evidence to arrest her – if she's a suspect, they'll keep her in for questioning. If they find nothing, they'll have to let her go. They can't keep her for more than a day or two without charging her, I think,' I said, hoping to reassure her and remove the worry from her eyes. She'd lost a family friend, her parents were distressed, and now her best friend had been arrested.

Anjoli shook off her concern. I was getting used to these mercurial changes in mood. 'Well, I've been working hard,' she said. 'We need to interview people to sort this out and, given my natural charm … I was best placed to set up the interviews. So, drumroll … Arjun has agreed to see us. He doesn't want to meet in his office though, so I've told him to come to the restaurant. More low-key.'

Perfect. Low-key worked for me. The last thing I wanted to do was bump into the police again.

As I gulped back the coffee, we rehearsed the questions we needed to ask. I had to do it properly this time. Without DC Ghosh's sway behind me, I would have to do all I could to convince Arjun to talk to me and to tell me the truth. Given his anger at my prying on the night of the murder, it wouldn't be easy.

Two hours later, Anjoli and I sat in a booth, talking behind menus so the other waiters, who didn't understand what we were doing or why I wasn't setting up the restaurant for lunch, wouldn't be able to stick their noses into our investigation.

'So, what does PinRak do?' I stage-whispered.

'I'm not sure, import, export … steel? Construction?' said Anjoli vaguely. 'They have a lot of business in India, I know that.' The name rang a distant bell – PinRak – I had seen it somewhere before.

Before I could ask any more, Arjun, dressed in a well-tailored navy suit, white shirt and sombre tie, stood framed in the doorway, the bell tinkling to announce his arrival. Salim Mian hurried up to him, sniffing a large tip.

'Anjoli,' I heard Arjun say to Salim Mian, who ushered him to our table. He paused for a second, staring at a framed photograph on the wall of the restaurant. I had seen it dozens of times over the last months – a photo of the Prime Minister of India shaking hands with a businessman. With a shock, I realised the businessman was Rakesh. Before I could think about what it meant, Arjun was at our table. 'Hmm, *you're* here,' he said, spotting me. 'Haven't you meddled enough?'

'Arjun, thanks so much for coming.' Anjoli gave him her most charming smile. 'Kamil and I are trying to help your family get to the bottom of this – he just has a few more questions. It won't take long.' As he shuffled into the booth, I spotted a gold signet ring on his finger glowing under the downlighting.

'Tea? Coffee?' Salim Mian asked Arjun, raising an eyebrow at me. He was never so polite with me but sitting with Arjun may have boosted my status.

Arjun shook his head and Salim Mian rushed away, disappointed at seeing his big tip evaporate but excited to inform everyone in the kitchen I had become a customer for the day.

'Right, this is a tough time for you, we won't keep you long,' Anjoli began.

'You're right, it is tough,' said Arjun shortly.

'I'm so sorry, Arjun. We will miss Rakesh Uncle. How're you and Pinky Aunty doing? Should you be back at work so soon?'

'We're okay,' said Arjun, his features softening as he sighed. 'It's a massive shock. But it's better to be there doing something, instead of moping around at home. All those well-wishers repeating the same things ... I couldn't take it. Mummy won't stop raving about Neha. Gold digger, witch, serpent ... you name it. I wish she'd stop, it's embarrassing. Look, it's always nice to see you, Anjoli, but as you said, today's not the best time. Do you need me here for long? I should get back soon.'

He sounded hyper. I wondered if he was on something.

'Kamil's running the show,' said Anjoli. 'I'm just helping.'

'I see,' said Arjun glancing at his watch.

'I was a Sub-Inspector in the Kolkata Police,' I reminded him, 'and Saibal-da asked if I'd look into this matter and try to make sense of it. We'll be quick.'

He looked at me expressionlessly. 'The police are doing their job and have arrested Neha, how are *you* going to help?'

'Just dotting the i's and crossing the t's,' I said. 'Can we start with when you last saw your father?'

Arjun rolled his eyes. 'I've told the police everything.'

'I know, Arjun, I'm sorry, but we are just trying to put together the facts,' Anjoli cajoled.

He shook his head and sighed. 'Twenty past one that night? He left the sitting room to show that Taania actress out. Then your parents left to get you two and Ma and I both spoke to Neha and apprised her of the situation with PinRak. Dad had kept her completely in the dark and the news hit her like a lorry,' he said with satisfaction. 'Then you came back and we said bye. Neha showed you out and around fifteen minutes later I heard her scream. Ma and I followed the noise to the basement and saw ... Dad. I pulled him out of the pool and then we came up to make the calls – I called the police and Neha called your father.'

'Neha had hurt her foot, she said?' I asked.

'Yes,' said Arjun. 'She got some glass in it or something. She pulled it out while we were waiting for you. Her foot was bleeding.'

I nodded. 'And your father messaged you when we were leaving?'

'Yeah, he said he was sorry. Probably the charade about the charity. I told him it was stupid – people would soon know the truth. But he insisted. You can't tell him anything. Couldn't.'

'And Pinky Aunty was with you all the time while Neha was looking for Rakesh?' asked Anjoli.

'Of course she was, what are you trying to say?' said Arjun, a note of belligerence entering his voice.

'Nothing, just confirming the facts,' I placated. 'Can you tell us about the financial problems PinRak was having?'

He continued to look at Anjoli. Did he think I was so low on the totem pole that he couldn't even look at me?

'You know about that?'

'Yes,' said Anjoli. 'Neha told us.'

He nodded. 'I need a drink.' He snapped his fingers and Salim Mian came running. Arjun barked his order, Black Label, no ice, and it appeared instantaneously. I'd never seen Salim Mian move so fast for other customers. As he sipped the whisky, Arjun gestured to the two of us, inviting us to order as though we were the guests and he the host.

Anjoli and I shook our heads in unison and Anjoli, unable to help herself, murmured, 'Ten-fifteen is early for me.'

'I'm grieving,' he said tonelessly. After a few more gulps, he added, 'Anjoli, you should ask *your* father about PinRak's money issues.'

She looked puzzled. 'Baba? Ask Baba what?'

He ignored her question and continued, 'Listen, my dad was an exceptional man. He pulled himself out of Basanti slum with nothing – got himself schooled and became a topper—'

'I know that, yes . . .' said Anjoli as Arjun continued his seemingly well-practised stump speech, '—can you imagine the combination of luck and hard work needed?' He waved his glass at her. 'He started his business forty years ago with a small cement shop in Howrah and now PinRak is one of the biggest real estate and construction companies in India and—'

'PinRak! Construction!' I interrupted as the connection became clearer in my mind. 'You had the Kolkata Metro contract – the signs were everywhere.'

Arjun stopped listing his father's achievements and mumbled, still not looking at me, 'That fucking Metro.'

'What do you mean?' I asked.

He took a lengthy pause, then said flatly, 'PinRak is no longer involved with Kolkata Metro.'

'Why? What happened?' asked Anjoli.

'We lost the contract,' he muttered.

'But why?' Anjoli persisted.

'These are confidential matters that I do not need to discuss with you.' He looked at his glass and swirled the whisky around.

'That's why PinRak was in trouble?' I pressed.

Arjun laughed bitterly. 'In trouble! Yes, you might say that, Mr Policeman. And not just PinRak. Others are coming down with us.' He glanced at Anjoli. 'We have to sell everything and even that won't be enough.' He took a gulp of his whisky, getting more agitated as he spoke. 'All our money was tied up in that bloody Metro. We were leveraged to the hilt. Borrowed money from everyone to take on that project. Thousands and thousands of crores of rupees. A charity! What a joke. Neha's fancy Bishops Avenue mansion – even that belongs to the creditors now. I told Dad to be wary – business in India is never straightforward. And when he pulled the plug on us ...'

'Who? Who pulled the plug?' I asked.

He didn't answer but stood and walked to the entrance of the restaurant, staring out at Brick Lane, clenching and unclenching his fist.

'Who pulled it? Why did you lose the contract?' I persisted.

'I said it was confidential,' he shouted. 'Leave it. Enough. I have to go now.'

There was silence as we digested his outburst. Then Anjoli rose, put a hand on his arm and led him back to the table. 'I'm sorry, Arjun, I truly am,' she said, gently. 'I know this is a painful and terrible time for you – the business collapsing, your father. Have another drink. You shouldn't leave like this.'

She waved and Salim Mian refilled Arjun's glass. He took a sip and muttered, 'You don't know the half of it.'

She continued, 'I have to ask, where will PinRak's collapse leave Neha? When the police release her, that is.'

Arjun snorted and looked at her. 'Who cares? Neha's no fool. That sweet pussycat has sharp claws. I know she's your friend Anjoli, but she knew exactly how to reel Dad in when she was his secretary. Made him leave his family. *And* made him take out an insurance policy – paid for by our company, I might add – so it pays out two million pounds on his death. To her. So, *she's* okay. I told the police.'

Anjoli and I looked at each other at this piece of news as he continued, 'Dad insisted she sign a prenup so she wouldn't get much if she divorced him but if he died? Different story. It wasn't suicide, that's for sure. She killed him. I wouldn't put it past her. That's what the police think too.'

'Arjun!' This was a bit much for Anjoli, especially with the waiters listening agog.

'Were you angry with your father for remarrying?' I pressed, wanting to find the root cause of his outburst.

'What the hell are you suggesting? I *admired* my dad. He taught me everything I know. He just made stupid choices in the end. Neha was one of them.'

'What happened to the business then? The Kolkata contract? Was it fraud?' I pressed again.

'Fraud!' he roared, standing up and leaning over me. 'Of course not. Who the hell do you think we are? We are a clean company. Always have been. Dad insisted everything we did was legitimate. We've won awards for company transparency and governance, so I don't appreciate you besmirching our reputation with this kind of accusation. And you … you …'

Anjoli gave me a slight shake of her head. I was particularly adept at annoying members of the Sharma family – diplomatic questioning was clearly not my strong suit. I thought back to the Asif Khan case – maybe it had never been.

'I'm truly sorry, Arjun. So, what happens now?' asked Anjoli, trying to calm things down. Momentarily mollified, he responded, his voice now at a normal level – the waiters, who had been staring in glee at the drama, hastily returned to tidying serviettes and place settings.

'We'll be in administration in a week. Poof! All gone! The office is crawling with lawyers and accountants, that's why we couldn't meet there,' he said, downing his drink. 'Okay, enough. You've got what you needed.' He walked to the door. On his way out, he turned and gave me a filthy look, 'Now leave me the hell alone.'

'That was *awful*,' Anjoli groaned. We left the restaurant to get some air and discuss what had just happened so the Tandoori Knights staff couldn't hear everything we said. 'He's under a lot of pressure – we shouldn't have bothered him.'

'We have to sort this out. Is he normally as rude as that?' I asked, feeling bad that I was shirking my job and leaving Salim Mian and the others to set up for lunch.

Anjoli looked thoughtful as we walked in silence down the street. 'To be honest, he was always a spoilt brat, growing up,' she said, finally. 'Only son of rich parents, father not around much, mum always at parties, brought up by nannies – you know the drill. The entitled heir to the business. He was nasty about Neha, wasn't he? Didn't realise he hated her that much. He's so obviously pleased that she's the number one suspect.'

'It lets him and his mum off the hook,' I mused. 'You should talk to Pinky. First rule of policing: corroborate everything. Although given they are mother and son, they would alibi each other.'

'I know her, I'll know if she's lying. I don't think she'll come to the restaurant though – I'll see her at home and pay my condolences. That insurance policy, it's another nail in Neha's coffin, no?'

I nodded as she continued, 'And I'm worried about Baba. Why did Arjun keep asking us to talk to him? Why was he arguing with Rakesh Uncle? How can he be mixed up in this? He's not involved with Rakesh's business; he's got enough to worry about with keeping the restaurant going.'

'No idea. Did Saibal-da have a business relationship with Rakesh? How did they become friends?'

'They met in Kolkata years ago at uni, long before he and Ma moved to London. God, must be forty years ago now – before Rakesh Uncle became this big shot. Ma and Baba were at his first wedding to Pinky. That was in Kolkata too.'

'There may be more to Rakesh's death than we think. Remember the argument I heard your dad having with him? It's time we asked Saibal-da what that was about.'

'All right,' Anjoli responded, despondently. 'He'll be in the flat. Probably watching daytime TV.'

As we turned and walked back to see if Saibal could unpick the situation, my memories caromed back to the OC's revelation in the Control Room that had changed everything.

The Detective

Kolkata. July. Tuesday.

I knew where to go to get the original 100 call recording. The Lalbazar Control Room. It was, as always, complete chaos. Phones ringing, computer screens flashing, operators dealing with calls ranging from shootings to lootings and routing them to the correct police thanas. Sick with worry at losing the NVR drive, I found the Officer in Charge, an old friend of Abba's, sitting at his desk, exploring his teeth with a toothpick, white turban glowing in the dim light of the computer monitors.

'Kamil!' The OC exclaimed as I walked in. 'Haven't seen you for a while, beta! How is CP Sahib?'

'Sat Sri Akal, Uncle, Abba is well. Do you have a minute free?'

'For you, always. Sit.'

I pulled up a chair opposite him, composing myself and marshalling my thoughts, which was difficult in the hubbub. 'I don't know if you heard but I am in charge of the Asif Khan murder,' I began.

'I did hear! Badhaion, my boy! This will make you!' He grabbed my hand and shook it vigorously. 'Why don't you look thrilled?'

I winced. That was an understatement. I certainly wasn't thrilled – my career was vanishing down the drain faster than one of Kolkata's cockroaches, all because I hadn't filled in a stupid form.

'Uncle, I screwed up. I had a vital piece of evidence in the malkhana and it has now vanished. Have you heard of this happening before? How can I get it back?' I said, clutching at straws. He ran the control room, not the malkhana.

'What was it?' he asked.

'A computer drive.'

He guffawed. 'You leave a computer in the malkhana? And are surprised when it disappears? Those subedars are a bunch of thieves. Keep nothing valuable there – always lock it in a safe or it will vanish. They treat the malkhana like their personal kirana shops!'

My despair returned, but I tried to put my professional face back on and address the reason I was here. The 100 call. 'You're right, Uncle. There's something else I wanted your super expertise on … I came to get the recording of the 100 call that reported Asif Khan's death.'

The OC's bonhomie slipped, and his face clouded over. 'Why?' he asked, carefully. I'd never seen him so serious before. He was Fun Uncle Singh.

'The person who reported the call is a person of interest and I want to hear what he said and how he said it. I need to build an accurate timeline because the response time was so slow. When exactly did you get the call? When did you pass it to New Market and when did they call DC Ghosh because it was a hi-pro case?'

The OC's eyes narrowed. He threw his toothpick into a wastepaper basket and leaned forward, beckoning me closer. I inclined my head across the desk as he whispered, 'We didn't send it to New Market. We routed it directly to DC Ghosh.'

'Not to New Market?' I whispered back. 'But the DC told me that New Market had called him?'

'DC Ghosh gave instructions yesterday that we should route all murders to him.'

'All murders? Not just hi-pro murders? Why?' I said, puzzled.

'*All* murders. How do I know why Deputy Commissioners do what Deputy Commissioners do? I am just the Officer in Charge!' He leaned back and picked up another toothpick.

A feeling of trepidation descended. What was the DC playing at?

'Has he done that before?' I asked slowly.

'No.'

'What time did he issue this instruction?'

'Around 0830.'

Mitra's call reporting the death had been at 1105. The DC had predicted a murder *before* it was reported! The feeling of trepidation was now a flashing red alarm. Where was this heading?

'Were any other murders reported that morning?' I asked.

'Yes, two.'

'And you routed all three to him?'

'Yes.'

'And what did he do?'

The OC looked around to make sure no one could overhear him. 'The Grand murder he said he would deal with himself, the other two he sent back and told us to inform the thanas.'

'So, you *never* informed New Market about the Grand killing?'

'No.' The OC sat back. 'Why are you worrying about this Kamil? It is good for you. You are in charge. Solve the murder. Get a promotion! Make Commissioner Sahib happy. Keep it simple. No need to go digging.'

I nodded dumbly and walked back to my desk, considering the magnitude of what I had just heard. This wasn't a 'simple' case. It involved the DC in a way I couldn't fathom.

'What the hell is going on?' I whispered to myself. My confidence of the previous day evaporated, and a sick, drowning sensation rose around me. All my dots had vanished in one go – my case was a blank Etch A Sketch.

No CCTV; nothing to connect Mitra to it if I couldn't prove he erased it; fingerprints that couldn't be matched with anyone; and an unknown man in a video. I was back to staring at a blank sheet of paper with no idea of how to proceed. And even less of an idea of what to tell my boss.

Then, as though he was watching my every move, I got a text to report to the DC's office. Now what?

I made my way reluctantly to the top floor.

'Rahman. The AC Cyber Crime has sent me a complaint about you. What have you been saying to him?' The DC looked at me irritably as I saluted.

'Sir, I am very sorry to say that the CCTV computer drive has gone missing from the malkhana. I got upset and I spoke out of turn. I will apologise to him.' I spoke carefully, bracing myself for the wrath of God that was to be unleashed on me.

'How can it be missing? I thought you were recovering the video?'

Voice trembling, I explained what had happened.

'I see,' he said, annoyed. 'You should have filled in the form, Rahman. Proper procedure is critical at all times. The AC-CC took great pleasure in informing me that I was not running a tight ship. I don't need this nonsense. Have you *seen* the media? Every TV station is going crazy. They are making all manner of speculations. Did you recover any of the footage from the drive? Was the hotel manager on it?'

'Why the hotel manager, sir? No, we recovered nothing. The drive disappeared before we could. I'm sorry sir, it won't happen again.'

'It had better not,' he said, brusquely. He continued with a milder tone, 'I've been thinking,' he sat back in his chair. 'This Mitra fellow. Have you interrogated him yet? With the CCTV being erased, he is the obvious suspect. You said his niece found the body? And there were condoms in the room? So, what if Asif Khan tried something with this housekeeper niece? And Mitra found out and took revenge? He knew the Kali statue could be used as a weapon and got rid of it before calling the police. Is it possible that the CCTV showed him with the statue, so he erased it? He had a pass key and could have entered the room unnoticed. There is motive here, as well as opportunity and means. You have no other suspects, so bring Mitra to the lockup, apply pressure and he will crack. Give him the full third degree. You yourself said he was suspicious. I think this is an open-and-shut case. And apologise to the AC and calm him down.'

He gave me a smile and returned to his paperwork. I felt an immense surge of relief. I had screwed up, but he had given me a lifeline. I considered what he had said about Mitra. It was plausible – I should have thought of it myself, I'd had my own suspicions about him. Yes, I *would* question Mitra forensically and have him admit to the erasure. He would tell me what he had seen on the CCTV or admit to the murder himself. I didn't need the actual drive! My confidence returned.

'I will do that. Thank you for your guidance. Sir, one more question?' I said, trying to be as circumspect as possible.

'Mmm-hmm,' he leaned back in his chair, report in hand.

'Sir, I was talking to the Control Room and they said you gave instructions to be called if they reported *any* murders yesterday? Is this right, sir?'

He continued to read the report. 'I told you I am notified on hi-pro cases. It is standard procedure. Now sort out that manager, I am busy.'

'But why did you ask for *all* murders to go through you yesterday, sir? Not just the hi-pro ones,' I persisted.

He put down the report, leaned forward and looked at me, eyes blank behind his glasses. He then rose deliberately from his chair, came around the desk and backed me towards a wall.

'Know your place, Rahman,' he breathed. 'I gave you a chance with a big case to make your name because I heard you were a high flyer. But first, you lose critical evidence because of your incompetence; then, you seem to have more interest in being rude to the AC Cyber Crime than doing your job; and now, you are questioning me instead of interrogating the obvious culprit.' My back was hard against the wall and he leaned towards me, face so close that I could smell the coffee and cigarettes on his breath. He continued, in the same controlled tone, 'Don't think I can't take you off the case and get your badge stripped for this level of ineptitude. I can replace you like this,' he snapped his fingers in my face. 'Now get the manager to confess, I don't care how. That is an order. If you are too squeamish to do what is necessary, you don't belong here, and I can get you transferred to be a subedar in a village somewhere. I think that might be your actual level. This is a dog-eat-dog world, Rahman. You decide if you want to eat or to be eaten. I do not care either way. Wrap. This. Up. Now, GO.' His eyes bored into mine until I dropped my gaze.

'Sorry, sir. Yes sir, I will do the needful, sir,' I mumbled.

He stepped aside and I gave a watery salute and scuttled out. Once outside his office I stood, panicked, shaking, taking deep breaths to slow my trembling. The DC's peon looked at me curiously. Even Abba had never dressed me down like this. The DC's friendliness had deceived me, he hadn't risen to his rank by being a nice guy. And I didn't doubt for a moment that he would make good on his threat if I didn't perform. I could imagine him calling Abba and the regretful tone he would use in saying it was such a pity I hadn't been up to my first big case.

I let the wall behind me take my weight and forced myself to calm down. The DC was right. Mitra was involved and I would prove it. I could not afford to be eaten. I had to get a result, or I was dog meat.

The Waiter

London. October. Monday.

We entered Anjoli's flat to find *Bargain Hunt* on the TV and Saibal fanning cigarette smoke out of the window.

'Ah, you're back, children. Come, sit,' he said with a forced casualness. 'This Madley fellow has got these idiots to buy rubbish from a car boot sale, thinking they are antiques. Cha khabé?'

Anjoli raised an eyebrow at her father and stared pointedly at the cigarette butt in the teacup in front of him – Maya did not approve of smoking in the house. 'We have to talk to you, Baba,' she said, turning the TV off and throwing herself onto the well-worn, faux-leather sofa under the calendar from the local garage.

'What are you doing, Anjoli?' said Saibal, surreptitiously, or so he hoped, throwing the butt out of the window. 'I was watching that!'

'Where's Ma?' Anjoli asked.

'She is having a little sleep before the dinner shift. What has happened?'

'We've been interviewing people, Baba,' said Anjoli. 'We met Arjun. He told us some interesting things. He mentioned your name a few times ...'

'Hain? Tell me.'

I took up the baton, knowing Anjoli shouldn't be in charge of interviewing her own dad. First rule of police work – keep the personal out of it. Besides, there was no point in being oblique with Saibal – he had always been straight with us and we owed it to him to do the same.

'He confirmed that PinRak was bankrupt and Rakesh had lost everything,' I said. 'He said you would know something about it. When did Rakesh tell you?'

He looked uneasy. 'I … I knew something had happened,' he said reluctantly, his eyes darting between Anjoli and me. 'I did not know the details until Arjun told me at the party.'

'Baba, what's going on? Kamil heard you and Rakesh having an argument …' Anjoli said.

'An argument? When?' He looked surprised.

'At Rakesh's party. You were on the patio outside,' I said.

'And where were you hiding and listening from?' he asked, waggling his head sarcastically. I could see where Anjoli got it from.

'He wasn't hiding, Baba, he heard you through the window when we were in Rakesh and Neha's bedroom, and …' she explained.

'What?' interrupted Saibal, face horrified. 'You were together in their room? Why? That is not right. Two of you in a bedroom?'

'Stop it, Baba. Kamil's like my brother, you know that,' said Anjoli, irritated.

That was a blow. I couldn't put my finger on why – we were close, but … brother? That felt different … Before I could analyse my feelings any further, she continued, 'Stop changing the subject, Baba. We need to sort this out.'

'It was a heated argument, Saibal-da. What was it about?' I asked.

Saibal looked uncomfortable in the ensuing silence. Finally, resigned, he said, 'You will find out eventually so I will tell. But I need a fresh cup of cha.'

'I'll make it,' sighed Anjoli and went into the kitchen.

She left us enveloped in a gloomy silence. Saibal stroked the cushion in his lap as I looked at the rain, thinking again about

Anjoli's 'brother' comment. I wasn't sure why it bothered me, but it did. She came back with a tray of tea with some jam biscuits and banged them on the table.

'Okay, here's your tea. Now talk,' she announced. I suppressed a smile at her 'bad cop' routine.

Saibal took a careful, slow sip of the tea and bit into his biscuit as Anjoli stared at him and exhaled to show her impatience.

'Okay, so …' he started. 'So, our business …'

'TK?' she asked.

'Yes. No. When we came to London all those years ago, before you were born, we had another business. A jewellery shop on Ealing Road with another partner. I opened it with our family money and loans from the bank. We imported gold and diamonds from India and sold it in showroom. Your mother was excellent at selling and keeping accounts.'

'What did the partner do?' I asked.

'He handled the India end, sourcing the goods. We were growing, doing well. Then Maya became pregnant with you, Anjoli. I told her she must take her time, step back from work.' His face dropped. 'I wasn't as vigilant as I should have been. Your mother was on top of it, but I was not. And then my partner … he stole the stock overnight, took all the money and absconded to India. We never caught him and lost everything. I was penniless and desperate and couldn't even pay back the money I owed the bank. Baby on the way, we didn't have anywhere to live, it was a terrible time.' He took another sip of his tea, Anjoli looking increasingly concerned.

He continued. 'But Rakesh stepped in. He was becoming successful and had been my friend since Kolkata, and …' Saibal's voice cracked and his eyes glistened, reminding me of his tears on seeing Rakesh's body. He looked away from us. 'He was kind, he lent us the money to start again. Very generous. He had given us another chance and your mother is an excellent cook, so we set up a restaurant. Tandoori Knights. Good name, na? *I* thought of it.' He beamed at Anjoli, eyes still watery. 'We would bring you into the restaurant and you would lie in your little basket all day as your mother and I worked. I remember the diners would go coo-coo over you. There was this lovely young girl who used to sing to you whenever she came in …' He smiled at the memory, then pulled himself together. 'It was not an easy time. But things got better. I could not pay Rakesh back but he was very good about it. Then I borrowed more money from him to buy the building so we could have the flat over the restaurant. All our money went into looking after the family and paying for your lessons and your tuitions. So, I still could not pay back his loan. But he was a millionaire now. Every time I told him I would pay him, he kept telling me not to worry. Technically he owned the business and our flat and I was indebted to him. Your Ma knows, of course, but I never told you, because I didn't want you to worry. I trusted Rakesh. I trusted him as a businessman, as an investor, as a friend. I never thought he might one day be bankrupt.

'All those years working so hard, I cannot get the smell of masala out of my clothes and what do I have to show for it? My batchmates have done much better than me while I … I … and Rakesh …' he looked down in distress. I felt a stab of sympathy for Saibal; I'd only ever thought of him as Abba's London friend, not contemplating for a second the struggles he must have gone through.

Anjoli sat next to him and held his hand. He smiled at her, stroked her hair and composed himself once again. He seemed somewhat unburdened.

'When did you first realise all wasn't well with Rakesh's business? And how did it affect the restaurant?' I asked.

'A couple of months ago,' said Saibal. 'He came to the restaurant and told me he had to sell the building, our building. PinRak was having money problems and they needed to liquidate assets. They had lost a big contract. He said he was happy to sell it to me but what money do I have? He wanted one and a half million pounds for the freehold and the lease for the restaurant. Brick Lane has become so upmarket that the people who used to live here cannot afford it now. I could not understand why but he kept saying he had no choice and had to do it. He gave me six weeks to find the money to buy it. The bank refused me – my record is not good because I'm still paying back the loan from when my last business collapsed. I have no idea where else to go. At the party I again asked him why he was doing this, and to give me more time, but he refused. That must have been what you heard, Kamil.' He took a morose sip of his tea as I nodded in empathy.

'So that is that. There is nothing I can do. Bad karma,' he said, dejected. 'I must have done something terrible in my past life to deserve this. I didn't want to worry you both until I knew what we could do.'

Anjoli's eyes welled up. 'I'm so, so sorry Baba, I didn't understand. Don't worry, I'll get a proper job soon. Things will get better – I'll do everything to help. You and Ma don't have to shoulder everything on your own anymore. I'll give you my savings.'

'Dhut! What rubbish you're saying!' said Saibal. 'I will not take one penny from you; you need to buy your flat. Don't worry, God will provide. I have been running this restaurant for thirty years. I can do something different now. Everything has changed. Brick Lane is different – all young people and tourists now, no regulars anymore. I have to worry about things like Trip Advisor reviews-sheviews and Instant-gram – complete nonsense. People going click-click at their plates all night long. Tweeting and twatting. Good food, good service is not enough. Now the food has to be beautiful so people can take pictures and put on the Google. How do you make a chapati look nice? Maybe Rakesh did me a favour.'

Anjoli looked stricken. 'Ma! Poor Ma. How is she taking this?'

Saibal's expression turned despondent. 'She is strong, she can take anything. We rebuilt once; we will rebuild again.'

'I suppose that's what Rakesh's WhatsApp meant?' I said. 'He must have been feeling sorry for himself because he was drunk. It was his attempt at an apology.'

'I suppose,' said Saibal. 'He was not a bad man, just in a difficult position. The contract he lost – it was out of his hands.'

'We'll help you,' said Anjoli, determined. 'We'll save the business.'

Saibal stroked her hair. 'Always a fighter. But Anjoli, you must realise that this fire in your belly only becomes heartburn as you get older. She never gives up, this girl,' he said, looking at me. 'She should have been a lawyer.'

'She's a tough one,' I agreed.

'Neha will get millions from an insurance policy,' mused Anjoli. 'She thinks of you as her own family ...'

'I am glad. But I will not go to her, cup in hand,' said Saibal at once.

Something was bugging me. What had caused this sudden collapse in PinRak's fortunes? I wasn't a financial expert but surely a multi-million-dollar company couldn't just crumble? And if they had put everything into the Metro, why had they lost the contract? I hadn't read of anything terrible happening with the construction – in fact the papers in Kolkata kept saying it was going to plan. Arjun had been adamant there was no fraud.

'Do you know why they lost the Metro contract?' I asked.

Saibal looked straight at me, his face confused. 'Rakesh never said. Some problem in India. It was a cause of much tension in our friendship over the last few weeks.' Then he remembered something. 'But he said one funny thing. Six weeks ago, when we were talking, he blamed you. He said they lost the contract because of you, Kamil. Because of something *you* did ...'

The Detective

Kolkata. July. Tuesday.

'You need to confess, Mitra.' I tried to keep the nerves, the doubt, from my voice. Mitra looked nervously around the dingy interview room. The floors covered with unidentifiable stains; the broken tube-light on the ceiling casting half the room into crepuscular gloom; the high-barred window on the wall that appeared to suck out the light as opposed to letting any in.

'Confess, Inspector Sahib? To what?' he said, choosing his words.

I hated myself for what I was about to do: put my scruples behind me and be ruthless. The DC had left me with no choice. He'd laid out a plausible case for Mitra being the murderer and I had to follow it up. I hoped I could get Mitra to cooperate without getting physical. I had never roughed up a suspect before but the DC expected a result and I needed his confession. Fast.

I mentally cracked my knuckles and got to work, 'You know what I mean. Sit.'

Hazra pulled the wooden chair out from under the bare table and patted the seat encouragingly. Eyes darting from side to side, Mitra sat gingerly on the edge, Hazra standing behind him.

I sat on the table's edge and, looming over him, said, 'I will ask nicely. Tell me the truth. What happened to the CCTV?'

He looked up at me and licked his lips. 'Inspector Sahib, I told you. It malfunctioned.'

125

I noticed a bead of sweat trickle down his temple. He was lying. I leaned closer. 'We have a team of tech experts, and we know you erased it, Mitra.'

He looked very old, small and nervous, sinking back into the hard chair.

'Why should I do that, Inspector Sahib? I want to cooperate with the police.'

I moved even closer as he tried to edge the chair back but Hazra put a foot behind the leg to keep it in place.

'Because, Mitra, it implicates you,' I whispered with all the menace I could muster.

He shook his head vigorously. 'No, no, sir ... '

I got up and stood over him, my legs now touching his knees, blocking out his view of the room with my body. We sandwiched Mitra between us, Hazra's hands resting on his shoulders. Speak, please speak, I implored internally. Hazra looked at me, as if to say, 'What are you waiting for?' But I was *not* someone who beat people up. Even though it was normal for cops in Kolkata, almost expected, I couldn't do it.

'No! It malfunctioned,' Mitra whined. 'I had nothing to do with the murder. I swear on my children!'

'Then why are you so nervous, ei?' Hazra hissed in Mitra's ear, trying to help me.

I leaned over Mitra, to show him I was boss, nose to nose. It had worked well when the DC had instilled the fear of God in me. Hazra's hands tightened on Mitra's shoulders.

'Nervous? I am not nervous.' His rapid breathing belied his words.

'Then why are you sweating so much?' With a finger, I wiped a rivulet of sweat off his face and showed it to him.

'It is hot. Humid. Monsoon season ...'

As if in echo, a clap of thunder sounded. I felt ridiculous – a villain in a cheap film.

'Last chance. Tell me the truth or I can't be responsible for the consequences. Did the CCTV capture you stealing Asif's money? Were you getting revenge for something? Did Asif Khan, with his power and privilege, hurt you or your niece? Is that why you erased it? Or did someone pay you?'

I saw a flash in his eyes as he blinked rapidly. I had touched a nerve.

'I know nothing about money, no revenge, nobody paid me, God Promise.'

He squeezed his eyes shut, unable or unwilling to meet my gaze. I straightened up as I considered what to do next. Mitra had something to do with this – I knew it in my bones. The next step was to do as I had been ordered and take direct action. I flexed my hands.

Hazra looked at me over Mitra's head, made a fist and raised a questioning eyebrow. I had to stop wavering. The stakes were much higher now. It was time for desperate measures. I took a breath. A look of pity in Hazra's eyes filled my resolve. 'What a sissy!' I imagined him thinking. I gave him a curt nod.

Hazra shuffled Mitra off the chair and, panting with effort, tried to punch him in the gut and, unbelievably, missed. This was turning into a farce. He looked embarrassed and tried another clumsy punch, which connected this time. Mitra yowled as he tumbled to the stained floor in his pristine suit. I winced, both at Mitra's pain and at Hazra's terrible pugilistic skills. Even I, pacifist that I was, might have done better than that, with what had stuck of Abba's boxing lessons … Hazra looked set to continue but I held up a hand.

'Tell me what I want to know, or … ' I pointed at Hazra who was clenching and unclenching his fist, face a mask.

'I swear, I know nothing about this!' Mitra groaned. 'The CCTV is so badly protected; anyone could have done this.'

Hazra looked for the all clear, his foot hovering over the man's ankle. Refusing to cause any more pain, but wanting to show that I had what it took, I leaned over Mitra, twisted his ear and shouted, voice shaking, 'Mitra, if I find out you were lying to me—'

'I KNOW NOTHING!' he shouted into my face, eyes teary with frustration and pain – pain that I had inflicted with Hazra's fists as my tools. He continued, wheezing, looking me straight in the eye, enunciating every word, 'I did not kill Asif Khan.'

I believed him. Looked away, unable to hold his gaze. He may have known something about the death but he was not the killer. The DC was wrong. If not the manager, then who?

The three of us sat in silence. Hazra tried to regain his composure, sizing me up, hoping I wouldn't tell any of our colleagues about his poor roughing-up skills just as I hoped he'd stay mum about my dithering. Mutually assured embarrassment.

Mitra might be useful in another way. I showed him the video clip on my phone of the mysterious man arguing with Asif at the party. 'Who is this man? Have you seen him in the hotel?'

'It is Asif Khan,' he whimpered.

'Not him. The man he is with,' I rasped.

Mitra looked at the video through blinking, watery eyes.

'It is Jaideep Sanyal.'

It took a second, then clicked. I knew I'd recognised him from somewhere!

'Jaideep Sanyal? The Chief Minister's son?'

Mitra looked up at me. I saw an unreadable expression in his eyes. Fear? Was he scared we would hit him again or ... was it something else?

'Yes,' he said, shortly.

I looked at him uncertainly. 'Is there something you want to tell me, Mitra?'

'No. May I go now?' he said, avoiding my eyes.

I nodded. He rose, walked stiffly to the door, clutching his stomach and not looking back as Hazra escorted him out.

Alone in that stinking room, I felt sick. I had let the pressure of the case and the fear of losing my job get to me and crossed a line I'd sworn I'd never cross. Rivers of remorse ran through me as I stared at the grey sky through the barred window. Abba was disgusted by the day-to-day violence he saw in the force and had always told me to solve crimes using brainwork and diligence, not brutality. Maliha spent her working life prosecuting policemen who killed suspects in 'encounters'. And now here I was, as bad as any of them. So much for being the person who kept the public from harm; I had crossed over to the other side.

My phone pinged – a WhatsApp from Ashutosh.

Been digging into Asif Khan's finances. Does not look good. He was overstretched and needed money. Also borrowed a lot and was having difficulty paying it off. Will keep looking.

* * *

I had to damp down the remorse I felt about Mitra so spent the rest of the afternoon drowning myself in mindless administrative tasks. I'd instructed Hazra to ask Sabina Khan if she knew of a connection between Asif and Jaideep Sanyal when he fingerprinted her but when the never-ending paperwork became too much, decided to do my own research and fired up my internet browser.

The facts I collected about Jaideep didn't tell me much but instead served to underline what a failure *I* was, given that he was my age and had achieved far more than I ever would:

- On *Time* Magazine's list of 'Ones to Watch'.

- The *best* education – St Xavier's School, Presidency College, MBA from Wharton in the US.

- The *best* jobs – two years with Goldman Sachs in New York, returning to India to set up JSRS Investments, a Media Fund in Mumbai with $100 million under management.

- The *best* family connections – the only son of Ranjit Sanyal, Chief Minister of Bengal who for the last decade had won landslide victory after landslide victory through his championing of the poor; although, given he was presumably the 'RS' in Jaideep's investment company, clearly had done well enough to bankroll his son.

- And finally, the *best* social life – hobnobbing with the global glitterati, exquisite actresses and models hanging off each arm.

Seeing all this success just managed to increase my depression – I had to get out of here or the walls would swallow me up. I switched off the computer and gathered my stuff when a WhatsApp came in from Hazra:

Sabina Khan offered me cha! No match of her fp's in room & party dress clean but she confirmed financial difficulties. Asif rcd Rs 10 lakhs in cash last month and was expecting another 10 this mth! No sign of Asif/Sabina/Jaideep in video after midnight. Did not know Jaideep Sanyal. Sabina's driver told me Asif would go to a low-key place called Voodoo Club when he was in Kolkata! Am off-duty tonight so cannot go myself to check it.

Typical Hazra – handing things over just when there was a potential lead. Leaving aside his hysterical overuse of exclamation marks, the cash was intriguing – that might lead somewhere. But with Sabina apparently cleared plus my lack of success with Mitra, I now had zero suspects. All I had to go on was the shadowy figure from the video, this Jaideep Sanyal, son of the Chief Minister. How could I get to him?

I called Hazra to get further details of his interview and informed him in no uncertain terms that as far as I was concerned, he was on duty twenty-four hours a day, seven days a week till the murderer was caught. He sheepishly offered to come to the club with me, but I figured I was better off going undercover as Hazra would only ever be able to blend into a 'come as your favourite policeman' fancy dress party. Maliha would be a better bet – we were due to meet for dinner and I could make her my Dr Watson for the evening.

She was waiting for me in a bar opposite what was supposedly the Voodoo Club, but it was so low-key it was totally unmarked.

'What's up with you? How come we're meeting here instead of in Tangra as we'd planned?' she asked as I sat down and ordered a beer.

'I need your help on this Asif Khan case. I need to check out one of those doors.' I pointed across the road. 'We need to get into the Voodoo Club.'

'I've never heard of any Voodoo Club. And you've never taken me clubbing before Sub-Inspector Rahman – is this an early life crisis?'

'We have been dancing before …' I started indignantly, then noticed her grin. 'Okay, okay, let's just keep an eye out for potential clubbers opposite – and if anyone turns up who looks like they're going to a secret club, let's head over there. So, here's the story …'

I gave her a quick run-down of the case, avoiding my treatment of Mitra and not mentioning Jaideep – I still wasn't sure how involved he was with the case. She'd be upset about Mitra, knowing I had done nothing to stop Hazra getting his fists out. If anything, I'd encouraged it. I still had to come to terms with my actions. Maliha was my sounding board for so much, especially when I wasn't confident enough to tell my father. She understood and never judged me. She was a sympathetic listener and gave the best advice. But this might push her goodwill too far, particularly given the recent spate of police attacks on innocent victims.

'I'm sorry, it's not a very romantic thing to do for our date night … but Hazra is a terrible date,' I finished as she rolled her eyes at me, then leaned across the table and gave me a peck on the lips.

We drank our beers and nibbled aubergine fritters, my mood lifting as Maliha told me about her day. She started to discuss potential guests for our wedding, when I had to interrupt: 'Maliha, look!'

Two smartly dressed men rang a doorbell across the road, spoke into the intercom and were buzzed in. We nodded in tacit agreement, downed our beers, threw some money on the table and stepped out into the street. I grabbed her hand and we dashed across the road, dodging traffic. I rang the buzzer by the side of the unmarked door.

'Yes?'

'Voodoo Club?'

'Who is this? Members only.'

'Erm … I am a guest of …'

'Asif Khan!' Maliha blurted out.

'Mr Khan is sadly no more.'

'We know,' said Maliha, winging it. 'And want to pay our respects. We came here with him once and saw how much he loved it.'

There was a slight hesitation and we were buzzed in. We parted a bead curtain and found ourselves in a warm, dark room with velvet banquettes, private booths and candles, with soft jazz playing. There were a few men swaying on the postage-stamp-sized dance floor and several others lounging and drinking. Doors led further into the building into other even more private rooms.

'Oh,' said Maliha, nudging me. '*That* kind of secret club.'

'Huh?' I said.

'No women, Kamil! This is a gay bar!'

I shook my head. That couldn't be the case, but as I looked around again and reassessed the tight T-shirts and the men dancing, I realised she was right.

What the hell was Asif doing hanging out here? Was it just because it was low-key?

We found seats at the horseshoe-shaped bar and ordered two beers from the good-looking young barman in another too-tight white T-shirt.

'Get one for yourself,' I said. He nodded his thanks and opened three beers.

'I'm Kamil, she's Maliha. Have you been working here long?'

'Couple of years,' said the barman.

'Cool, can I ask a few questions?'

'You can ask,' he offered.

'You heard about Asif Khan's death?'

'Yeah, I read. Tragic.' He nodded at a waiter and poured green liqueur into a cocktail shaker.

'He used to come here sometimes, no?' I asked.

He rocked the shaker vigorously. 'Sorry, this is a discreet place, man. I can't talk about other members.'

'Of course, I understand,' I replied, putting a five hundred rupee note on the bar. He put down the shaker and pocketed it.

'Yeah, I saw him here a few times. On and off.'

'Was he with anyone special?'

'Naah, not that I saw. Most people come in for hook-ups. Private rooms at the back. Not a place for couples.' He looked at us meaningfully as Maliha laughed.

He handed us our drinks and we migrated to a nearby booth that gave me a good view of the room.

'Do *you* come here often?' Maliha asked me, giggling. 'Anyone special you meet?'

I made a face and took a swig of my beer. 'Is it weird being the only woman here?'

133

She looked around. 'A bit. It's sad that it has to be so seedy and undercover in this day and age. That it's illegal to be what you are.'

'Well, Section 377 states that homosexuality is still considered a serious crime – law states it is an "unnatural offence" and they can jail you for life.'

She rolled her eyes, and I could see her passionate vehemence for the injustices in every corner of society bubble straight to the top again.

'That damn "unnatural offences" law was made a hundred and fifty years ago by the British! How is it even remotely applicable today? You police are turning ten per cent of the population into de facto criminals. We brought a case against it last year and the judge said overturning the law would lead to, and I'm quoting him now, "rampant AIDS and paedophilia". Bloody prejudice!'

She took an angry swig of her beer. The craziness of prosecuting and persecuting those who were gay was a view we both shared.

'I know, darling,' I began, 'but what can we—'

'Yesterday it was the untouchables, today it's gay people, tomorrow it'll be the Muslims, the day after ... who knows. This country is just ...'

'I agree,' I said vehemently, 'and ... Oh. My. God. Look who just walked in!'

Striding in through the beaded curtain, as if he owned the place, was the man I had been Googling a few hours ago. Things were getting interesting.

'Isn't that the Chief Minister's son, Jaideep Sanyal?' asked Maliha, who was more clued up on her politics than I was.

'It is. And I didn't tell you but he was at Asif's party. I think I might just say hello. Keep my seat warm.'

Emboldened by my fourth beer of the night, I slipped out of the booth and joined Jaideep at the bar, as he barked 'Black Label. On the rocks.'

'Jaideep Sir, hello.' I tapped him on the shoulder.

He spun around.

'My name is Sub-Inspector Kamil Rahman. I'm looking after the case of your friend, Asif Khan.'

Tall, well dressed, good looking, I clocked the brands that were subtle but apparent – slim-fit Diesel jeans, Burberry shirt, Dolce & Gabbana sunglasses, useless in the room's gloom. He looked remarkably cool, given the warmth of the club, making me uncomfortably aware of the large damp patches that had formed in the armpits of my printed Double Bull shirt, badly tucked into my no-name baggy chinos.

'Good to meet you, Sub-Inspector. A horrible thing,' he said, his deep, honeyed voice sombre, a slight American accent breaking through. 'I hope you can bring the killer to justice. What are you doing here?' He was playing it cool.

'I believe this was one of Asif's hangouts. But I can ask the same question of you?'

Jaideep was silent for a moment.

'Look Inspector, it's not what it looks like. I'm meeting someone here for business. I am well known in Kolkata so must find places that are ... discreet. You know what I mean,' he said with a conspiratorial, overfamiliar nudge.

'Yes of course. Can I ask, did you ever come here with Asif?'

I could see his brain whirring, wondering what I might have found out. Finally, he said, 'Yes, I met Asif here a few times to discuss the financing of the movie.'

'How many times?'

'A few.'

'Did you know Asif was gay?' I said taking a gamble.

A pause. Then reluctantly, 'Yes, I knew.'

His confirmation of what had been bubbling in my mind for the last fifteen minutes was still a shock. Asif Khan, the biggest sex symbol of our time, was not the lady-killer he appeared. That might explain Sabina's indifference to his sex life; she must have known.

'And you were at the party? The night before he died?'

'Yes, he invited me. I'm an investor in his films. I've put ten crores into this one and had a similar amount in *Jango*,' he said.

A hundred million rupees! Jaideep was not short of cash.

'There's a video of you and Asif talking at the party. You appear to be arguing? What was that about?'

'Arguing? Me and Asif?' He said, puzzled. 'No, not at all. We chatted that evening but didn't argue.'

'It looked like a heated discussion. What did you talk about?'

'Nothing special. The film. Usual party chitter-chatter.'

I couldn't tell if he was being evasive or genuine.

'And what time did you leave?'

'Midnight? A little before?'

Ah! Same time as Asif. Was this something?

'Where did you go?'

'I was tired and had an early meeting this morning, so I drove straight home. I have a house in New Alipore; my driver will vouch for me. I only heard about Asif's death this afternoon on the news – it was a terrible shock. I was at lunch with my father. The CM,' he said casually.

Didn't take long to drop that in, I thought as I continued, 'We found money in Asif's room. Any idea where that came from?'

'Did you?' he asked curiously. 'How much?'

'A sizeable amount,' I said. 'In a bundle of notes.'

He shook his head. 'No idea. Must have been Asif's, I suppose.'

I played my last card.

'We also found evidence of drugs and alcohol. And sex. Did Asif mention to you he was planning to have a party in his suite?'

Jaideep laughed. 'No, he didn't, the bastard – I might have joined him if he had. And now I'm afraid I need to . . .'

I went for the jugular. 'Mr Sanyal, was there anything . . . more than friendship between you and Asif Khan?'

Anger suffused his face and his genial mask slipped. 'Absolutely not, *Sub-Inspector*. I came here a couple of times for business meetings. I am not gay. It wasn't like that between Asif and me. I'm a reasonable man but don't think I will stand by while you besmirch my reputation with your slanderous claims.'

'No, no Jaideep Sir. I am not suggesting anything. I am just trying to determine the facts.'

'Well, I suggest you focus on actual facts and not make up bullshit that will get you into serious trouble,' he snarled. 'Now excuse me, I have to meet my colleagues. This is a private club and I'm sure you are not a member.'

He downed his whisky, slammed the glass on the bar and stormed off. I turned to the barman who had been watching our conversation with interest.

'Hey, did you ever see that man here with Asif?' I asked.

The barman stayed silent. I sighed, took out a five hundred rupee note, and the barman palmed it expertly. The DC would have a fit when he saw my expenses.

'Yeah. They were here a few times. Danced, took a private room,' he said with a knowing look as he moved to clear up Jaideep's whisky glass.

'Wait,' I said. Another five hundred rupees changed hands and the whisky glass, wrapped in a napkin, was mine.

I walked back to the booth where Maliha had polished off both of our beers. She raised an eyebrow quizzically as two sizeable men in dark glasses and black suits came towards us.

'I think Jaideep might have spoken to management,' I said, surreptitiously dropping the glass into her handbag. 'Let's get out of here.'

My mind raced as we walked out. I could see the contours of the case now. If Asif and Jaideep were gay, could the fear of the law and society have forced them to hang out here and live their lives in secret? Were they a couple? Was one of them blackmailing the other? It made sense – the money, the condoms, Jaideep's body language towards Asif at the party ... Jaideep was the missing dot in my picture. I was sure of it.

The Waiter

London. October. Monday.

'He said they lost the contract because of you, Kamil. Because of something *you* did ...'

It made no sense, I thought, as Saibal looked at me as though I had the answer. It must be a joke. I didn't always get Saibal's humour, so I smiled, pretending I'd got the gag.

Anjoli looked in shock at Saibal, then at me, and back and forth.

'What are you grinning about, Kamil? Baba, how could Rakesh lose his business because of Kamil? What did he have to do with it? You told me you'd never met Rakesh before the party, Kamil.' She looked at me puzzled, and I wondered whether, with this strange joke from Saibal, she thought I might be a suspect.

'What? Huh?' I said. 'Saibal-da, you are joking, no?'

Saibal scratched his head.

'It's not a joke. Rakesh came to see if I had raised the money to buy the restaurant. And he drank and drank. You know how he is when he gets drunk, Anjoli.'

I tried to draw my memory back – it must have been recently, and I had been working in the restaurant virtually every day since I'd arrived in London. There was one night I had seen Saibal having dinner with a drunk man, who I now realised was

Rakesh. I hadn't served them as it had been a busy night, but the man had given me a dirty look a couple of times I'd passed. I'd assumed he was just an obnoxious drunk – the restaurant got a lot of them. But what had Rakesh said about me?

Saibal carried on. 'He got drunk and that's when he started talking. How he had been betrayed. By the Government; by his old friend; by you, Kamil. He was furious with you. I didn't even know he was aware who you were. Kamil Rahman this, Kamil Rahman that, you don't do as you're told. Your father doesn't do as he is told. How this is your fault.'

'My father? But what did he mean?' I asked, perplexed now. 'How did he even know who I was? What does he have to do with Abba? I know that you were at college together, but I've never heard Abba talk of Rakesh Sharma even once. What has this got to do with me?'

'He wouldn't tell me. He was livid when I told him we had taken you in. He spotted you serving that evening, you see. I have never seen him so enraged. He stormed out and refused to talk to me anymore. It surprised me that Neha asked me to cater their party – I thought it was, what do you call it, an olive tree. I asked you to step in because I needed the help, but I wondered if he intended for me to bring you along so he could speak to you. Did he try?'

This was bizarre. I had barely even heard of the man or Pin-Rak until three days ago. What could connect me with the loss of a multi-million-rupee business? But the link with Abba, perhaps that made more sense. Abba was always closed about his business associates … Was Rakesh taking things out on me, when really, he had issues with Abba?

'Maybe that was why Arjun was angry with you?' Anjoli said.

'I had better speak to Abba,' I said, panicked. I didn't want to be implicated in the Sharma case. I couldn't afford to get involved with the police – could this make me a suspect? All they had to do were a few background checks and they could have me deported.

'Hain, you talk to Adil, he may have the answers.' Saibal rose and let out a sigh. 'Let me wake your mother. We have to get the restaurant ready for dinner. Put on your uniform Kamil. Ami Aaschi.' He left the room.

As I picked up my phone to call Abba, Anjoli's phone rang. She answered it. Her eyes widened.

'What? Oh, shit. Okay, calm down. I'll speak to Baba. We'll sort it. Promise. I'll call you back.'

She hung up.

'The police have formally charged Neha with the murder of Rakesh. She's in custody.'

Part of me had been expecting this. There was no other obvious suspect and I assumed the police had now found something concrete against her. I kept the thought to myself, seeing how hard it was for the Chatterjees to imagine someone they had known since childhood as a murderer. Saibal and Maya took it particularly hard. 'She is also my daughter,' Saibal kept saying to the desk sergeant in Kentish Town who refused to let us see her. Pinky and Arjun had (understandably) refused point blank even to consider the company paying for her defence so the CPS said they would allocate a duty solicitor to her case. But Saibal wouldn't hear of it. 'These people they provide are useless, we will pay for an excellent solicitor ourselves,' he said, and phoned his friends, relatives and acquaintances till he got someone who came recommended and appointed him, sight unseen.

Dejected, we returned to the restaurant where I finished my shift in a febrile state and drifted to bed for another sleepless night, tossing the covers on and off as I alternated between feeling too hot and too cold. My brain was overloaded, speculating about the evidence behind the decision to charge Neha and trying to comprehend how I could have been responsible for PinRak's collapse. The only tenuous link I could find between me and Rakesh was Taania Raazia. But I hadn't met her in Kolkata, merely seen her among hundreds of other people in the footage of Asif's party. It was perplexing, akin to those optical illusions that shift with your perspective – it seemed that no definitive solution existed. Till you saw things from the right angle. And that angle eluded me.

* * *

'Chef is off today,' Saibal said the next morning as Anjoli and I were leaving to see Neha's solicitor, hoping that he would give us positive news after having consulted with her the night before. 'So, Maya will need your help in the kitchen tonight. And Kamil, make sure you are back for the lunch shift.' That was annoying. Despite the questions raised by the case, I had to help cook, too! Saibal's expectations of me were high. I wanted to tell him murder cases didn't solve themselves; they took time, precision, deliberation. Frying onions wasn't any rule of policing.

But I nodded and we set off. Throughout the tube journey to the solicitor's office, my neck tingled, as though someone's eyes were on me. Every time I turned to look, there was nothing. I shook it off, but the feeling persisted.

'It doesn't look good,' the solicitor said. 'They fear she may flee the country, given Rakesh's connections in India so have charged her with the murder without bail. They have plenty of evidence. Rakesh died because of the blow to his head and smashing his skull on the pool edge – there was limited water in his lungs, so he didn't drown. The glass in the head wound matched the broken whisky bottle. The police found fragments of glass in the sole of Neha's shoe. Blood from her foot was on the scene. The ring they found in Rakesh's hand fits her finger, Rakesh probably pulled it off when she hit him. She swears it isn't her ring but nobody else has claimed it and it doesn't fit Taania or Pinky. They think that she dropped her shoe and cut her foot because she was trying to get the ring out of Rakesh's hand when he was in the water. The final clinching piece of evidence was that forensics found only her and Rakesh's fingerprints on the body of the whisky bottle.'

Anjoli's face grew stony as the solicitor continued remorselessly to add brick upon brick of evidence that would build a cell around Neha. 'She knew about the bankruptcy. The insurance policy was in her name. The evidence, although admittedly circumstantial, points to her – it is such that between the timing of the message to ...' he checked his notes – 'Mr Chatterjee and that of the scream denoting the "discovery" of the body, she is the only person who physically could have carried out the murder. The police theory is that she had suspicions about her husband's romantic assignation with Taania Raazia, lost her temper and struck him with the whisky bottle, which caused him to fall back and smash his head on the pool's edge.

'There are no other suspects. They have spoken to Taania Raazia and are satisfied it was not her. She says she left Rakesh in the pool at around one-forty, went up and called an Uber. It took around half an hour to arrive and she waited for it in the house. The driver and the CCTV confirmed it. They have interviewed the other guests at the party, including your family of course, and Mr Sharma's domestics – butler, driver, maids – and decided none of them had anything to do with the killing as they had left well before the murder.'

'Are you defence or the prosecution?' Anjoli burst out.

'I *am* her lawyer, Miss,' he said gently. 'But we have to be realistic. Listen, it's her first offence. We could reduce it to manslaughter, it was clearly not premeditated. She is young and will be out of jail by the time she is thirty-five or so, still have her life in front of her. But she has to admit guilt. Unfortunately, she is being stubborn and keeps saying she just found him dead.'

'That's because she did!' cried Anjoli.

When we left, Anjoli was fuming and muttering about incompetent Indian lawyers and how she should have taken up law herself. As always, I couldn't find the right words to comfort her. And I was inclined to agree with the police; however much Anjoli liked Neha, I didn't see how anyone else could have done it. The evidence was overwhelming.

'I'm not giving up on Neha. I've organised an interview with Pinky Aunty. I'd better go on my own, she's more likely to talk to me,' said Anjoli fiercely as we swayed on the tube back to Brick Lane.

I nodded. 'Yes, go and see Pinky, the police may have missed something, and we should eliminate her ourselves. First rule of police work, double check the evidence.'

'Your police work has a lot of first rules,' said Anjoli, irritably. 'Are there no second and third rules?'

'"In detection, all facts are equally important, you ignore the smallest clue at your peril",' I parroted my teacher in the Police Training School. 'It forces me to examine all the angles and not let something seemingly inconsequential slip through the net. So now, I'm trying to get to Taania. I want to know what Rakesh was doing with her in the pool.'

'It's bloody obvious, isn't it? That story of her waiting for an Uber sounds fishy to me,' said Anjoli, distaste spreading across her face as if she had eaten a rotten mango.

'Well,' I said, thinking back to the blind alleys I had travelled down in the Asif Khan murder, 'First rule of police work, don't trust the obvious.'

That made her laugh. 'First rule of Anjoli Chatterjee – her detective friend is a total gadha. All right, I've got to change here. See you back at TK later.'

She winked and left the train as I returned to the restaurant for my lunchtime shift, smiling – I had moved from being her brother to her donkey. That was progress.

Anjoli returned after lunch, grabbed me from the restaurant and took me to the flat to debrief me. She was deflated, feeling that she had achieved nothing. Pinky had corroborated everything Arjun had said and spent the rest of Anjoli's visit alternately ranting about and gloating over Neha's arrest. Anjoli had reluctantly decided that she wasn't involved with the death.

'I don't know, Kamil, she was adamant that she and Arjun had stayed in the sitting room that night. They were waiting for Neha to find him so they could say bye. I believed her. I've known her for years and if she was lying, I would know.'

It was out of our hands now. Taania was our last chance and I didn't know how to get to her. But there was one thing I needed to know, because even if it wouldn't solve Rakesh's murder, it would help put my mind at rest. Anjoli wandered off and I dialled Abba's number, heart beating a tattoo in my chest. We hadn't spoken in months, and I missed him. Did he miss me?

'Son?' His voice sounded just the same, but crackly on the WhatsApp call.

'You well, Abba?' I tried to keep the worry out of my voice and stay cheerful. I didn't want him to know what I would ask and prepare himself.

'Yes. You?'

'Yes, all well.' I paused, breathing deeply, before saying: 'Abba, there's something I needed to ask you.'

'Go on.'

'You heard about Rakesh Sharma's death? And PinRak's collapse?'

There was a scratchy silence. Then he said, 'Yes, I read about that. Saibal also called me to tell me of Rakesh's demise. Very sad news.'

'You knew Rakesh Sharma?'

'We were at college at the same time but were not really friends. He was close to Saibal, though. We had been in touch on and off, but I'd not spoken to Rakesh for at least a year. His death is a tragedy.'

'Abba, Saibal-da said something strange to me. Apparently, Rakesh told him I was responsible for PinRak collapsing. And something about you not doing what you were told? Why would he say that?'

'That you were responsible? How could you be responsible? What did it have to do with you?' He sounded genuinely puzzled.

'I don't know, that's why I'm asking you.'

'I do not know, either.'

'And what about you not doing what you were told?'

He laughed. 'Other than your mother, who tells me to do anything now that I am retired? Kamil, I can only tell you I knew nothing about Rakesh's business matters. We were acquaintances from college who occasionally got in touch – just to catch up, mainly speak about Saibal. I have absolutely no idea what he could have been talking about. It is possible he mixed us up with someone else or someone is spreading nasty rumours? I'll speak to Saibal.'

There was shuffling in the background, and Abba said 'Here, your Ma wants to speak to you.'

Ma and I had the same conversation we always did – was I eating properly? Was I praying? I should visit the Masjid, it was right next door to the restaurant. As usual, I told her what she

146

wanted to hear. I missed her but felt that things in London had got much darker since the last time we'd spoken, and I couldn't fathom where it would end. She ended by telling me to ask Maya to call her, she had a shortlist of eligible boys for Anjoli.

Picturing Anjoli's apoplectic reaction to that piece of news cheered me up for a second then I returned to the mystery of Rakesh's words. Abba was as baffled as I was. But there had been genuine fury in Rakesh's face when he'd met me and even Arjun couldn't bring himself to look at me. I had to understand what was happening. Neha wouldn't be of any help, she had introduced me to Rakesh and clearly hadn't known he had any animosity towards me. Pinky might know something. I should have asked Anjoli to check with her.

Something else about the party was bugging me. A creeping sensation in the back of my head. Something someone had said that evening ... a false note ... what was it? Try as I could, I couldn't bring it to the surface. I had to let it germinate till the time was right for it to emerge into the light.

Anjoli and I trotted back down to the restaurant where Maya was perched on a high stool behind the bar, filing receipts into a book as a few desultory diners finished their meals, waiters hovering and eager to close the restaurant so they could start preparing for the evening. The lunchtime stragglers were annoying – of course they deserved to take their time since they were paying customers, but they made life more difficult for us. Salim Mian would start removing the tablecloths from the other tables while tutting under his breath in a none-too-subtle way, but that was too Basil Fawlty for me. The dreaded late-night lingerers were much worse. They took their time over their desserts and coffees as I kept a smile adhered to my face, desperately willing them to pay the bill and leave, so I could wash up and collapse into bed upstairs.

'What did the lawyer say, Anjoli?' Maya asked as soon as she spotted us. 'Saibal said you spoke to him.'

Anjoli conveyed the events of the morning to her mother, whose face fell as she heard.

'Terrible,' she said, when Anjoli had finished. 'I don't believe it. Not that girl. But he is a talented lawyer, well worth the money we are paying. He will find something and show she didn't do it.' Anjoli reached across the counter and squeezed her mother's hand.

'That's so nice, Ma. But ... but can we afford him? With the business and everything?'

Maya shrugged. 'We will manage. We have to help the girl. It is our responsibility. She is the sister you never had, Anjoli, and like a daughter to us. Kamil, you must be able to show it was an accident.'

I couldn't bear the false hope. This was no accident, someone had killed Rakesh and the likely perpetrator was Neha. 'I'll try, Maya-di,' I said. 'But the evidence is strong. And the Met rarely make mistakes.'

'Well, they *have* in this case,' said Anjoli stubbornly. 'And we will get her off. What do you want us to help with, Ma?'

Maya let out an enormous sigh and became her usual business-like self. 'Okay, go to the back. You can both chop vegetables for dinner.'

The stress returned – I was exhausted, the thought of spending the afternoon prepping in the kitchen followed by hours of waitering was overwhelming. It meant I would have no time to sit and get my brain around what had happened.

I followed Anjoli into the kitchen, trying to hide my involuntary frown and unhunch my shoulders. As soon as I entered, the smells, the familiarity, soothed me. The rack of deep stainless-steel pans in front of us contained spadefuls of multi-coloured spices – salt, turmeric, fenugreek, coriander, cumin, garam masala, tandoori masala and black pepper. These magic powders were the foundation of virtually any Indian meal and a superb chef like Maya could make food sing with them.

On the other wall hung similar racks waiting to be filled with chopped onions, garlic, ginger, tomatoes, green and red chillies, fresh coriander, fresh peppers, butter and oil. Two cookers with eight hobs dominated the space and dozens of pots, pans and other utensils were hung around the kitchen. And in the corner was Saibal's pride and joy: a naan oven, imported from India, that made the most deliciously soft and pillowy breads.

The entire kitchen was spotless as Maya was meticulous about cleanliness and inordinately proud of the five-star food-hygiene rating the restaurant got every year – *Highest in Brick Lane,* she informed me on my first day in the restaurant, *Don't let us down.*

We went to work, side by side in the kitchen. Anjoli wordlessly peeled onions, ginger, garlic and potatoes as I chopped and swept them neatly into the steel pans for cooking later. Most of the other restaurants on the street used bags of pre-cut, pre-puréed, pre-prepared foods but Saibal liked us to be as authentic as we could. *I have been doing it this way for thirty years, why should I change now? Old is gold.* Luckily the restaurant had only a dozen tables, so we could just about manage.

'There must be another explanation,' said Anjoli breaking the silence. 'I just can't believe that Neha would ...'

'People can do desperate things,' I said dicing an onion. 'Taania's our last hope. She was obviously with Rakesh at the pool, from 1.15 to 1.40. We need to reach her and find out what she saw that evening. And check that she waited half an hour for the Uber.'

Anjoli moodily threw the peelings into the organic recycling bin. 'If we can ever get to her. But if she left before the murder it makes it even worse for Neha.'

149

Anjoli had tried to get Taania's number, but no one wanted to give it to us. Bollywood stars were, unsurprisingly, difficult to reach. I did have one more idea and had sent a text that morning. It hadn't born fruit yet, but we would see.

When we were done in the kitchen, we went to the front where Maya was helping the waiters set the tables. She smiled when she saw us.

'All done?' she asked.

'Yes,' I said. 'Are you all right, Maya-di?'

'Oh, I've been so busy today. I have not had one minute to stop,' she said, rolling her shoulders back and forward.

'Relax, Ma, we'll do it,' said Anjoli, straightening cutlery on a table.

'Thank you, sweetie.'

'Ma, Dad told us about Rakesh's demands for payment,' said Anjoli quietly.

'Oh?' said Maya.

'I'm so sorry I didn't know, Ma. Are you okay? Will we have to sell?'

Maya paused, then sat heavily at a table.

'Ah, I am so tired of this, this stress, these problems. Maybe it is for the best – there is no community left here anymore. When we came to England forty years ago, we moved to Brick Lane because this was the only place in London where we were accepted. We were strangers in this unfamiliar, rainy country. But here we were amongst our own and so this is where we built our tiny village. Now, little by little, the rest of London has taken over our village. The sweet shops have become wine bars, the mosques have become food markets. Nobody can afford to live here except these technology people and everyone has had to sell and scatter. Maybe it *is* time for us to find a new village. We will be okay, Anjoli. I trust your father. You don't worry.'

'Well, this is my home and I'm not moving,' said Anjoli firmly. 'Have you eaten today, Ma?'

'Don't worry about me, I am fine. You two go and enjoy the evening, looks like it will be a quiet night. You have helped me lots.'

'Okay, Ma,' Anjoli hugged her and the two of us walked into the evening light of the street, the lamps and restaurant signs starting to buzz into life, blotting out the lilac twilight.

We walked out of the restaurant and Anjoli giggled. 'The neon's gone again!' I turned to look at the restaurant's sign which now proudly proclaimed in glowing hot orange letters TANDOORI NI TS.

I smiled as Anjoli said, 'I told Baba not to waste his money on that sign. I guess the punters will think we do a very specialised sort of cuisine!'

We wandered to the park, heading down the always bustling Brick Lane. As Anjoli expounded on the changes in the street over the last fifteen years, I felt a prickling sensation again, as if something was about to pounce. It persisted as we walked through the Bengali Arch into Altab Ali Park. I swivelled around a couple of times but didn't see anyone in the mass of people on the pavement. Lack of sleep could do strange things to the human psyche, I thought.

It was a chilly evening, but people were sitting and chatting on the small patch of green. I liked this bit of grass in the East End, loomed over by tall buildings. The park was named after a man who had been murdered in a racist attack; it felt an appropriate place to discuss our present preoccupation.

I found a tree, shooed away pigeons that had chosen to rest their wings on the grass under it, and Anjoli threw herself down

next to me, pulling her coat close around her. I thought of Maliha in the Botanical Garden and had to physically shake off the
memory. It seemed so long ago. Another life. Another lie I had
thought was true at the time.

'We need to save Neha, but Rakesh's death has brought so
many other worries with it. I need to look seriously for a job.
Otherwise I'm literally just a burden on Ma and Baba,' said
Anjoli, tearing a blade of grass into bits and staring out at
nothing.

'You're not a burden. Not literally. You're pretty light.' She
threw me a look. 'What would you like to do? Work-wise, I
mean,' I asked.

'Not a clue. Another market-research gig I guess?'

'How about printing and selling your tops?' I said, looking at
her current one that read *Don't you DARE read this T-shirt* under
her cardigan. I had been impressed with the inventiveness of
her personalised apparel. I hadn't seen one slogan repeated.

'On Etsy! That would be fun!' She perked up. 'But no ... too
much hassle for not enough money.'

'How about becoming a psychiatrist? People can lie on your
couch and you can tell them what's wrong with them. They
would pay you! You'd love that. And you have a psychology
degree.'

'I'll tell you what's wrong with *you* for free,' she said gleefully.
'Anyway, that takes years of training, no one tells you that at uni.
But I met this guy the other day who works for a marketing company and he said they hire people with psych degrees to do
market research, which helps them design new products to sell
to people.'

'Sounds dodgy?'

'It's a reputable firm. Pays well. It sounded interesting, so I'm
going to contact him. What are you planning to do? This investigation hasn't gone as we'd planned so detective work may not

come thick and fast ... and it doesn't look like you want to be a waiter.' She gestured to me, as always in my waiter's outfit, waiting to jumpstart my life.

'My visa runs out soon,' I said, gloomily. 'I must head back and start again. No idea what I'll do. Believe it or not, working for your dad as a waiter pays more than the five hundred pounds a month I earned as a Sub-Inspector in Kolkata police.'

She looked at me, surprised. 'Five hundred a month? Is that all you earned?'

I grimaced. 'Yeah. That's why everyone takes bribes. But on the other hand, you don't pay one pound for a single samosa in Kolkata, so I suppose it's more than it sounds.'

'Did *you* ever take bribes?' asked Anjoli, curious.

'No. Never. Abba would have been so ashamed. The occasional free meal, but that was it.'

We lapsed into silence. I pulled up tufts of grass and scattered them around as Anjoli gazed across to the moss-covered gravestones in the corner. Her phone pinged, she glanced down.

'It's Massimo, I'll call him later.'

Her barista. In the excitement and stress of the case, Neha's arrest, it had slipped my mind that Anjoli was seeing someone. 'Oh yeah,' I said casually. 'Ma said she had a shortlist of eligible boys for you back in Kolkata. Lucky you!'

She didn't disappoint. 'For fuck's sake!' She yelled, causing a panicked pigeon to ping off the grass. 'What are these people doing interfering with my life? Honestly sometimes I just ...' She fell into a moody silence.

'How come you're going out with this guy when you can't introduce him to your parents?'

'It's not that I don't want to introduce him to them. I do ... But they wouldn't approve. They've always wanted me to go out with an Indian guy – hence the head-hunting call to the rellies around the world.'

She sighed and continued, 'I just don't feel at home anywhere, I'm out of place everywhere. I mean, don't get me wrong, I am Indian. I love Indian food and songs and embarrassing Bolly-wood movies but sometimes it seems my Indianness is ... I don't know, a sari I wear over my jeans? Ma's always telling me off about these "English" habits I've picked up, that I'm not a "good Indian girl". Telling them about Massimo would just prove her point – even if she's entirely wrong.'

The sadness in her voice made me want to reach out and hug her.

'So, what *do* you want?' I said, instead.

'I've no idea. If I have to have another "What are you going to do with your life" conversation with them, I'll scream! Honestly, I'd like to move out and get my own place.'

'Why don't you?'

'Thought I'd save up to buy when I had the job and obvs can't afford it now. London is so crazy expensive. Anyway, with this Rakesh business it'll never happen. I'll have to give literally all the money I was saving for a deposit to Baba now.'

'We will figure something out,' I whispered, not sure if it was a promise I could commit to making, since they could ship me out any day.

'We will,' she said. 'I have faith in you. What types of cases did you work on in Kolkata? Anything like this?'

I couldn't tell her about the past I'd left behind. 'I don't like to talk about it, Anjoli,' I said, hoping she would let it go as usual.

This time she didn't. 'You never want to talk about what hap-pened in Kolkata. But if we're going to be partners on this case,' she raised her eyebrows meaningfully, 'there needs to be a degree of trust. So, tell me about it. I won't judge you for it, I promise.'

I looked at her serious face gazing at me. It *would* be a relief to unburden myself. If Anjoli was my friend, she deserved to hear it and know who I was. Saibal and Maya were like parents to me, and I knew how little I had told my actual parents ... And she was right, she wouldn't judge. *Keep talking, I'm diagnosing you* – I remembered her T-shirt. Maybe a diagnosis was what I needed to help put my guilty conscience to rest.

So, everything tumbled out in a confused jumble. Asif Khan's murder, my battles to bring the killer to justice, the crimes I had committed on an innocent man, the death on my conscience, my terror and helplessness when I was beaten, the impact it had on Maliha and me ... everything. I didn't whitewash it or leave anything out – from my initial excitement to how incompetent I felt later. And how talking to Arjun had brought those emotions back. It was like I wasn't even worth *his* time, and everything I'd worked hard for, respect, status, had vanished. How I desperately needed to be my own man. To get out of Abba's massive shadow. Everything I had done was to make him proud, to get a smile from him, a pat on the back. To be the son he deserved. And I had failed him.

I felt cleansed after I finished. The bitterness and anger that had been buried inside me for the last three months dissolved as I told Anjoli my truth, there amongst the anonymous gravestones of Altab Ali Park as the lights on Adler Street elongated the shadows of the passers-by.

There was a lengthy silence. Anjoli impulsively leaned over and took my hand. She said nothing, just held it lightly in hers, fingers entwined. Then her inner psychologist emerged.

'Thank you, Kamil. I think you've been grieving.'

'Grieving? For what?' I asked.

'For the lives that were lost and for the loss of *your* life. But maybe you can put it behind you. Move on. Can I ask you a question?'

'Yes,' I said hoarsely. Was there more to say? What other questions could she have?

'What do you believe in?'

'Pardon?'

'What do you believe in, Kamil?' she repeated.

I couldn't answer this strange question. What *did* I believe in? If she had asked me four months ago, I might have said justice. Now I knew from bitter experience that justice was an illusion and neither victims nor villains got what they deserved. Truth? Well, that fell by the wayside as soon it became inconvenient. Family? Abba, my rock, had proven himself to be made of sand when I needed him most. Love? I had torn that into pieces and thrown it away.

I heard myself say, without thinking, 'Kindness. I believe in kindness, Anjoli.'

Which was a joke, given how I had treated the people in my life. And how it had rebounded on me. I felt a chill as the terror I had felt lying on the sawdust-covered floor in Kidderpore Docks swept over me.

The Detective

Kolkata. July. Wednesday.

At 11 p.m., after a day of calm weather, the monsoon teased her usual evening entrance with spectacular peals of thunder, although the rain still held off. Abba's driver dropped me at my flat in Kidderpore Police Quarters and raced off into the night, trying to beat the deluge. I had given the glass I'd filched in the club to Hazra to analyse against the prints we had found in Asif's hotel room. Given Jaideep's position, I needed hard evidence before I could go to the DC. I'd also spent the day trying to see if I could get more information on Jaideep's investments in Asif Khan's film or about their relationship but had come up empty-handed.

Frustrated with my lack of progress, I took Maliha to my parents' place for dinner and spent the evening with Ma, talking about the wedding. I'd liked to have discussed the case with Abba but he had sequestered himself in his study, working. Perhaps he didn't want me to tell him too much about it; he wanted this to be mine, and I respected him for that, although I could have used his advice. Even though I had no evidence, Maliha believed that I should speak to DC Ghosh the next day and tell him my theory. After mulling this over, I decided it was good advice and I could use the DC's experience to point me in the right direction.

position, expecting a kicking. Instead he hauled me up by my collar till I was on my knees and waved a photo on his phone in front of my watering eyes. Through the blur, I saw with a shock that the picture was of Maliha, entering my parents' house with me, a few hours before.

'This time it is a warning,' he said. 'But this is nothing. We know where your pretty lady lawyer lives.'

I nodded, silent anger bubbling up inside me. At myself more than anything. How had I been stupid enough to bring Maliha into this? I'd put her in harm's way.

'Tell me you understand,' he said, gripping my neck with his hand like a cat holding a kitten.

'I understand,' I whispered, with difficulty.

The man released my throat, slapped my face twice, then pushed me back onto the floor, leaving me crumpled amongst the towers of tea, swimming in my guilt.

Maliha. I had to get to Maliha and warn her.

The Waiter

London. October. Wednesday.

'How on earth did you get Taania to agree to see us?' asked Anjoli, peering into her compact, applying colour to her eyelids as we sat in the overground on the way to Watford Junction where Taania Raazia was shooting her new film, *Din Ke Baad Din*, at Leavesden Studios.

'I can be very persuasive.' I said, raising an eyebrow suggestively. I looked around the carriage, checking every passenger. The free-floating anxiety about being watched the previous day hadn't left me. Once again, I dismissed it as my imagination. The stress of the past few days was playing with my mind but my confession to Anjoli had lightened my burden and I could see a path to daylight ahead of me.

'Shut up and tell me.'

'Okay, no need to be rude. Remember I told you last night that I met Sabina Khan in Kolkata?'

'Yes, Mr Big Shot, I remember,' she said.

'Well, I had a brainwave. I texted her yesterday to ask if she would make an intro to Taania. She was happy to help me since I'd been the inspector on the Asif murder and had helped get her husband's body released in time for the funeral. I think she may have thought I was still a cop and I didn't disabuse her of the notion. And Woy-La!'

'It's literally Vwah-la, not Woy-la,' said Anjoli, acidly. 'Anyway,' she continued, tapping me on the shoulder, 'well done. She's our last chance to prove Neha is innocent.' She was being a tad patronising, but I knew that she was impressed. I hadn't been aware of *her* texting Bollywood stars ...

The train trundled through the fading greenery near Watford. The trees were shedding the last of their leaves, silhouetted against a sky as grey as my bank balance. There was a stark beauty in the landscape hurtling past us and I let myself sink into it, the rhythm of the train calming my mind.

'So apparently this film's a big budget blockbuster remake of *Groundhog Day*,' said Anjoli, interrupting my trance.

'Do you have groundhogs in the UK?'

'No. They're probably using a hamster or something. I don't think realism is the hallmark of a Bollywood film.'

She bit into a Jaffa cake and turned to stare through the window at the scenery whizzing by, absently brushing crumbs from her coat.

We arrived at Watford Junction, then took an Uber to Leavesden and made our way to the main gates of the studio complex where we were ticked off a list and given lanyards with passes as guests of Taania Raazia. Anjoli took a few selfies with her pass, but I warned her not to post them anywhere. This was an active investigation – and I didn't want the police to know we were poking around.

'Sound Stage Four,' said the security guard.

They ushered us into the thankfully warm hangar with an admonition to be quiet. The enormous stage was set up as a big Punjabi wedding with hundreds of extras milling around, decked in technicolor outfits. The set was the exterior of a gigantic mansion ('Sharma Manor' mouthed Anjoli) covered with flowers, bunting and fairy lights ('How many unicorns threw up in here?'). A harassed-looking choreographer was trying to marshal the extras into a big dance number – 'No, luv, you go right there, not left. RIGHT NOT LEFT' – as they leapt back and forth in a metronomic fashion. It was organised chaos.

'Let's see if we can find Taania,' I said, steering Anjoli away from the spectacle.

An assistant director, overhearing, pointed us to a table at which Taania was sitting, sipping an orange juice. Tall, slim with long black hair, high cheekbones and eyes ringed with kohl, she was dressed in a skimpy pink ghagra and light blue choli, her jewelled navel winking as she moved in her chair. She looked up as we approached. I introduced myself, 'Kamil Rahman. I think Sabina Khan mentioned ...'

'Yes, she did,' said Taania, examining us with interest. 'She said you wanted to see me about Rakesh's death? That you were an Inspector in the Kolkata Police? Why are they interested?'

'The family have asked me to look into his death,' I said, dodging the query. 'There are still unanswered questions. I'm aware you've spoken to Scotland Yard, but I was wondering if you wouldn't mind helping us?'

Her eyes wandered to my left and I realised I hadn't mentioned Anjoli. 'And this is my assistant,' I said before she could say anything, 'Anjoli Chatterjee.'

Cottoning on, Anjoli nodded hello as Taania motioned us to sit, saying to Anjoli, 'Oh yes, I saw you at the party. You were sitting with Neha, right?'

Luckily, she hadn't recognised me as the waiter who had served her champagne. I had been invisible, just another bowtie with a tray amongst a multitude of bowties with trays.

Anjoli nodded again, then suppressed a giggle as I started, 'Well, Taania Madam ...'

'Please, call me Taania.'

'So, Taania,' I began again. 'How did you know Rakesh Sharma? Did he invite you to the party personally?'

'Yes. He had financed one of my movies. The big hit, *Jango*?'

I looked up from my notebook, startled.

'You mean *Jango* with Asif Khan?'

'Yes, the last movie he made before his … passing. Terrible about Asif … but *Jango* became a super hit after he was no more. It's what Asif would have wanted,' Taania said with exaggerated sincerity.

'And Rakesh Sharma financed it? I thought Jaideep Sanyal financed that movie?' Just hearing myself say his name out loud made my stomach tighten.

'Jaideep Sahib was the chief financier, but Sharma Sahib also put money in. I got to know him on the set when we were shooting *Jango* and last week he heard I was in London for this movie, so he rang and asked me to come to his party.'

I considered this, wondering how I could get onto the meat of my questioning without offending her. The stakes were high – if Taania was innocent of Rakesh's murder, Neha's jail door would slam shut.

'Did you spend much time with him at the party?' I asked, feeling my way.

'Not so much,' she said nonchalantly. 'We danced; I heard his speech. What a magnificent man, giving that money to charity. And such a tragedy what happened.'

'I saw you talking to him in the sitting room late that night?' said Anjoli, helpfully. 'May I ask what you were discussing?'

'Oh, this movie; other projects I'm involved in; was there any movie I wanted to do.'

'And was there?' I asked, curious if this was how movies got made – rich financiers being importuned at parties by actresses.

'I told him I was passionate about making an alternative version of the *Kama Sutra* from the woman's point of view. Tasteful, you know. Not too much sex or nudity or things like that. A spiritual *Kama Sutra*, about the power of a woman,' Taania said with some emphasis, seeing a flicker on Anjoli's face. 'He was very interested and offered to finance it for me. We agreed to meet the next day to discuss it in more detail, but he didn't turn up. I later heard what happened. Terrible. He was a kind man.'

'The police mentioned you were at the pool with him before you left the party?' asked Anjoli, as delicately as she could manage.

Taania was silent.

'We know you had no involvement with his murder, Taania Madam,' I said. 'But we need the facts. We will be extremely discreet with whatever you tell us. I understand the difficulties in the film world. As I said, I am acquainted with Sabina and . . . Jaideep Sanyal. In fact, I was the lead inspector on the Asif Khan killing,' I said, praying she hadn't seen the articles about me being fired.

This piqued her curiosity. 'Wow. You know Jaideep as well?'

I was rising in her estimation, so I swallowed and lied. 'Indeed,' I said as coolly as I could manage. 'So, what was your relationship with Mr Sharma? You knew him for a while?'

'It's always good to be friendly with the producers . . .' Someone called her name and she rose.

This circumspection was getting nowhere.

'I'm sorry to push, Taania Madam, but what happened when you were with Rakesh Sharma at the pool? You're not a suspect because the police cleared you, but we need to find out what took place.'

She looked at us for a second, expressionless. Then sat again. 'All right. I told the police, so I may as well tell you. I have done nothing I'm ashamed of. If you must know, Rakesh and I had a thing. He had been line-maaroing me since we met in Mumbai. It's normal, all the producers do. On Saturday night he was blatant. This was his birthday party, his wife and ex-wife were sitting at the other end of the room and he was flirting with me.

But he didn't care. That was Rakesh, he believed he had the licence to do what he wanted.'

'So why did you ...' Anjoli started then trailed away as I shot her a warning look.

'Why did I?' said Taania, curling her lip. 'Listen, it is hard to be an actress. Specially in Mumbai. We are all disposable, most of us have a shelf life of three to four years. Unless you are lucky and make it big. And I plan to make it big. But you have to make your own luck in this world.'

'And ... Rakesh Sharma was lucky for you?' I asked, softly.

'Sure. And I was lucky for him. I had made him money in *Jango*. And if what it took for him to finance my new movie and show my acting talent to the world was for me to be ... nice ... to him – usme kya nuksan hai? – what's the harm in that?'

I could feel Anjoli tensing by my side. She chipped in, 'But he was giving his money away to charity. Did you honestly think he'd be financing another film?'

Taania laughed. 'Get real! All these crorepatis have money squirrelled away. There was no way it was all going to kids in slums. That was PR!'

'So, what happened in the pool?' said Anjoli, too aggressively for my liking. I prayed that Taania wouldn't shut down.

'We are not judging, Taania Madam,' I clarified.

'To ab aap mujhe judge kar rahein hain? I don't mind. You can judge me all you like but this is the actual world women have to live in.'

'I understand, Madam, I do,' I placated as Anjoli bridled and interrupted again, 'Hasn't #MeToo reached India?'

I groaned inwardly. Anjoli was a resourceful sidekick, but interrogation was not her strong point. I'm not sure it was mine either, from past experience, but we were so close to getting Taania to tell us what happened, I couldn't afford to spook her. Although Taania didn't look in the least intimidated as she stared at Anjoli like a tigress about to rip an antelope into very tiny pieces.

'That is easy for you to say, Miss Hashtagtivist. Yes, we are aware of the Weinstein business. All those successful stars shouting METOO-SHETOO. You know what, for those of us still trying to make it in this profession, unless the system changes, the Rakesh Sharmas of the world will keep getting what they want. Zindagi to lena dena hain. Life is give and take, *Miz* Chatterjee. You may be a psychologist,' she said pointing to Anjoli's *Hug a Psychologist, We're Conditioned to Respond* T-shirt, 'but you need to learn about the real world. Asif Khan knew that. You think only minor actresses like me have to do things we don't want to? Believe me, even mega stars like Asif Khan do things *they* don't like.'

'What did Asif Khan do?' I asked, now curious.

'Let me just say, producers were not just after the actresses. Asif is dead, let me not speak ill of him. The power in the Mumbai film industry is not with the stars as you might think. It is with the money men. Jeevan bhar ke liye. So, this is a long answer to your question but superstars like Asif Khan *and* other struggling actors are out for the same thing you are – to make a mark on the world. And Mr Rakesh Sharma also wanted the same thing. So, I accompanied him to the pool, was "nice"' – she made air quotes – 'to him, then left. Happy now?'

I was awe-struck at her forthrightness. Anjoli looked away and said nothing. 'Thank you for being so honest, Taania Madam,' I said. 'I appreciate it. What time did you leave?'

'I left Rakesh at the pool around 1.40 or so. I called an Uber, but it was late on a Saturday night and there was a long wait for them to come to Hampstead. Half an hour or something.'

'And where did you wait?'

She stared at me.

'If you must know I went to the guest bathroom and … freshened up. Till the Uber came.'

She stared at Anjoli challenging her to say something. Who didn't oblige.

I probed, 'You waited in the bathroom for half an hour? Why not join the others?'

'What? In the living room? I heard them talking as I left but I could hardly go back in there after … being with Rakesh. And it was pouring with rain so I couldn't wait outside. It was a relief just to chill out – being a celebrity at a party where everyone wants a part of you is exhausting. The bathroom was comfortable, so I sat and made a few calls to LA. The police checked my phone.'

I nodded. That made sense.

'Did you see anyone when you left?'

'No, I didn't.' She hesitated, then continued. 'But when I came up, I got the impression that there was someone in the dining room. I could have been wrong, or it might just have been the butler or a server … but it felt like someone was waiting there.'

This was something. Had the police followed up on it?

'Did you tell the police this?' I asked, trying not to show my eagerness.

'No, I only just remembered. Anyway, the police seem convinced it was Neha Sharma. Open-and-shut case, they said.'

This sent a shiver down my spine. The Asif Khan case – DC Ghosh had called it that too. I knew that the obvious answer wasn't always the right one.

I decided to test something.

'Taania Madam, were you aware that Rakesh had lost his money? That PinRak was bankrupt?'

'What?' She couldn't have faked the shock on her face.

I nodded. 'Yes, the charity was a sham. All the money was gone.'

She went silent then whispered to herself, 'That bastard, that complete chutiya. He had no intention of doing the movie. Just wanted one last ...' Her voice trailed off. 'I have to go.'

'May I contact you if we have any other questions?' I asked.

'No, I am done with this nonsense. Today is the last day of the shoot. I'm returning to Mumbai tomorrow.'

I watched as she strode off, leaving the scent of roses in her wake. I turned to Anjoli, 'I believe that was Bollywood Hustler – one; Brick Lane Liberal – nil.'

'Yeah well, whatever, you can stop staring at her backside now,' Anjoli muttered. 'Why did you tell her about the bankruptcy?'

'It was the only motive I could think of. If Rakesh had taken advantage of her and then told her he was bankrupt, that might have pushed her to kill him. But she didn't know, so I'm not sure she had a motive. She thought he was funding her film.'

'Hmm,' said Anjoli, unconvinced. 'So, you believed her? What about what she said about the person in the dining room?'

'Yes, that was interesting, but who could it have been?'

'The butler, maybe?' said Anjoli, looking mutinous.

'He left with the TK crew, Anjoli, I saw him. Why are you so obsessed with this butler? Do you think he was Rakesh's long-lost twin brother separated at birth and had to kill him before he gave his money away so he could claim it after Rakesh's death? You're right, I'm sure that was it!' I winked.

'Stop it,' said Anjoli. 'It's not funny. Could a guest have stayed behind in secret?'

'It's possible I suppose. But the police questioned them, and we didn't see anyone else leave on the CCTV.'

She took a deep breath.

'Then that's it for Neha?'

'I'm sorry, Anjoli, but it looks like it. The police would have checked when Taania ordered the Uber and when it arrived, as well as the calls she made to the US. She'd have had to be a seriously cool customer to kill Rakesh then call an Uber and sit around waiting for it. She had no motive. The ring didn't fit her finger, nor were her fingerprints on the bottle. You were with me in the kitchen. Your parents were with Pinky, Arjun and Neha in the living room. So, it looks like the police theory is right. Taania came up, Rakesh cleaned up, sent his texts and after we left, Neha went to the pool and struck him with the whisky bottle in a rage. We have to accept that we can't do anything for her now.'

We made our way back to the station, despondent, and arrived to see our train in the distance. I headed to a spot near to where I thought the doors would open, Anjoli beside me. As I watched the train approach, I felt a hard shove between my shoulder blades and stumbled. I teetered on the platform, the train only a few yards away from me. I started to fall forward, almost in slow motion, seeing the driver in his cabin staring at me, utter shock in his eyes. The train moved inexorably towards me accompanied by a low rumbling that cascaded into my ears. My foot slipped below the platform but Anjoli grabbed my coat and yanked me back, just as the front of the train shot past me, an inch from my face.

With no control over my balance, I fell back and collapsed on the platform, my shoulder in agony. Anjoli bent over me in distress, the other commuters looking at me in consternation.

The horror of what had just happened hit me and I could barely breathe. I had almost died! I was underwater, I couldn't make out the voices trying to reach me. I tried to rise but my legs were jelly and couldn't hold me up. Passengers walked around me to board the train as Anjoli put my arm around her shoulder and dragged me to a bench where I collapsed in relief. I could still feel the hand that had pushed me on my back burning through my coat.

That wasn't an accident. It was deliberate. Someone had just tried to kill me. I thought about the shadowy figures I'd seen, the strange presence I'd felt around me for the last couple of days. *Just because I was paranoid, didn't mean they weren't after me.*

And there, near the exit, eyes boring into me, vape in hand, wearing a smart suit, was Biren – the vaping muscleman who had threatened me in Kolkata. When I caught his eye, he smiled, raised a hand in an ironic wave and disappeared through the exit.

I stared in a state of stunned shock at his shadow walking away. Why was *he* here? How had he found me?

The Detective

Kolkata. July. Thursday.

I spent Thursday morning in bed, recovering from my beating in the tea warehouse. Maliha tried to persuade me to tell my parents what had happened but, out of a perverse combination of stubbornness and shame, I refused. She looked after me as best she could, but every so often burst into tears. She crawled into bed with me after making me porridge, giving me Crocin for the pain and carefully rubbing Arnica on my bruises.

'Oh God, Kamil. What have you got yourself into? And this is all because of your case?'

'I'm so sorry,' I repeated endlessly. 'I'm so sorry to have brought you into this.' My words rang empty and hollow and I could tell that Maliha had seen something die inside me. What was I, if I couldn't protect her? I had put her in danger – those men could return at any time. One wrong move from me and ... I couldn't bear to think about it.

The memory of Mitra curled on the floor of the interview room returned, doubling my shame and guilt. This was karma paying me back. I had to be honest with Maliha. Hesitantly, I told her about what we had done to Mitra and how I deserved what I had got. 'So now you know the man you're going to marry. I won't blame you if you call it off.'

She took my face in her hands. 'You're a fool, Kamil Rahman. This case has destroyed you in just three days. You couldn't have done anything about those men. And what you did to that man-ager ... well, no, that wasn't your finest moment, but it was understandable. And the reason I love you so completely is that it matters to you. You have this guilt because you are an honour-able man. You have ideals. And the tragedy is that you've discovered ideals aren't enough. Phone Mitra, apologise, then let it go. He'll recover and you'll recover and we can live our lives. Tell the DC everything you have found out and ask him to find someone else to take it forward. It's the only way to keep us safe. Let's put it behind us.'

She stroked my aching head and I swallowed the tears that threatened to well up. She didn't want to go to work but had to leave to defend a case. I tried to persuade her that it might not be safe, but she said she couldn't let her client down and prom-ised to be vigilant. Reluctantly, I kissed her goodbye.

On my own, with just my guilt and fear for Maliha to keep me company, I decided to take her advice and call Mitra. I *would* apologise for what I'd done. Maybe he could tell me more about Jaideep. One thing the beating had done was to convince me I was on the right track. Jaideep had to have been behind it. Who else 'far above me' would I have created a problem for?

I dialled. Someone picked up the phone but didn't speak. 'Hello, Mr Mitra? Are you there? This is Sub-Inspector Rahman.'

Continued silence at the other end.

'Hello? Speak up, I can't hear you,' I said.

'Hello, Inspector.' The man's voice was soft. Mitra.

My breathing calmed. 'Mr Mitra. Thank you. I wanted to apologise and say that I am extremely sorry about what we did in the police station. It was uncalled for. I was under stress ... it should never have happened. How are you?'

'I am okay. Thank you.' Then, after a pause, 'I appreciate that.'

'Again, sorry. If I can ever do anything for you, just ask.'

Silence. Then, 'Yes. Thank you. I will.'

How do I ask him about Jaideep? 'Would it be possible to meet so I can apologise in person?' I said, ashamed at my deception.

Silence again.

'Mr Mitra? Are you there?' I said.

'Yes,' he whispered. It was getting increasingly difficult to hear him. 'Yes, we can meet. Actually, there is something I have to tell you. I'm at the hotel.'

My pulse quickened. 'Can you tell me now?'

He paused again. 'Someone may overhear me. Come and see me in room ... four-fifty-five. I will be there.'

'Okay,' I looked at my watch. 'I'll be there in half an hour.'

'Inspector,' he whispered, 'in case the time ... my knees locked.'

'Sorry, please repeat,' I yelled, 'what about your knees?'

But he had hung up. My phone buzzed again with a Whats-App from the DC – *Report Rahman*. Good. It was time to tell him my theory about Jaideep.

I dressed, which was a painful exercise, and limped out as quickly as I could. When I reached the DC's office, he was standing behind his desk and seemed calmer than he had the last time we had met. I dove straight in.

'Sir, I believe I may have solved the case and have discovered the killer. Asif Khan was in financial difficulties and sir, he was gay. Sir, I questioned Jaideep Sanyal ...'

The DC interrupted in surprise, 'Jaideep Sanyal? The CM's son? What has he got to do with this?'

'Sir, he was a person of interest, a friend of Asif's and an investor in his movie. And sir,' I said in a rush, not wanting to be interrupted again, 'I believe he was Asif's lover. Illegal under Section 377. If it came out, Jaideep could go to jail. Asif Khan needed money desperately and I believe he blackmailed Jaideep.

Jaideep is a high-profile person and couldn't afford to be outed. So, he paid Asif ten lakhs last month and was due to pay him another ten this month to keep his mouth shut.

'I have a video of them arguing at the party. I believe that Jaideep went up to Asif Khan's room that night to pay him and they had sex. Then, in a fury, he killed Asif. After murdering him, he wore Asif's clothes and left, taking the cash, not realising he had dropped a bundle of notes. If we check the notes and condoms for fingerprints, I am certain they will be Jaideep's. I would like to bring him in for questioning.' I ground to a halt and stood back, waiting for my strong investigative work to be appreciated with a congratulatory handshake.

The DC stayed silent, deep in thought. 'I see,' he said, finally. 'Do you have any corroborating evidence or is this speculation?'

I explained how I had seen Jaideep at the club but, even as I was speaking, realised I had nothing concrete. Suddenly my claims sounded thin.

'Hmm,' said the DC, uncertainly. 'I'm not sure, Rahman. Sanyal is a VVIP. We have to tread carefully. If you have nothing concrete, I don't see how ...'

This time I interrupted.

'There is one other thing, sir. They ambushed me last night, and ...'

A note of concern entered his voice. 'Who ambushed you? What happened?'

'Three goondas were waiting for me at night outside my flat. They took me to a godown in Kidderpore Docks and threatened me with force and violence.'

The DC looked appalled.

'Sit, Rahman. We cannot have this happening to our officers,' he said, sitting opposite me. 'What happened?'

I described what had happened.

He listened carefully then said, 'A terrible business. All the more reason to get this wrapped up. I will sort out these goondas who came after you. Are you okay to continue with the case?'

This was my way out. I considered it for a moment but heard myself saying, 'Yes, sir, I am fine and want to see this through to the end. I won't let you down. But sir, what I was trying to say was that the beating was also related to Jaideep Sanyal. I was explicitly told it was a message and I should stay away from important people in the case. He is the only important person I have interviewed.'

The DC considered this, took off his glasses, pinched the bridge of his nose and remained silent for another long minute. Then, snapping his eyes open, he leaned over and put a hand on my shoulder.

'But he is not, is he? You interviewed Sabina Khan. And who knows, maybe the hotel manager thinks himself important. Listen Rahman, this is a complicated business,' he murmured. 'Kamil' – it was the first time the DC had used my given name – 'Kamil, listen to me. Find hard evidence and we will act. Now, file the report about your kidnapping. Give descriptions. We will bring the men who did this to you to justice. I will not stand for my officers being hurt in my city. It is not acceptable.'

'Yes, sir.' I saluted again and left.

I understood where the DC was coming from; given his position, he had to be careful. Deep in my bones, though, I knew that Jaideep was involved. Mitra might give me more about Jaideep and the DC could then take action. There had been something in Mitra's eyes when I had shown him the video of Jaideep and Asif.

I suddenly realised that I had one other clue. Jaideep's whisky glass! I'd forgotten to tell the DC about that, and it might yield the proof I required. My beating had made me sloppy. I texted

Hazra to fast-track the forensics on the glass, got into the car and told my driver to rush me to the Grand.

Twenty-five minutes later, I was in front of room 455. I ignored the Do Not Disturb sign on the door and knocked. 'Mr Mitra?' It swung open.

The light in the vestibule was on, leaving the room in shadow, curtains drawn against the grey day. I could make out a single bed against the wall, bedclothes balled up in a mess, and next to it, a chair. As I walked into the room I gagged, cudgelled by an overwhelming stench of faeces. Dry heaving, I switched on the light to reveal a body hanging from the ceiling fan. I stared in shock at Mitra, the polite man, swaying in front of me, lifeless.

No. No. Not this. Not Mitra. Not now. What was happening? Had I driven him to kill himself? Was this my fault?

The Waiter

London. October. Monday.

Rakesh Sharma had been dead for over a week, though it felt like a lifetime ago. Today was the day of the funeral. The investigation was over and, after the incident at the train station, Saibal insisted I take it easy at work, so I was on delivery duty rather than being a waiter. I hadn't been badly hurt but was grateful to have my days to myself with evenings pootling around in the van, dropping off foil-covered takeaway cartons as far afield as Hackney and Limehouse – Tandoori Knights had its regular diners in distress all over East London.

I tried to work out how Biren had found me – and why. My involvement with the Asif Khan case was in the past. What did he want from me now? Was it a coincidence? Was the shove onto the tracks a last vicious expression of revenge for what Ashutosh and I had done in our final desperate act before I'd got fired?

I shared my fears with Anjoli, since she was now au fait with the Kolkata affair. She listened intently but was sceptical. 'Kamil, how likely is it that a vaping musclebound villain from India followed you from Kolkata to London to Leavesden and then back to Watford to push you under a train? This isn't a Dan Brown novel! It must have been someone else you saw.' And while logically I knew she was right, I was certain I hadn't mistaken that venomous sneer, etched in my mind. I *might* have been able to convince myself I had imagined it, if it hadn't been for the hand between my shoulder blades and the wave before he vanished. This was no coincidence.

When the news got out to the press that the police had charged Neha for the murder of wealthy industrialist Rakesh Sharma, they knocked themselves out. BUSTED: GOLD DIGGER MURDERS MILLIONAIRE HUSBAND, blared one of the headlines. The *Financial Times* published an in-depth analysis of the case and, according to their investigations, PinRak was totally leveraged, with the Metro contract being its only hope of survival. The company had lost the contract because Ranjit Sanyal (Jaideep's father no less!) the Chief Minister of West Bengal had been re-elected on an anti-corruption platform and had investigated all large contracts. He found that PinRak had won the Metro contract via an elaborate labyrinth of bribes and back-handers. Civil servants were fired, and the Government pulled the contract. So much for Arjun claiming the company was 'completely clean'.

Had Rakesh known about Jaideep's connection to Asif Khan? I was going crazy – wishing connections into existence.

'You're not wearing that are you?' asked Anjoli, dressed suitably for a Hindu funeral in a white top with white trousers as she shook the Tower of London snow globe she had put in my room when I had arrived, to remind me of my previous trip to London ten years ago.

'Yes, why? Is it not proper? It's a dark suit.'

'No, the suit is fine, the tie is a little ... loud for a funeral?' She tossed the globe from hand to hand, watching the snow drift onto the raven perched on the battlements.

I looked at the bright red tie with fir trees I was holding in my hands. Ma had bought it for my London trip, not realising it was a 'Christmas' tie. 'I don't have any others. I'm not a suit-and-tie person. I can't wear my TK bowtie to the funeral, can I? People will expect me to produce a tray of samosas.'

She chuckled. 'Hang on, I'll get one of Baba's.'

She reappeared a few minutes later with a navy tie which she placed around my neck and knotted. 'There you go,' she said, finishing with a flourish, 'you could be on the cover of GQ. "What the modern Muslamic wears to a Hindu funeral".'

I laughed. 'You look pretty good yourself.'

'Yes, I do, don't I?' she said, adjusting her hair in my mirror.

'Children!' shouted Saibal. 'We have to go.'

'Children!' she grimaced. 'You're thirty, I'm twenty-seven and we are still kids in their eyes.'

'It's nice, I like it,' I said, remembering the formality that had pervaded my family life. Ma had always thought of me as her little boy and Abba had insisted on keeping a distance between us – sometimes we felt more like colleagues than father and son. My time with Saibal and Maya was my first experience of being part of a *proper* family.

My replacement parents were waiting at the bottom of the stairs dressed respectively in a dark suit and white sari. We piled into the Volvo and drove off to Shanti Funeral Home, adults in the front, 'children' in the back. As I'd taken to doing over the past week, I checked the street before we left for anything suspicious. To my relief, I saw nothing out of the ordinary.

We drove in silence for a while, until Anjoli spoke up: 'Would the police normally release the body so rapidly, Baba?'

'I don't know Anjoli,' Saibal replied. 'The lawyer said Arjun was vehement and insisted; the police have arrested who they think is the killer so ...' His voice trailed off.

We drove on glumly, knowing what that meant for Neha.

'So, is this your first Hindu funeral, Kamil?' Saibal said eventually, trying without success to lift the atmosphere in the car.

'Yes, Saibal-da,' I said, wondering where this was going.

He nodded.

'Bhalo. Good. First, we go to the funeral home for last rites then to the cremation. Muslims do not cremate, no?'

'No, we bury.'

Anjoli and I smiled at each other, knowing what was coming. And right on cue, Saibal proceeded to educate me. 'Hain. We Hindus call it Antyesti. The last sacrifice. We believe in rebirth. So, the body is nothing. The atman, the soul, is everything. When you die, you sacrifice your body, but your atman is reborn in another being – could be human or animal – it depends on your karma and how much good you did on earth. So, Rakesh is not really gone – he will be reborn.'

'Probably as a cockroach, back in his Kolkata slum,' said Anjoli acidly.

'Anjoli! Take that back. Rakesh helped us so much; he was our friend for many years and today is his funeral!' said Maya, voice cracking.

'Sorry, Ma,' said Anjoli, contrite. 'I just didn't like the whole Taania Raazia business. It was disrespectful to Neha. And what he did to our family.'

'No one is perfect,' Maya said.

We parked and piled out, hurrying to the tiny waiting room of the funeral home to see Pinky, sitting in the corner, looking desolate and Arjun gazing at a strange three-dimensional picture on one wall, showing a ferocious goddess Durga riding a tiger. Rakesh's other relatives were also present, their whispers drowned out by the dirge of the bhajans keening over the PA system.

'Not very cheery is it?' Anjoli whispered, as everyone air-kissed, murmuring platitudes of condolence.

'Well, it is a funeral,' I murmured. 'What do you want? Ed Sheeran? I'm going to see if I can speak to Arjun, it might be my last chance. I need to see if he knows why Rakesh had it in for me.'

But before I could accost Arjun, the funeral director opened the door to the main parlour and we trooped in to see a dhoti-clad priest in a white kurta tapping on an iPhone that he shoved into his pocket as we entered.

An open coffin containing Rakesh Sharma's body, clothed like many of the guests in a smart suit and tie, lay on a stand in the centre of the room. We arranged ourselves around him as the priest said, 'Please to pay last respects to the deceased.'

After you die you become the 'deceased', I mused. Or 'body' or 'corpse' or 'cadaver'. You stop being a person and become a thing. I had used the same language – I recalled telling Hazra to 'cut the body down' when I'd seen Mitra hanging in that hotel room. I reminded myself to be more careful with my speech and remember the individual for who they were and not what they had become.

One by one, the family approached Rakesh, each lost in their thoughts. I followed, trying to see their reactions in case I learned something. Arjun walked up to his father with a set face, blinked a couple of times and walked back. Pinky wept nonstop and Anjoli, Maya and Saibal visibly tried to control their grief. When it was my turn, I stared at Rakesh's pale, lifeless face – it looked unreal, like a badly taken photograph – and tried, without success, to imagine the successful man that Saibal and Arjun had described. The wound on his head had been expertly covered up by the undertaker but strangely, his mouth was slightly open.

'Oldest son, please come,' intoned the priest.

Arjun obeyed, serious and determined. The priest gave him a small brass cup with water in it and a handful of leaves. 'Ganga-jal and Tulsi leaves. Please pour in mouth.'

As Arjun did this, the priest intoning Sanskrit verses from the Upanishads all the while, Saibal whispered in my ear, voice shaking, seemingly compelled to continue his lesson, perhaps to take his mind off his friend lying dead in a coffin a few feet from him. 'They purify the body.'

Anjoli was trembling, unable to take her eyes off Rakesh. I gave her shoulder a squeeze.

'I can't believe they wouldn't let Neha attend her own husband's funeral,' she said in a choked voice. Maya nodded, tears trailing down her cheeks.

'Now rice in mouth, oil on forehead,' said the priest.

'Feeds him for the journey ahead,' explained Saibal, brushing away a tear and holding Maya's hand.

'Flowers,' said the priest. 'Walk around, please. Quickly.'

The mourners collected handfuls of red petals that were lying in a basket near Rakesh's feet and circumnavigated the coffin scattering them around and on the body. Pinky was in a daze, tears falling from her eyes, which she ineffectually wiped at with her sari as she continued her circling.

We scattered our handfuls of petals in the coffin, then backed away to the edges of the room, trying to get as far away from Rakesh as possible. As the priest continued to perform the last rites, I smelt something burning. Would they cremate him here too? Surely not!

'Hey! What are you doing?' shrieked Pinky.

Everyone turned away from the priest to see Anjoli hitting Pinky's substantial backside with her palm.

'You're on fire, Pinky Aunty!' gasped Anjoli. Pinky had backed into an incense stick and her sari had started to smoulder.

Crisis averted, we stifled our laughter, the tension broken. Pinky grimaced and moved away from Anjoli. The priest looked on disapprovingly and raised the volume of his incantations till we fell silent.

He gestured to the funeral director, who fetched the coffin lid that had been standing upright in the corner of the room and placed it on top of the casket, after which he and Arjun screwed it on with large brass bolts. Anjoli put her arms around her mother, who cried into her shoulder.

'Thank you. The ceremony is finished. All please go now to crematorium. We will follow in the hearse.'

We arrived at Hoop Lane crematorium half an hour later to find the car park full of scores of Rakesh's friends and colleagues who had come to pay their last respects. I saw several who had been at the fateful party, save for Taania Raazia. 'Guess she's had enough of Rakesh,' Anjoli said.

'She returned to India, no?' I responded.

'Oh, yeah, I forgot. Well, they can have her.'

The mourners shook hands and took their place inside the church-like crematorium, which was all dark brown wood and brick walls. A large photograph of Rakesh had been placed at the front of the chapel and on it hung a garland of fresh flowers. This memorial was finished with a flickering LED candle, the kind I had seen on offer in my local Cash & Carry. The whole tribute was surprisingly moving. *Now* I could picture Rakesh as the father and husband, instead of Rakesh the philandering, bribe-taking CEO. The family were seated in the front rows; the other attendees filled the entire room, spilling out at the back. Rakesh had been popular.

I sat next to Anjoli in the third row as the flower-decked coffin was carried in by the bearers – Arjun, Saibal and four other friends and relatives of Rakesh's. The priest stood in front of the lectern and greeted the congregation in Hindi. He stepped down and Arjun took his place.

'Thank you for coming,' he said. 'Dad would be so happy to see you here. He told me when *his* father died, there were only four people at his funeral in India. Dad made his own way in the world and taught me that was what I had to do. And I will have to do it without his guidance now.

'Dad was exceptional. Generous to a fault. He sacrificed a great deal to get to where he was. When I was growing up, I didn't see as much of him as I would have liked, since he was always working so hard. But his influence was always there. He made me what I am. Thanks for everything, Dad, we won't forget you. You have left a great legacy.'

Tears swam in my eyes. Arjun could have been speaking for me – this was how I had felt about Abba, before he'd abandoned me when I'd needed him the most. I squeezed my eyes shut, unable to stop one lone tear escaping down my cheek.

The priest rose and spoke again, his voice fading as the plaintive refrain of a Hindu religious song played. He nodded to Arjun who pressed a button and, with a quiet rumble, a door in the wall opened and the coffin slid away on a conveyer belt. The door shut after it, leaving us lost in our thoughts.

We walked out of the exit of the crematorium and stood under a long, covered walkway, with arches looking onto pretty gardens on one side. Wreaths and flowers with condolence messages for the day's earlier funerals were placed on the floor, lining the wall. Rakesh's arrangements were by far the largest and gaudiest – each well-wisher trying to outdo the last. Arjun and Pinky stood opposite the wreaths laid for Rakesh as the congregation filed along, hugging, shaking hands and expressing their sympathy. I followed the mourners, shaking Pinky's hand and, when I got to Arjun, shook his hand and offered what words of consolation I could find, hoping I might have time to speak to him alone. But after the condolences were over, every time I tried to catch his eye, he would move on to talk to someone else.

Back in the car park, Anjoli and I found Saibal and Maya saying their goodbyes to Pinky, who said 'Come and have dinner, the two of you. And you also, Anjoli.' They nodded as Pinky continued, 'I am glad they caught that woman. I have cried all the tears in my body for that man. First after die-vorce and now after death. I cannot cry any more. The good news is the administrator cannot touch what I got in the die-vorce. Rakesh was generous. So, Arjun will at least be okay. In a funny way I suppose I should be thankful to Neha. If she hadn't seduced him and Rakesh hadn't die-vorced me, we might have lost everything. God is great and sometimes there is light when you do not expect it.'

I had failed in talking to Arjun but wanted to see if Pinky knew anything about Rakesh's animosity towards me.

'I'm sorry for your loss, Mrs Sharma,' I said.

She gazed at me with a blank expression. Arjun had clearly not mentioned me to her. Saibal, realising we had never been introduced, said, 'Pinky, this is Adil's son, Kamil. He has been lodging with us.'

'Oh! I thought you were one of Saibal's waiters. I was wondering why you were here.' She smiled at me. 'How are Adil and Rehana? I haven't seen them in so many years.'

'They are well, Aunty,' I said. 'I was wondering. Do you know if Rakesh said anything about me or Abba to you recently? Any reason he might have been upset with us?'

'Upset? No. He mentioned nothing. Why?' she asked, a puzzled look on her face.

I could see what Anjoli had meant about knowing if Pinky was lying. This was a lady who didn't hide any emotions.

'No reason,' I said. 'Again, my condolences.'

She air-kissed us and sailed off to say goodbye to another well-wisher. Another dead end.

'Wonderful,' said Anjoli watching her leave. 'So, Arjun and Pinky have half of Rakesh's money from the "die-vorce" ... Baba and Ma lose their business and home and Neha goes to jail. Yeah, God is really great.'

'It is karma, Anjoli,' said Saibal philosophically, patting the pockets of his jacket to find his car keys. 'Our actions determine our lives. We must have done something bad in an earlier life. But don't worry. Ami tomara Baba, nai? I will always be there to take care of you. Rakesh is at rest and, God willing, we will help Neha.' Saibal unlocked the car.

'I know Baba, I know,' said Anjoli sliding into her seat. My phone pinged with an email as I opened the door for Maya, and she smiled her thanks.

I read the email. Anjoli looked at me through her window. 'Everything okay?'

'It's an email from UKVI,' I said slowly.

'UKVI? What is that?' asked Saibal.

'Visas and Immigration,' I replied. 'They want to see me tomorrow at four with my passport. They have raised a question about my immigration status.'

'Huh? Who's raised?' asked Anjoli.

'It doesn't say,' I said. My fears had become a reality.

'I'll come with you. Baba, nobody knows about Kamil working for you on the wrong visa, do they?'

'No. Just the people at the restaurant and they won't say anything,' said Saibal, looking troubled.

Now what? I couldn't catch a break. Just as I was getting back on to my front foot someone hurled another missile at me to knock me back. I walked around Saibal's Volvo to get in, when, across the top of the car, with a shock I saw a face I recognised. It was unmistakeable, even in shadow under the peak of a cap. Biren. Vape in hand he was leaning against a blue BMW 7 Series, staring straight at me.

Without thinking I slammed the car door shut and raced towards him. He took off, weaving through the parked cars and out the entrance of the crematorium. I dodged the few remaining mourners and hurtled to follow him. He darted in front of a car to cross the road, the driver giving him a loud blast of his horn. He looked over his shoulder at me, then vaulted a low wall into a cemetery opposite. I felt the rough brick under my hands as I did the same and saw him, now just a few yards ahead of me, zigzagging through gravestones. I was gaining on him, my determination to find out why he was here tormenting me, giving me reserves I wasn't aware that I had. But as he heard my thudding footsteps behind him, he found fresh impetus as well and the distance lengthened between us. By now the sprint was taking it out of me and I was panting, my legs starting to feel stabs of pain and I started slowing down. No, I thought, I cannot let him get away. He turned to see where I was, tripped over a low grave at his feet, and fell face first into the dirt. Before he could scramble up, I reached him and threw myself over his body, covering him like a blanket. My hands scrabbled to pin his arms down as he thrashed beneath me, his cap flying off.

He wriggled out from underneath, rolled to his feet and stood, facing me. I looked into the red eyes that had haunted me since that night in Kidderpore docks – I had lost so much because of this man. We both launched at each other simultaneously, our heads colliding with a painful crack and we landed in a heap. I leapt on him and we wrestled, tumbling and rolling like two children in a playground – he stood up as I scrambled to my feet and I landed a punch to his stomach. It was rock hard, and my fist rattled with pain. But it appeared to have an effect as he staggered back.

I looked around to see if I could find something to hit him with when, with a roar, he charged at me and got his arms around my waist. I tried to cuff the back of his neck with my hand but staggered and fell back onto a grave, my head smashing against a gravestone. I felt fiery blood spurting down my cheek. He grabbed my tie and lifted my head with it, making me choke.

I heard shouting in the distance – 'Kamil, Kamil!'

Biren looked up, gave me a look of utter contempt, let go my tie and stumbled off, limping through the gravestones. I got onto my hands and knees as Saibal and Anjoli sprinted up to me, eyes filled with fear and concern.

'It was him,' I managed to say. 'It was him. And I hurt him.' I held my fist up with a look of pride.

Then I collapsed.

The Detective

Kolkata. July. Thursday.

I rushed to Mitra's hanging body, jumped on the bed and tried to unknot the sheet from around his neck in case he was still alive. The cloth was tight against his windpipe and I couldn't get my fingers under it but as I looked at his eyes, staring blindly into mine, I realised I was much too late. I let him go, covered my nose to avoid the stench and tapped a text to Hazra. As I looked up from my phone, I spotted, on the bed next to my feet, a letter, in an unsealed envelope. I pulled a pair of latex gloves from my pocket and opened it.

THE GRAND HOTEL

I am sorry. I cannot live with myself anymore. I killed Asif Khan. I saw his money when he checked in and could not resist it. I went to his room thinking it was empty and when I saw him there, I panicked and hit him with the statue. I am sorry.
Abhijit Mitra

I looked up at the body in confusion. My first thought was an overwhelming sense of relief that the beating I'd inflicted on him hadn't resulted in this. But did this mean Mitra was the killer after all? Had the DC been right all along?

Bullshit. I didn't believe it. It was much too convenient. The man I had spoken to an hour ago had not been about to take his own life. What had he said to me on the phone about his knees? With trepidation, I approached the hanging corpse, gagging at the smell and avoiding Mitra's staring eyes. I crouched and focused on his knees, hoping for something obvious to jump out at me, but couldn't see anything strange.

I looked around the room, taking photographs. A pad of paper on the desk, pen next to it. I could see the imprint from the note on the blank page on top. Had someone else written the note? Or forced Mitra to write it? I imagined him sitting at the desk as someone stood over him, dictating. I'd have to check his handwriting. Or did I just not want to accept what was dangling in front of me?

The shock of everything returned and my legs turned to water. I sat on the floor, not wanting to disturb the crime scene, and waited for my energy to return. I kept my eyes off Mitra as I tried to get to the truth. CCTV. I needed to check the hotel CCTV and see if that revealed anything. I hoped they had replaced the drive I had confiscated.

As I rose, the door slammed open and Hazra and the team ran in.

'It is the hotel manager!' exclaimed Hazra, looking up at Mitra's dead face.

'Yes,' I replied. 'Cut the body down. Get FFPS and forensics to do a full sweep. I want a complete picture of everything that happened in this room. Stand guard outside.'

'Yes, sir.'

'Oh – and get forensics to check his knees carefully.'

'His knees, sir?' Hazra tore his eyes away from the swaying corpse and looked at me uncomprehending, as if I had suggested we eat Mitra for dinner.

'Yes, both his knees. See if they are locked.'

'Locked, sir?' he repeated, convinced I had gone mad.

'Yes, see if you can bend them. Or something. He said it to me on the phone. Knees locked.'

I took a last look at the grotesque sight and walked out of the room.

At the front desk, I introduced myself to the assistant manager and gave him my card. I wouldn't tell him Mitra was dead; I needed to get the facts first. Who knew who was involved in this? Who I could trust? My paranoia was real; the case was getting to me.

'Have you replaced your CCTV drive?' I asked.

'Yes sir, why?'

'I need to see the CCTV footage of this morning. Police business.'

He looked at me quizzically.

'Only Mr Mitra has the authorit—'

'NOW!' I banged my fist on the desk, unwilling to waste any time on niceties.

'Yes, of course.' He looked around. 'The police impounded the old NVR so we are using our backup one.' He shepherded me to the security room and left.

I logged in with 'CCTVpassword' – clearly the hotel's security consciousness had not improved since the last murder. I fast-forwarded through various bits of footage, not sure what I was looking for. Then a shock rippled through me and my hand froze on the mouse. There, walking into the lobby just over an hour ago, were the three men who had attacked me – the vaping muscleman and his two henchmen. I closed my eyes, heart racing as I breathed to calm myself. Here was the proof I needed for the DC. Mitra had been murdered. On Jaideep Sanyal's instructions.

In other clips I saw the men in the elevator, exiting the lobby, and, a few minutes later, a video of me entering the hotel. I took out my phone and recorded the footage from the computer, ensuring I captured the time stamps. The hotel would have to do without its CCTV. I disconnected the drive and carried it to room 455, where I found Hazra standing outside keeping watch as forensics swept the room.

'Are they working in there?' I asked.

'Yes sir.'

'Okay, this is the CCTV footage from the hotel. Take it to Ashutosh in Cyber Crime. Make *sure* you fill in the paperwork and log the footage yourself. Keep the computer under lock and key – no one must have access to it. Do *not* store it in the mal-khana – understood?'

'Understood, sir.'

Hazra trotted off with the drive and I walked into the room. The body had been cut down and laid on the floor. The forensics officer photographing the room looked up. 'Looks like suicide, Sub-Inspector. Open and shut. He hung himself with his own tie from the fan.'

I grunted and pointed at the pad and pen on the desk. This was neither open nor shut, it was a twisted snake pit of murder, black-mail and cover-ups. And I was right in the middle of it, the snakes crawling over me, deafening me with their furious hissing.

'Take everything in the room as evidence,' I told the forensics officer. 'I want to see the chance prints. Did you check his knees?'

'Yes, sir. Knees normal, sir. Were you expecting something?'

What the hell had Mitra meant? Was he on his knees, pray-ing? What did *knees locked* mean?

'Check the knees of his trousers for fibres.'

'Yes, sir.'

My phone rang. DC.

'Yes, sir?'

'Rahman? I have some thoughts about Sanyal. Come and see me.'

'I am at the Grand, sir. We have just found the body of the manager Mitra – he was hanging from the ceiling fan in a hotel room.'

'My God,' he said after a moment. 'The manager?'

'Yes sir.'

'Was it suicide?'

'We found what appears to be a suicide note, sir, but ...'

'I knew it!' he said, satisfaction in his voice. 'That scoundrel. He killed Asif Khan, and—'

'It was a set-up, sir,' I interrupted. 'The men who beat me up were at the hotel at the same time. I have them on CCTV.'

Silence again.

'I see. Come and see me at the office. At once.'

I rushed over to Lalbazar and was in front of the DC thirty minutes later, showing him the video of the men in the hotel.

'This proves it was Jaideep, sir!' I said, my voice steady. 'They beat me up yesterday to get me to stay away from him and now they have killed Mitra to set him up for the murder.'

The DC contemplated the video for a minute. Then turned to me.

'Do you have Mitra's suicide note?'

I showed him the picture I had taken. 'Here, sir, but they forced him to write it. Jaideep ...'

'Listen to me Rahman,' he said in a low, solemn rumble not unlike the sound of rolling thunder in the distance. 'I will say this once and only once. This case does *not* involve Sanyal. This suicide note proves it was the manager. The case is closed. You will drop Sanyal. Am I making myself clear?'

I stood in silent confusion. Didn't he understand what I had said? 'But sir, the men ...'

The DC got up from his desk and we now stood nose to nose.

'AM I MAKING MYSELF CLEAR?' he yelled in my face, spraying me with spittle.

'Yes, sir. Completely.'

He returned to his desk, opened a folder and leafed through its contents, as I wiped my damp face with my sleeve. Without looking up he said, 'I will convene a press conference tomorrow to say we have wrapped up the case. You will attend.' He gave me a thin smile, 'Remember there is no "I" in team.'

No, but there is a 'U' in fucker, I thought as I gave him a trembling salute and left his office, heart a jackhammer in my chest, my field of vision disorientated by the DC screaming at me and my mind a confused blur. What the hell had just happened? I tried to replay the last few minutes in my mind. Regardless of any evidence, the DC did not want to hear anything about Jaideep. Why?

Instantaneously, the true picture came into focus. I felt like throwing up. My dots were connected, but the image differed from anything I had expected. I shut my eyes to control myself, furious at my stupidity. How had I not seen it earlier? I had been a complete and utter moron! DC Ghosh had orchestrated everything from the beginning! My revelation that Jaideep was the killer hadn't surprised him – he had known all along!

I steeled myself, mustering the self-control it took not to yell and punch the wall and instead sat down at my desk to examine the timeline in my notebook. Jaideep had killed Asif at 01.45 and then, in a panic, had told his father. The Chief Minister or a shadowy figure in his office had called the DC and told him to sort it out. The DC had waited for the 100 call to come through, then chose me to run the case. I had foolishly thought my talent was being recognised, but all they wanted was an inexperienced sucker who would do as he was told to make sure Jaideep was in the clear. I was now coverer-up-in-chief. My job was to pin the killing on Mitra. I would deferentially do the DC's bidding while he reported back to the CM. And the CCTV computer – it must have been the DC who had organised its disappearance, who else could have? The investigation had been a sham from the start!

I was in despair. Trapped. And now this bloody press conference the DC had sprung on me. What the hell? A part of me felt responsible for Mitra's death. Picturing myself standing in front of dozens of journalists and lying about the perpetrator made me sick.

This case was much bigger than me – much more dangerous. There was only one other person who would understand, maybe even help. I called Abba. I needed him to be in on the full picture. Abba would have the answers. I told him everything.

After I finished, there was silence on the line. Then he said, 'Sounds like a busy case. But resolved now?'

I was speechless. Hadn't he understood what I had just been saying? Ten seconds of silence followed and then he said, 'Son?'

I responded with, 'Yes, Abba. All neatly tied up. An old man like Mitra could definitely overpower a fit, muscular man like Asif Khan and kill him. And basically, an amazing coincidence that the men who attacked me were in the hotel at precisely the time Mitra died. And somehow Mitra took his tie, attached it to the fan and hanged himself in pitch darkness. Very impressive.'

Abba only mumbled his agreement, with a few lines of 'Well done, your first big case sorted.'

'Abba, wake up!' I was frustrated. I needed my father now, to understand me, and to be fair. 'Mitra was told to meet someone in the hotel. These three turned up, forced him to write the note – or wrote it themselves – then killed him. They are working for Jaideep Sanyal! Mitra was a loose end. Jaideep had instructed him to erase the tape and I was getting close to him – and now that thread has been neatly snipped. What do I do? Abba, please. I need your advice.'

More silence. I continued.

'Can you speak to the DC and tell him he has the wrong man? Surely, they don't want the actual murderer running free? ... Abba, are you still there?'

'Yes, son, I'm still here,' said my father, a deep weariness in his voice. 'I am sorry about what you had to endure. I cannot imagine how horrible an experience this has been for you. What can I say to you? This kind of attack is not unheard of when rich and powerful people are involved. You are right, I'm sure. But what can I do? I am retired now, I cannot interfere. You have no hard evidence against Jaideep. Thik achhé, listen, you want my advice? Here it is. Go to the press conference, do what DC Ghosh wants, close this case in the eyes of the press. After that you and I will talk to Ghosh and find the men on the video. I will not let the men who beat up my son and threatened my future daughter-in-law get away with it. This, I promise. Okay? Kamil?'

His words stunned me. For the first time I saw my dad as a coward. We may never have got on – but I had always looked up to him. Now, he just sounded weak. Weaker even than me. I hung up. I couldn't rely on Abba. I was completely alone.

* * *

Besides the Deputy Commissioner, several other senior officers had turned up for the press conference including the Joint Commissioner, the Additional Commissioner, the Special Commissioner and the exalted Commissioner of Police himself, Abba's replacement. My direct superior, the Inspector and *his* superior the Assistant Commissioner also joined them. I was familiar with the hierarchy in the force, but it was interesting to see a visual representation of what an insignificant satellite I was in this galaxy. Not even that, a satellite of a satellite. I squeezed in at the end, hoping to stay inconspicuous. Fifty or sixty journalists packed the room.

My phone pinged and I thumbed it onto silent. A WhatsApp from Hazra: *Prints on whisky glass match chance prints on money bundle and condoms sir!!! But they are not Mitra's! Whose are they?*

So, I finally had my hard evidence – Jaideep's prints were on the money and the condoms. He *was* Asif Khan's killer. Instead of elation, however, sitting there amongst the top brass, all I could feel was despair. What the hell could I do? Grab the microphone from the DC and announce that Jaideep was a murderer? Or jump off Lalbazar roof screaming Jaideep's name as I plummeted to my death? Chances of Jaideep facing justice in both scenarios was precisely zero.

'Ladies and gentlemen, thank you for coming,' the Commissioner began. 'I am pleased to say that after excellent police work by Kolkata Homicide under Deputy Commissioner, Detective Department, Ghosh, we have found the culprit for the murder of Asif Khan in record time. DC Ghosh will give you the details.'

The DC stood and took the microphone. 'As you are aware, Mr Asif Khan was found murdered in his hotel room at the Grand Hotel on Monday July tenth.

'We put a crack team together to find the murderer, under Sub-Inspector Kamil Rahman. These heroes worked round the clock and we discovered the culprit was the general manager of the hotel, one Abhijit Mitra, who was deep in debt.'

Deep in debt, first I'd heard of that! The set up was now watertight.

'We now know that Mr Mitra entered the hotel room to steal a vast quantity of money from Mr Khan and, on being disturbed by Mr Khan, bludgeoned him to death. Aware we were closing in on him, this Mitra committed suicide, leaving a full confession. When we searched his quarters, we recovered a substantial quantity of the stolen cash – a full eight lakh rupees. The case is therefore classified as closed as the culprit has met his end. Only God will judge him now. I will take questions.'

A cacophony of demanding voices arose, with the various commissioners kicking in with answers as they saw fit. Thankfully, they didn't call on me to say anything.

They brought the press conference to a close and the reporters were given a takeaway box of biryani as they left. The DC came to me and shook my hand. 'Outstanding work, Rahman. I will watch your future career with interest.'

'Thank you, sir, do you still need me or am I dismissed?'

'Yes, go back. Celebrate.' He moved away to speak to the Additional Police Commissioner, ignoring my salute.

Numb and empty, I walked in a daze to the canteen and ordered a lassi and a pyaza. I stared at my phone as I chewed and swallowed the crispy onion bhaji, tasting nothing. The news about Mitra was all over the internet. I was the hero of the hour, just when I didn't want it.

Ping. A WhatsApp from my father. *Well done, son.* I deleted it. I just wanted to be with Maliha, draw the curtains and shut out the world. The video of the killers in the hotel and Jaideep's fingerprints at the murder scene weren't enough to achieve justice. It all only revealed how naïve I'd been for years, defending the force to Maliha against corruption allegations. I had been blind. And now that I could finally see, I had to let it go. I felt a deep exhaustion and took out my phone to call Maliha when it rang, displaying a number I didn't recognise.

A panicked voice, 'Inspector, I am the Assistant Manager at the Grand. Mr Mitra's brother-in-law just called to speak to him – he didn't know the news about Mr Mitra's death! Three men just broke into his house and abducted his daughter! She is a housekeeper here.'

Now what? Why would the muscleman turn his sights on Mitra's niece? Was there something she'd held back when I questioned her that first day? Or did she know something about Mitra's 'suicide'?

'Has he called the police?' I asked.

'Yes,' said the assistant manager. 'Sir, he said the men kept asking her about what Mr Mitra gave her. When she said she didn't know, they took her. What should I do?'

What could Mitra have given her? My pulse quickened. 'Leave it to me. I know where they have taken her,' I said, grimly.

I rushed to the squad room, grabbed my Glock from the weapons safe, gathered Hazra and four armed policemen and piled into the Sumo.

'Kidderpore Docks, full siren,' I shouted.

Thirty-five long minutes later, the driver switched off the siren just before we reached the docks and the car rolled to a halt in front of the godown. We slipped out of the SUV and I gestured the team to draw their guns. I positioned one policeman on each side of the closed godown door and, at my signal, they slid it open and we launched ourselves into the warehouse, screaming 'POLICE', weapons drawn.

As my eyes adjusted to the dim light, I saw three men scatter and take cover behind the boxes of tea. In the centre, sitting on a stack of pallets was Mitra's terrified niece, seemingly unhurt. I dashed to drag her out of the way as my men slid along the walls to find the goondas.

A shot rang out as Hazra bellowed, 'They are armed, sir!' and my team took cover.

I crouched, sheltering the girl, and shouted, 'You are out of options. Show yourself and we won't encounter you. Otherwise you will be dead.' The response was another wild shot. Now what? I needed a plan. There were six of us and three of them. Our odds were good.

I felt alive, every sense intensely alert, my instincts and training taking over. Poking my head around the boxes, I surveyed the godown. The pallets were arranged in straight rows, wide aisles between them to allow forklifts through. Faint sunlight shone through the open doorway we had used. Hoping this was the only exit, I motioned one of my team members to stay hidden with a view of it and prevent anyone from escaping. I signalled two policemen to make their way down one side and two down the other. Flattening themselves against the walls, they crab-walked, peering round the corners of the carton towers.

Another shot rang from the goondas, instantly followed by smashing glass and darkness. 'They are shooting at the lights,' shouted Hazra, grandmaster of the obvious. So much for my plan.

The housekeeper trembled in my arms. I sat her down and whispered, 'Don't worry, I will get you out.'

I drew my weapon and as I crept along the wall to the first aisle, I heard a shot near the entrance followed by a scream. 'Got him, sir!' shouted the cop I had positioned there. 'You,' he yelled at the man writhing on the floor, 'drop the weapon or I will shoot.'

The man tossed away his gun and the cop dragged him to one side, handcuffing him to a water pipe.

'Excellent work,' I shouted. 'Now, you two others. Come out or it will be worse for you.'

There was no response. I carried on further down the side of the godown, trying to damp the crunching sound of sawdust under my feet. Feeling my way, in the dimmest of light, along the rough wall, I stopped dead at the sound of a faint rustling close by. Almost blinded by the darkness, I picked up a large box of tea and threw it in the direction of the noise, the gun in my other hand. As it landed, a shot went off and I fired at the flash, experiencing a grim satisfaction at the screech. I fired again, a little higher, in the same direction. All was still.

A hush descended over the warehouse as both sides waited for the other to make a move. The loud whine of a motor shattered the silence. I ran towards the light of the entrance to see a forklift trundling towards the open door, my team firing wildly at it. As it reached the entrance, the vaping man jumped out of the cabin and sprinted out of the godown, two of my men in pursuit, Hazra wheezing after them.

I helped the housekeeper to her feet, 'You're okay now. Don't worry,' and told the cop at the door to bring the handcuffed goonda into the Sumo. As I reached the warehouse entrance, Hazra ran back with the others and croaked, 'We lost him, sir,' as he leaned against the car, gasping for breath. 'He had a Jeep with a driver. I got the number.'

'Well done, Hazra. You all did very well. Take a torch and find the last man.'

They entered the godown and a few minutes later, re-emerged, empty handed.

'Sorry, sir, he must have got away.'

'Station,' I said. This was no time to feel sorry for ourselves. I had work to do.

Back at headquarters, I sat the housekeeper down in an interview room and gave her a cup of hot cha and a biscuit. 'Drink,' I said, gently. 'We have called your father and he is on his way. Tell me exactly what happened.'

She took a sip and said, 'It was my day off and Daddy was home with me. These three men came into our house and started shouting that Uncle had given me something and where was it. I said I didn't know what they were talking about, but they tied up Daddy and kept asking and asking and then they took me away and were threatening the most terrible things if I didn't tell them and …' she broke down, crying.

There was nothing more she could tell me. I left her in the care of a lady constable and went to see the injured goonda. It was the thug who had held me from behind as the vaping man had taunted me. He was sitting in an interview room, handcuffed to the table, blood dripping from his leg, while Hazra perched on a chair in the corner, eating a sandwich as usual.

'Doctor . . .' the goonda moaned.

'Yes, like I needed a doctor when you beat me up on Saturday,' I retorted. 'What did you want with the girl? We have you on CCTV before you murdered Mitra, so you will hang.' I dragged a chair and sat across the table from him. 'Talk.'

After a moment, he saw he had nothing left to lose, so he did. '*They* killed manager – the other two. I did nothing. I just stay outside and make sure no one come in. But manager killed Asif Khan, so he deserved it,' he added defiantly. 'I heard manager say he has insurance so we can't kill him. That if he dies, information will come out. What information, I don't know.'

'Then what happened?' I said. 'Why did you take the girl?'

He looked at me and continued. 'They hurt him, and he say girl has it. Then they kill him.'

'Who was giving you these orders?' I barked.

'Biren.'

'Biren was your boss? The vaping fellow?'

'Yes. Doctor, please!' His voice trailed away as he looked at the pool of blood on the floor under his leg.

'Who did Biren work for?'

'Some big shot. I never saw him. Biren was his bodyguard and took the orders. Biren hired us this week when we took you.'

Hazra raised his palm and the goonda screamed, knowing what might come, 'I swear on my life! Biren works for VIP, that is all I know! Now please, doctor!'

I wouldn't get any more out of him. I nodded to Hazra. 'Have him bandaged up and put in a cell. Under guard, I don't want anything happening to him.'

I returned to my desk and cleaned my gun, trying to make sense of what had just gone down. I had finally done something useful on this case, rescuing the poor girl before they had assaulted her, or worse. What did they want from her? She had sworn Mitra had given her nothing. I felt sure she wasn't lying.

I locked my Glock in the weapons safe with a click. And something clicked in me. Maybe she didn't *know* that Mitra had left something for her.

I knew what 'Knees Locked' meant.

The Waiter

London. October. Tuesday.

My nerves were jangling. Why had Jaideep sent this vaping man, Biren, after me in London? He was clearly here to harm me – first by trying to push me under the train and now smashing me against a headstone in the cemetery. It seemed Jaideep had a long memory and an even longer reach. He wanted me out of the way. Was he nervous that I was holding proof of his involvement in Asif Khan's death?

I had to be extra careful. I couldn't afford to put Anjoli in danger and would never forgive myself if she got hurt. Biren had ruined my relationship with Maliha; I wouldn't let him take away anyone else close to me.

Was the immigration letter another part of this plan against me? The Asif Khan case was closed ... but could Jaideep be involved with Rakesh's murder too? Even though Neha had been charged? I was spinning in circles.

In the crowded waiting room of the UKVI, a host of different nationalities surrounded Anjoli and me. Couples dandling children on their knees, children dandling babies on their knees and men dandling iPhones. All wore a similar expression of forlorn nervousness that mirrored my own. I could sense their apprehension in the pit of my stomach, like a hunger. There were notices on the walls explaining in bold capital letters about the dangers of outstaying your visa and urging people to inform the authorities if they knew anyone working in Britain without the correct documentation. Other posters warned that medical treatment required in hospitals would be administered only after payment in full. Yet more posters showed the penalties for hiring illegal immigrants as cleaners, tradesmen or in businesses.

Everything I read just heightened my tension that was now verging on panic. We'd both read the news stories – even people who most deserved to be in this country had to fight for their right to remain. What hope did I have, here on a visitor's visa, working illegally? I was about to get deported. I wouldn't even be allowed to pack. What would I tell Ma and Abba when I skulked my way back to Kolkata? And would it even be safe there? Would Biren follow me back there to finish the job?

'Look, your name has come up on the appointment board. Room seventeen,' Anjoli said piercing our silence.

We made our way to room 17 where we were met by a small, dusty-looking man. It reminded me of my squad room in Lalbazar. I guess civil servants are the same all over the world, I thought as I looked around the bare, windowless space and wondered what it must be like to spend eight hours a day dealing with nervous immigrants when you had the power to destroy or transform their lives with the blithe scribble of a biro.

'Mr Rahman, I am an immigration officer. Do you speak English?' he said, barely looking up from his forms let alone bothering to rise and shake my hand.

'Yes of course I do,' I responded as Anjoli and I sat opposite him.

'Good. May I see your passport, please?'

I handed over my precious navy blue booklet, trying to keep my hand from trembling. He leafed through it, page by page, then compared it to a form on his desk.

'You're here on a visitor visa and arrived … nine weeks ago?' He asked, nose buried in his paperwork.

'That's right, visiting and staying with friends of my parents,' I smiled weakly.

He looked up. 'You are a Muslim?'

'Yes. Non-practising.'

'Why does that matter?' asked Anjoli, pugnaciously. The immigration officer ignored her.

'And do you visit a mosque here?'

'No, I told you I was non-practising.'

'And have you travelled to Pakistan?'

I had assumed they had wanted to see me in case I was working illegally; this line of questioning seemed to put an altogether different slant on things.

'No. Indians aren't allowed to travel there for tourism,' I replied, trying to keep any worry out of my voice.

'Why are you asking these questions?' Anjoli interrupted. 'He's here legally and has every right to do what he wants as long as he doesn't overstay his visa and, as you can see, he has another three months.'

'And you are …' The immigration officer looked at her, stifling a smile at her *Harry would have been nothing without Hermione* T-shirt.

'I am Anjoli Chatterjee, a friend of Kamil's. And a British citizen,' she retorted.

'May I see your ID?' he asked politely.

Anjoli bristled. 'No, you may not. We don't live in a fascist state. Yet!'

'Anjoli, please …' I said.

She ignored me. 'Please tell me why my friend is being interrogated like this? He's done nothing wrong.'

'There have been questions raised about his status and we have to investigate,' said the immigration officer, calmly.

'Questions raised by whom?' she asked.

'I can't tell you I'm afraid,' he responded. 'Have you had any paid work in the UK?'

There it was. They *were* investigating me working illegally. But how did they know?

'Work?' I said. 'No, of course not. I'm a police officer. Where would I get work as a policeman?'

I laughed. He didn't.

'So, you are not working as a waiter in ...' he looked at his form, 'Tandoori Knights restaurant in Brick Lane.'

I tried to respond as nonchalantly as I could. 'No, I've just been relaxing and seeing the sights. I *am* staying with my parents' friends in the flat above the restaurant. Maybe that's where the confusion arose?'

He gave a non-committal nod. 'Please excuse me, I have to make a copy of your passport. I will be back in just a moment.'

He closed the file, put it in his drawer, and left the room.

Anjoli glanced at the closed door, then scooted round the desk and pulled the file out of the drawer.

'What the hell are you doing Anjoli,' I whispered, horrified, eyes dashing between her and the door.

'Shh!' said Anjoli, rifling through the file.

'Stop it. They'll throw me out of the country,' I said.

With her phone, she took a quick picture of the form the immigration officer had been looking at, then thrust the file back in the drawer and sat back, all innocence, on our side of the desk just as the door opened and the officer came back in.

He sat down, pulled the file out and carefully put the copies he had made of my passport in it.

'We will investigate and come back to you. Thank you for coming in,' he said, handing me my passport back.

'What do you think will happen now?' I asked, heart thumping, as we walked out of the immigration centre onto the street.

'I've no idea. But no one in the restaurant will say anything about you working there. Don't worry, I'll marry you and you can be my kept man if there are any ...'

'Show me the picture you took?' I interrupted.

I zoomed in and scrutinised the form scrolling down and across. It was a printout from the British Gov.uk website reporting Kamil Rahman, a Muslim in the UK, working illegally in Tandoori Knights restaurant in Brick Lane. It had been submitted by Arjun Sharma of PinRak Industries. I handed the phone back to Anjoli.

'Arjun!' hissed Anjoli. 'The bastard! Why would he do this? Do you think it's connected to the murder? Maybe he's worried you're getting close to something?'

'Look at the date,' I said. 'It was submitted five weeks ago. Before I even met him. Before Rakesh's death.'

And before I could even consider what this might mean, my phone rang. It was Ma.

'Ma? Isn't it late there?'

'Kamil, come home.' Ma's voice was croaky. I could tell, even thousands of miles away, that she had been crying. 'Your father has had a heart attack.'

The Detective

Kolkata. July. Friday.

*K*NEES LOCKED.
     KNEES LOCK.
NIECE'S LOCKER.

An inspired guess. There was only one place to look now.

At the Grand, the assistant manager gave me the master key to the housekeeper's locker and stood nearby as I rummaged through its contents – a uniform, bits and pieces of makeup, film magazines and shampoos from the hotel bathroom. Right at the bottom, under an old copy of *Stardust*, I found an envelope with my name on it. I opened it to find a scrawled letter.

Sub-Inspector Rahman,

If you have received this letter, I am no more. I am scared for my life. I received a call on the afternoon Asif Khan's body was found and was told to erase the CCTV footage. They promised me Rs. eight lakhs to do this and that if I did not, they would kill my family. I did as I was told and the next morning, they delivered the money to me. I am ashamed to say I took it and lied to you. Now the same man who delivered the money has phoned to say he wants to see me in the hotel tomorrow morning. I am frightened. So, I am putting this letter in my niece's locker and if something happens, hopefully you will find it. I am sorry.

A. Mitra.

PS. I attach something you may find useful.

I shook the envelope and a USB stick fell into my hand.

My heart broke for Mitra. They had dragged this poor guy into the middle of something not of his making and he had lost his life. And the same could have happened to his innocent niece. I trembled with rage at Jaideep, at the injustice wrought by people in power, and at my own impotence. I vowed that I would do all I could to get justice for Mitra, in whatever form I could manage.

Back at the station, I plugged in the USB and clicked on the first of two files. My eyes widened as I saw a video of Jaideep and Asif laughing with each other in the hotel lift – Jaideep carrying a blue gym bag and dressed in the tan trousers and blue shirt he had been wearing in the party video. The timestamp was five past midnight, Monday. I clicked on another. 2.43 a.m. Jaideep, alone, going down in the lift, carrying the same gym bag, which seemed bulkier. Now clothed in Asif's jeans and shirt. As the video ended, leaving a black screen, I realised I'd been holding my breath.

This was it. Incontrovertible proof. Jaideep had killed Asif because Asif was blackmailing him. He had his goondas bribe and threaten Mitra into erasing the CCTV. He had me beaten up because I was getting too close and then had Mitra killed. I had the proof, including Jaideep's fingerprints on the condoms and the cash.

I thought for a second whether to take this to the DC, but realised immediately that the evidence would conveniently go missing in the malkhana again. It was all down to me. I knew what I had to do. Time to stop being the DC's pawn and take control. Even if no one wanted to know, even if the justice system was corrupt, I would force them to look the facts in the face, I would live by my ideals, damn the consequences. Abba might be furious, but he would know I had fought for what was right.

I would avenge Mitra and Asif Khan. Use a thorn to remove a thorn, as Ma used to say.

I walked over to Cyber Crime. 'Ashutosh, do you have a sec? It's personal.'

He removed his headphones, was about to make a sarcastic quip but saw my grim look and just nodded. We walked to an interview room and sat across from each other. I hesitated for a minute. Could I bring him into this mess? I had no choice.

'Listen, I'm in trouble and I need your help.' I told him everything, ending by showing him the videos and Mitra's letter to me. He listened in total silence without interrupting and after I finished, said, 'Fuuuuuck. This is crazy, Kamil.'

'Yeah. So, here's where you can help. I want you to set up a website, upload the evidence and send the link to the newspapers. Someone is bound to pick it up. Can you do that?'

He looked stunned. 'Are you crazy, man? This will be the end of your career. And possibly your life!'

'I don't care,' I insisted. 'Two people have died. They can't get away with it. Don't worry, I'll keep you out of it. You won't be involved.'

'I'm not worried about that, dude. I can make sure nothing is traced back to me. But are you certain, Kamil? This is dangerous!'

Ignoring the doubts bobbing up and the thought of Biren still on the loose, I blurted, 'Yes, I'm sure.'

'It's your funeral, man, but okay ...'

Two hours later, Ashutosh had created asifmurder.in. There, I laid out everything I knew about Asif's murder and set up an anonymous email for the newspapers to ask me for more information. I emailed the link to the top three newspapers in the country.

Now all I had to do was wait.

* * *

I spent Saturday scouring the web every hour to see if anyone had picked up my story but ... nothing. I checked asifmurder.in for views – there had been a few, not many. I calmed myself down. This was an explosive story. These were reputable newspapers. They would need to check the facts, do their own digging, they couldn't just link to my site. But doubts nagged me. How deep was Jaideep's influence? The newspapers would surely call him for a comment. And the CM could and would shut them down. Had I thought this through properly?

Then I saw that @Bollysizzle had tweeted:

Was Asif murdered by a crazy suicidal hotel manager or was weird voodoo at work? Did our heartthrob have a wicked secret? And was another handsome rich Bong financier partying with him that night? Bollysizzle is soooo curious! #Asifdeath

So, someone had seen my post. It only had three likes and no retweets but maybe this would start something. More hopeful, I got my driver to pick up Maliha from her work. Abba had told Ma about my assault and she had insisted we rush over so she could feed us, always convinced her cooking could make everything better. In the car, I told Maliha everything that had happened, bar my online adventures. She listened, then just said, 'It's over now, Kamil. Let it go.' Exactly the advice Abba had given me. I brooded silently for the rest of the journey, her hand resting in mine.

'What a terrible thing to happen, how dare they touch my son! Bloody bastards! My poor Kamil ... ' Ma kept repeating. 'I have homoeopathic for the pain, Kamil, here please take it. Adil, do something – bring these villains to justice and have them hanged.' To calm her down, Maliha expertly changed the subject. 'Aunty, we have made plans about the wedding, can I discuss them with you?'

Abba beckoned me to his study, and I watched as he poured our whiskies. There he stood, straight and weathered as a banyan tree, in his habitual well-cut suit and tie, grey hair, trimmed moustache and beard. I looked around at his decorations, commendations and awards for bravery, long service, merit. There were dozens of them, as well as pictures of him with various dignitaries. Being in here had always made me feel inadequate but his weak response to my cry for help had left me confused. I would give him one more chance to help me get justice.

I told him about the housekeeper's kidnapping, how my team had rescued her, showed him the videos I had received from Mitra and ended by showing him the website Ashutosh and I had created. He listened silently, expression sombre, gripping the whisky glass in both hands.

When I finished, he spoke. 'I am truly sorry you are mixed up in this, Kamil.'

'I need you, Abba. I need guidance now.'

He looked down at the glass in his hand. 'It is my fault,' he said. 'I should have warned you when I saw things were getting nasty. You are playing with fire here, Kamil. This is a dangerous game. You need to take that site down.'

'Abba, I have the concrete proof you asked for!' I said, mutinously, the situation and surroundings making me feel as though I was eleven years old, trying to get my way. 'You've seen it with your own eyes. How can you ask me to let it lie? You know it's not right. Please! Can't you go to the CP? How can they cover this up, Abba?'

'Kamil, I know it upsets you I am not helping more, but this is hazardous territory,' he said. 'These are dangerous people. They have assaulted you, threatened Maliha and killed the manager. You cannot imagine what else they can do. You'll lose your job. Or worse. I am only looking after your best interests, son.'

'Abba, I am a member of the police force,' I said, righteous indignation pouring out of me. 'A Homicide Sub-Inspector. I can't stop. Remember what you said at my graduation? Ensure those who do evil are punished and victims get their justice? Was that just bullshit?'

His face flushed then he slammed his glass on the table.

'LISTEN TO ME KAMIL! This is not a game. Don't you bloody understand your lives are at stake? Do you want to get killed? Do you want something to happen to Maliha? To your mother? Take that site down and stop this nonsense at once!'

I was shocked at this reaction from Abba, who usually showed his anger in a quiet and measured way; it took only a stern look from him to make me experience extreme regret, contrition and repentance. He had never yelled at me before. Ever. I found I was shaking.

Ma and Maliha rushed in on hearing the shouting.

'What's happening? What is this yelling? Adil, remember your blood pressure, what are you doing?' said Ma, worried.

My dad turned away.

'Pah! Talk sense into this stupid boy, Rehana. He is putting himself and Maliha in danger. He has solved his case, received the credit, but he keeps pushing. I can't talk to him anymore.'

Ma looked shocked.

'What are you doing Kamil? What is he doing Maliha?'

'I don't know,' said Maliha. 'What *are* you doing? I thought it was over?'

I regained my composure and showed them the site, knowing I knew I wouldn't like their reaction. And I didn't. Maliha's face went white and Ma's eyes were filled with incomprehension.

'Maliha,' I mumbled, 'I had to do the right thing.'

'And when were you going to tell me this?' she asked, eyes glistening. 'Never? The right thing? This was not it, Kamil. Your father is right.' She turned and walked out of the room. Seconds later, I heard the flat door slam shut.

Ma and Abba gazed at me, waiting for me to say something. Had I made a terrible mistake? Was Abba right? Was this worth Maliha being hurt? Had I put her in greater danger now with my rashness? My mind was in a whirl. But I *had* to do it. Jaideep *had* to be punished. Without saying another word to them, I left, running after Maliha.

On Monday morning, I got a WhatsApp: *Report to DC Ghosh*.

I stood erect in front of him as he stared at me without expression. Then he spoke. 'You are dismissed from the Kolkata Police forthwith. Hand over your ID. Are you carrying your service revolver?'

It was a body blow.

'No. What?'

'You are sacked for dereliction of duty. Effective immediately.'

'But sir, I ...'

'ID.'

I put my police ID on the DC's desk.

'Phone?'

'Sir?'

'Give me your phone.'

'It's my personal phone, Sir.'

'You will get it back. Unlock it and give it to me.'

In a daze, I did as I was ordered.

The DC scrolled through my videos and the CCTV footage. He erased them and handed the phone back.

'Go.'

I left in a state of utter shock. It had never occurred to me that they would sack CP Adil Rahman's son. Had my story got out? Had Ashutosh told the DC? Had they traced the email address back to me?

I navigated to asifmurder.in on my phone.

It was gone. As was the @Bollysizzle tweet.

It was over.

Now what? What would I tell Maliha and Abba? As I walked out of Lalbazar, my eyes landed on the large Kolkata Police seal above the door with its motto in big Sanskrit letters: *Satyameva Jayate, Truth will Prevail*. The irony. I leaned against the wall of the station, afraid I would collapse.

My phone pinged. A text. Number withheld. Pictures attached. I clicked them open.

Pictures of Maliha. Leaving her flat. On her way to work. Entering court.

And a message.

After I have finished with her, you are both dead.

* * *

It was a cold, grey August morning when I stepped off the Jet Airways flight at Heathrow Airport.

The previous weeks were a blur. After being dismissed in disgrace from the police force, I'd moved in with my parents. In response to the menacing message, Abba had contacted a security firm and hired round-the-clock protection for us. He drew upon his contacts in the police to find Biren, the ringleader of the gang who had threatened our lives, but his influence came to nothing. He had said nothing to me directly, but I could tell the loss of his power and authority had hurt him. In my darker moments, guilt seared through me and I felt responsible for this as well – Abba's lifetime of earned respect destroyed in a week by one stubborn son.

Interest in the Asif Khan case dwindled. With the killer identified, the public and press had moved on to their next scandal. A small article appeared in the *Telegraph*.

Khan Cop Sacked

TNN: July 31, 2017 02:37 IST

KOLKATA: Sub-Inspector Kamil Rahman, son of Retired Commissioner of Police Adil Rahman, has been sacked from the Kolkata CID for corruption. Rahman was the officer leading the Asif Khan murder and only two weeks ago was the darling of the Kolkata Police. He has been accused of taking bribes from the Kolkata Mafia and of trying to kill one of them in Kidderpore Docks in an encounter when he asked them for more money and was refused. The Commissioner signed his dismissal order two days ago. A further investigation is underway, and more action may be taken.

Ma hid the newspaper the day it came out but Hazra thoughtfully Whatsapp'd a screenshot to me. My despondency deepened. I would never get a job now – the DC had seen to that.

As I was picking at my dinner that evening, Abba said, 'Kamil, we need to talk.'

'Hain, Abba?'

'You have to get out of here. I have spoken to my friend Saibal in London. I think you should shift there and stay with him and his wife for a while. He can give you a job in his restaurant. With you gone, Maliha may be safe. I think this is best.'

The first thought came into my head was that he was ashamed of me and couldn't bear to have me around. Could I blame him? The more I thought about it, though, the more appealing it seemed. A clean break before a new beginning. Away from my failures.

I broached the topic with Maliha at the Someplace Else pub in Park Street. Relations between us had deteriorated. I resented the fact that she was busy at work while I lay in my childhood bed watching terrible TV. When we met, I was taciturn and sullen, burdening her with the entire conversation. I was behaving terribly and hated myself for it. The London trip offered us a lifeline. I allowed myself a spark of hope.

'This is it, Maliha,' I said. 'A fresh start. For both of us. Saibal is a good friend of Abba's. We can stay there, let things die down and then come back – maybe shift to Mumbai.'

'Kamil, I can't,' she said with as much gentleness as she could muster. She looked tired and drawn. 'My life is here. My job is here. My parents are here. I like Kolkata. There are things I want to do. Things I care about. Even more so now, after . . . after everything that has happened. I can't let men like that get away with this shit.'

'Do you mean me?' I said, getting angry.

'Of course, I don't mean you, what are you talking about? I meant those men who attacked you. Jaideep and his goons.'

'So how can we live here with that threat hanging over us, Maliha? My parents can't afford to pay for protection forever.'

'The threat is over, Kamil. It's been a while, and nothing has happened. The case is closed. What will they gain by hurting us now?'

'I don't know.' I ordered another whisky.

'Maybe you shouldn't have any more of those?'

'It's only my second.' It was my fourth. 'I'm fine. Listen, I can't hang around here anymore. I need to start again. Abba is right. Six months in London could be the break I need. He has made the arrangements with Saibal, all you have to do is pack. Please come.'

'Oh. So, you've decided? You're going?'

I took a big gulp of the whisky.

'Yes, I am.'

'Well, there is nothing to say then, is there? Ami Aaschi.'

She took off her engagement ring, put it between us on the table and left. That was it. I didn't see her again.

* * *

I spent the next few days sorting out tickets, buying clothes and gifts, saying the few goodbyes I had to say. I remembered Saibal and Maya with affection. We'd met a few times when I was younger; I vaguely remembered visiting them in London when I was nineteen or twenty. I recalled their rather irritating daughter, Anjoli, a gawky, talkative seventeen-year-old with braces and long plaits. She'd barraged me with information about bands I'd never heard of (*You haven't heard of The Killers? Or White Stripes? Are you that backward in Kolkata? Are you still listening to the Spice Girls? That's literally mental!*). I'd bought her a Tower of London snow globe and it had amused her, creating her own tiny blizzard wherever she went in the house.

I hadn't packed much for this trip. Whatever fit into my wheelie bag plus the several boxes of sandesh and spices Ma had put in for Maya. 'Don't worry, I'll send whatever you need,' Ma assured me. 'I need to buy you a proper, warm coat. London winters are killing!'

I walked through immigration, picked up my bag and went onto the concourse, looking for Saibal and Maya.

The Waiter

Kolkata. October. Wednesday.

The next day, after a fifteen-hour journey, Saibal, Anjoli and I arrived exhausted at the Netaji Subhash Chandra Bose International airport in Kolkata – Saibal hadn't wanted to leave Maya alone in London but she would brook no disagreement, saying that someone had to look after the restaurant and insisting he had to see his sick friend and that Anjoli should meet her Kolkata relatives. Anjoli suspected she would be subjected to a stream of potential suitors that the 'rellies' had lined up but decided the chance to visit India couldn't be missed.

I was nervous about seeing Abba; we hadn't parted on the best of terms. But I needed to rebuild and restart. I would make the effort. I was also worried that Biren, the vaping man, might follow me to Kolkata and try to exact revenge there – although for what, I was still in the dark.

After collecting our luggage, we fought through the crowds and, from the dozens of drivers offering 'AC Car, Good Price', chose a yellow Ambassador taxi to take us to the hospital. The driver lashed Saibal's suitcase to the roof of his car with three different ropes as it wouldn't fit in the boot with the rest of our bags. I closed my eyes and breathed in the familiar warm, dusty smell of Kolkata, enjoying the cries of porters touting for business, mingled with the incessant honking of cars. I was home.

The nostalgia dissipated in the first ten minutes of the crawl through thick Kolkata traffic and the liquid heat ('AC not working' the driver informed us mournfully). After two painful hours, the taxi juddered to a halt and we spilled out to see Ma waiting at the hospital entrance, having WhatsApp'd us every ten minutes to see when we would arrive. She threw her arms around me in joy. 'It has been so long, Kamil. You never call, you never email, your father has to almost die before you answer a message!'

She finally let go of me to hug the others. 'So nice of you to come, Adil will be happy to see you. He is sleeping right now, but much better. We can take him home today. Such a scare. Come and see him. He is in a private ward. I have a surprise for you, Kamil,' she added with a sparkle in her eye.

We trundled our luggage down the dingy green corridors to the private ward, which looked the same as the other grimy areas of the hospital.

As we walked into a room with 'Adil Rahman' scribbled on a dry-wipe board on the door, a familiar figure rose from Abba's bedside and my heart leapt into my throat.

'What are you doing here?' I asked, astonished.

'I told you I have a surprise, na!' said Ma smugly.

'How are you, Kamil? You look well,' whispered Maliha, kissing my cheek.

'He has become a stick, he is not eating enough,' Ma butted in.

'I'm ... fine, how have *you* been?' I stuttered back. How could I be so nervous in front of someone I had once known so intimately? Why would the words not come?

'I came to see how Uncle was and, when I heard you were coming, I thought I would stay and hello-hi.'

'Oh ... Hi! Thanks ... I mean ... It's good to see you. Sorry, I'm in a daze. Lengthy flight. So glad Abba's all right.' I stood, not knowing what to do next.

'I should go,' said Maliha, after a pause. 'We'll meet before you go back to London?'

'Yes, of course … I'll text you,' I said, aware that Anjoli was examining her, as Maliha quizzically took in Anjoli's *Proud to be Everything the* Daily Mail *Hates* T-shirt.

Abba was asleep on the bed, attached to a monitor sounding intermittent beeps and tones. I bent and gave him a faint kiss on the forehead. How small and frail he looked. Where was the imposing figure who had so dominated my life? I realised with a shock that he could have died. I couldn't imagine life without him, however distant he might be.

Anjoli hung back but Saibal neared the bed, whispered some words and laid his palm on Abba's cheek, who blinked and opened his eyes. Saibal took Abba's hand as Anjoli approached and kissed him on the cheek.

'Hello Uncle Adil, you look good!' she whispered.

'Who is this lovely girl?' Abba said weakly, smiling at Anjoli. 'You were only a child with a long pigtail last time I saw you.'

'Tui bhebechilish tui more jaabi are amader shobaike chere chole jaabi? You thought you would die and leave us, Adil? Not so easy, not so easy, my friend. Chalo, let's get you home,' said Saibal, tenderly.

'I am indestructible, you know that, Saibal,' Abba smiled back. He turned to me.

'Ah, Kamil. You have come. How are you, son?' he asked, extending a shaky hand.

'Fine, Abba. I'm glad you are better,' I said, squeezing his hand.

On the way home, Ma broached the subject everyone had so far avoided.

'Very sad news about Rakesh,' she said. 'You were there when it happened? Why didn't you tell us, Kamil?'

'Yes,' replied Saibal, shaking his head. 'Terrible accident.'

Abba said nothing. This wasn't the occasion for a full dissection. And that was that. For now.

We reached my parents' flat in half an hour, the traffic having thinned. Ignoring our protestations that we were exhausted and needed to sleep, Ma laid out the meal of rice and fish curry the cook had made for us, which we picked at, trying to make conversation. Anjoli was impressed with our home, decorated as it was in traditional Bengali motifs. 'Only been in Kolkata for a few hours and I'm already learning a lot. Maybe you're a little more sophisticated than I thought, Monsieur Parrot!' she told me before I went to my room and collapsed into bed.

The next morning, logey with jet lag, I woke to find Saibal drinking tea with Abba and Ma while Anjoli had gone to visit her mother's family. I had a dutiful breakfast with them, giving my parents gifts I had bought from the Duty Free in Dubai. A scarf for Ma ('This is so beautiful, Kamil! You have such excellent taste!') and two boxes of golf balls for Abba ('Thank you, son').

'So, retirement is suiting you, Adil?' said Saibal. 'Golf and time with Rehana?'

'He never stops working,' grumbled Ma. 'Likes to think he is indispensable. And the office doesn't behave as if he has retired – they keep calling him, especially that Ghosh.'

An electric current ran through me. 'You're still in touch with DC Ghosh, Abba?'

'Not really,' said Abba. 'He calls every now and then and asks after you. I think he regrets what happened.'

I wasn't sure I believed him but, seeing him sitting there, old and wan, decided not to push it.

With nothing planned for the day, I took Maliha up on her offer and texted to see if she was free. She had a meeting at 10 a.m. but was available before so we met at Café Coffee Day in

Park Street, Maliha greeting me with an awkward peck on the cheek.

Her hair was longer, she seemed to have coloured it, and she looked as beautiful as ever in her jeans and simple red top. The familiar sharp pain returned. There was so much I wanted to say and so little I could.

'So, how have you been?' I asked, taking a sip of my black coffee to avoid showing any emotion.

'Yes, good. You?'

'Good. How're your parents?'

'Fine. Good.'

So, we were all good. That was good. The conversation ground to a rapid halt. Maliha stirred her cappuccino, destroying the perfect feather motif in the foam.

'So, are you ... seeing anyone?' I asked, not wanting to know the answer.

She avoided the question.

'Are you?'

'No,' I replied.

'Anjoli's beautiful, no?' Maliha said.

I didn't know how to respond to this non sequitur so just took another sip of my coffee, which was followed by another pause.

'How's the job?' I asked, frustrated at our staccato conversation.

'I quit. I've joined another firm that is fighting cases against the police. For underprivileged Muslims.'

'Oh wow, that's what you always wanted to do. If I were still here, you'd be fighting against me. Only joking. I'm so happy for you, Maliha.'

I tentatively took her hands, holding her smooth fingers under mine. She didn't pull away. My emotions were a complete jumble. I couldn't place what I was feeling, other than overwhelming sadness, mixed with self-pity. I was genuinely happy that Maliha had a fulfilling job, yet I couldn't help but compare it to the aimlessness of my life in London. I felt like I'd fallen in her eyes, although the rational part of me knew that she would never judge me.

Her face softened. 'How are you, really, Kamil?'

'I'm so sorry Maliha,' I stuttered. 'I was in a grim place earlier in the year. And after those threats and those goondas I couldn't stay. I was horrible to you. I was ashamed and angry and ...'

'Yes. I know, Kamil,' she said. 'It wasn't easy. For either of us. I wish ... I just wish we could have discussed it more. After ... you left the force ... you ... you went into yourself and I couldn't reach you and ...'

'Yes. You're right. I'm sorry. Abba thought it was best I shift to London and I ...' I trailed off, dejected.

We held hands, looking at each other. I said hesitantly, 'I ... I ... still haven't got over it ...'

'Got over what?' she asked, gently.

All the hurt I'd hidden away for months came pouring out.

'I pretend to myself that I have. That it's behind me. But every now and then I see that bastard Jaideep in the press. At parties. All over Instagram. Pretending nothing has happened. Literally getting away with murder. And then it all comes back. And I miss you. I miss you so much. And London, it's demoralising waiting on tables, wearing a stupid bowtie and ... I still blame myself for Mitra's death. And that I let everyone get away with it. You don't understand Maliha, it's still all here! Not finished!'

I didn't tell her about Biren following me to London – I couldn't bring that up again and terrify her.

Maliha looked at me, eyes glistening.

'Kamil, it's hard. But it will fade. It must. You just have to give time a chance to do its work.'

'I'm sorry. It's just ... coming back here has brought it all back.' I held her hands to my face. 'I do miss you. So much,' I repeated.

'Yes, me too.' She drew her hands away and sat back. 'But we have to move on. We'll always stay friends, I hope. But since you asked, I am seeing someone else.'

My heart closed in on itself.

'Oh, who?'

'You don't know him. A lawyer in my firm. He's a good guy.'

She stared at me, trying to gauge my reaction. I didn't want to give her any reason to feel guilty or sorry for me. So, I smiled.

'Good for you. I'm so glad things are working out for you, Maliha. You deserve it.'

'Really?' she said, brightening. 'I was a bit scared to tell you.'

'Yes really! I am happy for you.'

And I meant it. We sat silently for a minute. Peaceful.

'How long are you here for?' she asked.

'Not long, till Abba is better.'

'He'll be better soon,' she said confidently. 'But don't rake it up again Kamil, leave it in the past. That's where it belongs.'

I nodded.

'Anyway, I'd better go to my meeting,' she continued. 'It was lovely to see you – take care of yourself.'

She stood up to leave and stopped.

'Do you know what date it is today?' she asked, hesitating.

I glanced at my watch.

'Yes, October nineteenth … oh …'

Tears shone in her eyes.

I stood and hugged her tight.

'I'm so sorry, I'm so very sorry,' I mumbled into her hair.

'It is what it is.' She looked around. 'It would have been a nice day for a wedding, no?'

'Yes, it would have,' I said hoarsely.

She kissed me on the cheek, turned on her heel and walked away. I watched her move off with her familiar rapid march as I touched my face where she had kissed me. I felt a strange combination of sadness and calm. A feeling of something lost, something resolved, something gained. I knew what I had to do with complete clarity. Kolkata was my home and I needed to be here. I would begin by forgiving Abba and asking for his help to find a new job. I would be the bigger man. Mend my fences with him. Apologise. Make everything right. If Maliha could start again then so could I.

By the time I got home, Saibal had gone to join Anjoli at their relatives and Ma and Abba were watching a technicolour Indian serial about the Mahabharata. It was the perfect opportunity. Filled with my newfound optimism, I was about to launch into how sorry I was for everything that had happened and ask if he could help get me a new position, but Ma insisted on getting me a drink.

'So, how is London, son? Saibal is looking after you?' asked Abba, as Ma fussed in the kitchen.

'Yes, Abba.'

He nodded and relapsed into his habitual silence.

Ma came back with nimbu pani and, as I took a sip of the tart lemoniness, said, 'Adil, would you like something?'

'I will have a Scotch,' he said. 'Black Label.'

'Are you mad? At eleven in the morning? You cannot drink so soon after a heart attack. Anyway, the Black Label is finished. Don't you remember you and Rakesh emptied the bottle when you had that huge argument last month?'

Abba flushed. 'Oh yes,' he mumbled.

Her words took a few seconds to sink in. When they did, my resolve disintegrated into ash. I looked at Abba in shock, almost feeling myself go white, my breathing become shallow. I drained my glass, carefully placed it on a coaster, and said, the words coming out with some difficulty, 'Can I have a word please, Abba? In your study?'

'I'm tired now, Kamil. Later,' he muttered.

'It's important, it won't take long,' I insisted, getting up.

'Talk to your son, Adil. You haven't seen him for so long,' Ma encouraged.

Reluctantly, he followed me into the study and sat in his leather armchair as I perched on the footstool in front of him.

I looked at him through narrowed eyes. 'So, Rakesh Sharma was here last month. In your house. Drinking with you. You told me on the phone you hadn't seen him for a year. Why did you lie? What's going on? What were you arguing about?'

A pause.

'Terrible what happened to him. You were there that evening, no?' said Abba, evading my question.

'Yes, I was. How well did you know him?' I persisted.

'I knew him,' he muttered.

'He was your friend?'

Pause.

'Yes,' he replied. 'I was his senior in college. I didn't see him too often. After I became Police Commissioner, he got in touch again.'

'How come I didn't meet him?'

'You weren't living here.'

I tired of his forward defence to my questions. I needed to treat this as though it were a suspect's interrogation; forget he was my father.

I raised my voice. 'What is going on? No good will come from keeping me in the dark. I will not stop till you tell me, so please, save yourself the bother and just come clean.'

Another pause. 'All right. First, get me water – I have to take my tablets.'

I stood, controlling my irritation and went to the kitchen. This was Abba being Abba – always had to be in command.

I returned with a glass of water, set it on the table and stood over him, trying to intimidate him in some small way.

'Well?' I continued, annoyed now. 'What's this about? I need to ...'

He raised a hand as he carefully decanted two tablets from a bottle saying, 'For my BP,' then popped another one from its foil, adding, 'cholesterol.' He took the tablets with two gulps of water, cleared away the medicines, looked at me and said calmly, 'So what can I tell you, Kamil?'

I swallowed my exasperation. 'What was your relationship with Rakesh Sharma?'

'All right,' he nodded. 'Rakesh, Saibal and I were at college together. When I became Police Commissioner, Rakesh did me ... favours.'

'Favours?' I repeated, an uneasiness descending over me.

'Meaning ... he was well connected, and it was useful for me to have knowledge of dealings he had with politicians in Kolkata. In return, I would make him aware of certain facts that might be helpful for his business. Then he called me that morning ...'

'Called you which morning? For what?' I asked.

Abba closed his eyes, drank some water. Then, quietly, 'The morning of Asif Khan's murder, Rakesh called me and said that there was a high-profile murder case coming up. He suggested I call DC Ghosh and get you assigned to it. I did. The DC was my man, so he obliged.'

I staggered backwards, collapsing into a chair, as if a truck had hit me. *Abba* had got me on to the Asif Khan case! And pretended to be in the dark when I spoke to him about it! What was going on? Was he in cahoots with the corrupt DC? And what did Rakesh have to do with Asif's death?

'Did Rakesh tell you that Asif Khan was dead when he called?' I asked.

'Yes,' said Abba reluctantly.

'And you didn't think that was suspicious?' I said, incredulous.

'Of course, I did. I thought that he or his son may have something to do with the death,' he admitted.

I was in shock. Abba. Covering up a murder. I couldn't take it in.

'You *wanted* me to be part of a cover-up?'

He looked away and didn't reply.

'So *that's* how the DC knew the call was coming that morning. *You* told him! That's why he asked the Control Room to route all murders to him? So he could assign the case to me?'

He nodded.

'But what had Rakesh to do with Asif Khan? How was he involved? It was Jaideep!' I asked.

'Rakesh didn't mention Jaideep Sanyal when he called me. I only found out about Jaideep's involvement when *you* told Ghosh your suspicions about Jaideep after seeing him in that gay club.'

'I see,' I said, slowly joining the dots. 'DC Ghosh got worried when I told him about Jaideep and called you for instructions.'

'Yes. That's when I realised we had an enormous problem. Rakesh was not protecting himself – he was covering up Jaideep's involvement to protect the Chief Minister. This would put you in genuine danger.'

'*You* were the one who told DC Ghosh to let Jaideep off?' I whispered. I knew the answer but wanted to hear it from him, as if it would grant me clarity and wisdom, vindicate my suspicions and justify everything I had been through.

'Kamil, I *had* to. Things were spinning out of control. I know how things work, okay,' he said. 'Ami khali tomar bhalor jonyo chinta kori. I was just looking out for you. The direction you were going in ... You were too good at your job, Kamil. You're a fine officer with high principles. But it would not go well for you. I could tell that when I saw the big picture.'

'Why was Rakesh doing this for Jaideep?'

'Listen,' Abba said wearily. 'Rakesh was a dangerous, well-connected businessman. He was a fixer for the West Bengal politicians. PinRak won the massive Metro contract because Rakesh was friends with the Chief Minister and Jaideep. Rakesh even bankrolled Jaideep's investments in movies to stay close to his father.'

I shut my eyes and pieced it together, speaking slowly as things fell into place. 'JSRS Investments! Jaideep Sanyal *Rakesh Sharma* Investments. The RS didn't stand for Jaideep's father Ranjit Sanyal! I've been such a fool. Jaideep killed Asif. He panicked and asked Rakesh – his friend and his father's fixer – to make it go away. And Rakesh called *his* friend Police Commissioner Adil Rahman to get his son onto to the case. Because I was inexperienced and would do as I was told. But I got to the heart of the matter and discovered Jaideep was the killer. Those goondas who attacked me, they were Rakesh's men, right? Not Jaideep's. Rakesh was the hidden hand behind it all. The goondas worked for Rakesh!'

Abba look at me, worry in his eyes, then nodded. 'When the ... beating ... happened I was furious and called Rakesh but ... he wouldn't listen. He was so angry that you had found out about Jaideep.'

The disparate dots were converging into a full, IMAX-3D picture.

'*Rakesh* was the one pulling the DC's strings. Through you! He was supposed to shield Jaideep, but he failed. When I discovered Jaideep was the killer, Rakesh framed Mitra for the murder and the case was closed. But then I posted that video online *proving* Jaideep was the murderer, and ...'

'And they fired you for it. Kamil, it broke my heart when that happened. You had done nothing wrong, just used the talent you were born with and the skills you had learnt ... from me.

And you suffered because of it. I will live with that for the rest of my life,' Abba said, his voice breaking.

I ignored his self-pity and continued.

'So, Jaideep's father was furious that his son's association with Asif's death had become public and pulled the Metro contract, causing PinRak to collapse! *That's* why they said I was responsible – because if I had shut up and played my part, the murder would have been swept under the carpet and everything would have been fine. Now I understand! I was so blind. And *that's* why they tried to finish me off in London.'

'What?' said Abba, shocked. 'What happened in London?'

'The vaping goonda, Biren, tried to push me under a train. I couldn't understand why Jaideep would have done that but if Biren was Rakesh's man … now it makes sense. Rakesh and Arjun blamed me for the collapse of PinRak and Arjun wanted his revenge!'

Abba looked at me, pained.

'Kamil, I swear on your mother's life I did not know. When PinRak collapsed, Rakesh blamed me for everything. For not being able to control you. I tried. When things got … difficult, all I wanted was for you to escape unscathed. That's why I told Ghosh to get the video taken down. It was too dangerous for you. I *told* you that.'

By now I was numb to this conveyor belt of betrayals – they kept coming, one after another.

'Why didn't you back me up?' I asked. 'I had hard evidence that Jaideep killed Asif. If you had spoken, people would have listened. For God's sake, Abba, Rakesh called and asked you to have me assigned before the housekeeper even discovered the fucking body!' It was all I could do not to explode.

'I was trying to protect you, you stupid boy, why can't you bloody understand?' he said, his voice rising.

The problem was, I just *couldn't* understand. My heart had given up. I felt defeated. 'Why, Abba? Why were you doing so much for Rakesh?'

'I owed him,' said Abba, now resigned. 'Look around you, Kamil. We live a good life. Have you never asked yourself how we lived like this on a police salary? Holidays in the UK and Dubai? The best schools and colleges for you? Has it never crossed your mind that sometimes I had to do favours and that I got them in return? So your mother and you could have what you wanted? What you needed? How do you think we can afford this flat on a policeman's pension? Rakesh was very ... generous. He made a lot of this possible. For you. So, what choice did I have but to help him? After it collapsed, he came over for dinner and ended up just screaming at me and your mother. How ungrateful we were ...'

He seemed to shrink inside himself as I took in this new bombshell. Abba, who had always seemed the personification of rectitude had been on the take – like any cheap two-bit Indian constable – for years. I looked around at his awards dotting the room and laughed. This was unbelievable. And ridiculous. Abba, taking bribes ... Abba!

'I am tired now,' said Abba, his voice shaking. 'Let me rest, Kamil.'

I had one last question. 'Was Ma aware of this?'

'No,' he said, emphatic. 'She knew nothing of this. When Rakesh came that night, she had no clue what he was talking about, it upset her. Please don't tell her. Do that much for me.' His voice became weaker. 'Kamil, there is one last thing. All your life you have wanted to be like me. Son, I was proud of you when you refused to give in. Yes, it was a stupid thing to do and I was scared for you, but also proud. Keep doing the right thing.'

He raised himself up to embrace me for the first time ever, but I pulled away. It was too little, too late.

I looked into his eyes and said, 'I always thought you had the high morality of a Nakhoda Masjid Imam, Abba, but now I see under that righteousness was just another Sonagachi pimp.'

I turned away from the shock on his face, left his study, returned to my room and lay down in my familiar bed, vibrating, unable to control my thoughts. Adil Rahman, Commissioner of Police, corrupt! In the pay of Rakesh. And God knows who else. But he was right. Somewhere inside, I must always have known he was crooked – I'd had a good, luxurious life and just chosen not to think about it. A random memory came to me: my dream of being drenched in the goat's blood and how it had troubled me. Ibrahim had been ready to sacrifice his son Ishmael on the word of Allah, yet Abba had been prepared to ... I couldn't take any more. I swallowed two sleeping pills with a glass of whisky and, even with my mind in such turmoil, before I knew it, was asleep.

I woke, six hours later, in the evening, strangely rested and with an even stranger sense of freedom. What I had heard was shocking but I no longer had to live up to my father. That brought a sense of relief I had needed for years.

I went into the drawing room to find Saibal and Anjoli (in a *You can take the girl out of Kolkata but you can't take Kolkata out of the girl* T-shirt) having yet more tea with my parents, Abba not meeting my eyes.

'Kamil, finally you are up,' said Ma. 'You missed lunch, you must be starving, you poor boy! We didn't want to disturb you. Now, what will you eat?'

After the revelations of the afternoon, I couldn't face a painful family dinner so I said, 'Actually Ma, do you mind if Anjoli and I go out to dinner? I want Nizam's Kathi rolls and she doesn't believe that they are the best in the world,' I replied.

'Here for such a little time and he doesn't want to eat his mother's khana,' Ma grumbled.

I immediately felt guilty but controlled myself. 'Sorry Ma, you know I love your food, but I promised Anjoli.'

'I don't mind staying . . .' started Anjoli, but I enveloped Ma in a huge embrace. Mollified, she nodded her assent and muttered, 'Don't make her sick.'

'Oh, I've got a cast-iron stomach, Rehana Aunty. Have to with the food Baba serves at his restaurant,' Anjoli chuckled, elbowing her dad in the ribs. She kissed him and we walked towards the door.

'Don't be back too late,' called Ma.

I wanted to tell Anjoli what had happened with Abba but couldn't do it with the driver listening. He dropped us off at New Market and I started to say, 'Anjoli, I have to tell you someth—' but she interrupted me and said, 'Oh my God, this place is *amazing!*' as she looked around in exhilaration at the crowds out for their evening shopping; the rickshaws being pulled by muscled, sweating men; the hundreds of stalls selling everything from toys to watches to saris to household utensils. Street hawkers recognised her as a foreigner and besieged her, trying to flog their fake perfumes, knock-off handbags, sunglasses. Suddenly I saw New Market, which had been so commonplace to me for years, through her eyes and felt I was experiencing it for the first time – the food stalls selling delicious-looking chaats with yoghurt and tamarind; spirals of bright orange fried jalebis; shaved-ice lollies covered in different coloured syrups; kababs of different flavours and hues. Anjoli seemed intoxicated and dizzied by the sounds and smells and the wealth of food on offer and her joy momentarily took me away from my troubles.

We arrived at Nizam's (the sign proudly declaring 'Inventor of Kathi Kabab Rolls, no Beef') and walked past the decorative latticed doors into the basic cafe with fake marble plastic tables and wooden chairs. The fluorescent tube lights cast a bright cold glow that rendered romance dead.

'Goodness, what a magical place, Mr Rahman. You are exceptional at treating a girl like a princess,' commented Anjoli as a waiter in dark trousers and a T-shirt brusquely showed us to a grubby table covered by a blue plastic tablecloth.

'Yes, all right, just sit and wait till you taste what's coming. Let me order, then I need to tell you what I've just discovered,' I replied as the waiter tossed two menus the size of encyclopaedias on the table.

'Sigree kababs, Guldasta rolls,' she said, perusing the tome. 'I've never heard of half this stuff and I thought I was a foodie, being the daughter of a restaurateur and all. Fine, you order.' She slammed the menu shut.

'Ei! Duto mutton Kathi roll ebam dui nimbu pani,' I told the waiter. 'Listen, Anjoli, I …' I said, but she wandered to the counter to watch them make the Kathi rolls. The cook gave her a brilliant white smile out of his dark face and I saw her watch in delight as, with balletic, well-practised motions, he fried the flaked paratha on a tawa in oil till it was a perfect golden brown, cracked an egg on it, expertly turning it over so the yolk was marbled with the white and the egg perfectly cooked. He took pieces of goat off a skewer roasting over flames emanating from hot coals, coated them with a thick, dark, aromatic sauce and ladled them onto the eggy paratha. He added chopped onions, tomatoes and chillies, rolled the whole thing up, wrapped it in paper and handed it to her with a wide grin, earning a radiant beam in return.

'Ooh, hot, hot, he was a proper artist!' she juggled it between her hands and brought it back to the table as the waiter brought me my roll, together with our sweet and salty lemon water drinks.

Following my lead, she unwrapped the top of her roll and blew the steam away before taking a small bite. She closed her eyes in bliss and chewed. I bit into mine too. It was just as I remembered – hot and spicy, the smoky tartness of the meat complemented by the crisp flakiness of the paratha, the unctuousness of the egg and the fresh, cool tang of the raw onions, tomatoes and chillies.

'Amazing,' she said, her mouth full with her second, larger bite. 'Okay, I take it back, you do know how to give a girl a marvellous time, Mr Rahman.'

'This is a Kolkata institution and I wanted to share it with you,' I said, pleased.

'So, what did you want to tell me? Is it about Maliha?' she asked casually, taking a sip of her nimbu pani and wiping her mouth with her napkin. 'Your mother said you saw her?'

'No, that's not it. But she was fine,' I said. 'I left things badly between us last year. I needed to make sure there were no hard feelings. For either of us.'

'And how was it?'

'It was fine. We're good. Happy for each other.'

'I'm glad. So, what's on your mind?'

My face hardened.

'The Asif Khan killing. It runs much deeper than I thought. My father was not the innocent he appeared. I've found out that he and Rakesh were the hidden hands behind what happened in Kolkata last year. And it explains why Arjun wrote to the Home Office. But you know what I realised? I don't have to be the perfect son for him anymore. He certainly isn't the perfect father.'

'Rakesh was behind it? And your dad? Tell me,' she said, agog.

So, sitting in Nizam's, I told her the entire story as the sounds of New Market at night and the warm, earthy smell of kababs grilling on coal washed over us.

The Waiter

London. October. Sunday.

'Well, that was quite a trip,' said Anjoli, in the cab back from Heathrow, three days later. 'Baba, the rellies are something! "Anjoli you have grown so much!", "There is this bhery nice bhoy in my bhilding – he will be porfect phor her!" It was endearing and suffocating at the same time.'

'Not *the* rellies, your rellies … relatives,' said Saibal absently, looking out of the minicab window.

'Ooh! I got an interview tomorrow!' she exclaimed, checking her mobile.

'Interview with who, Anjoli?' he asked, turning to look at her from the front passenger seat.

'I applied for this job with a company looking for psychologists to do research. That's exciting! I'd better get a haircut.'

'Congratulations!' I said, trying to summon some enthusiasm while absorbing the grey day crawling by outside, a sharp contrast to the searing sun in Kolkata. The previous two days had been difficult. I had to put on a smiling face for Ma while trying to avoid Abba as much as possible – just seeing him around the house crushed my heart. Ma suspected something was wrong but said nothing. To her annoyance, I spent the bulk of the time away from home, showing Anjoli around my favourite parts of the city – the dusty book shops and coffee houses of College Street where I had argued politics with my university chums; the nostalgia of a time long forgotten in Tagore's home at Jorasanko; the shops where we would buy Eid presents in Rajabazar filled with their gilded Korans, multi-coloured waist-coats, colourful hookahs and mounds of dates and pomegranates; the white-uniformed waiters in Tollygunge Club, a little slice of colonial Britain in the middle of this insane city; and the silent peace of Rabindra Sarovar lake – I looked up at a familiar sky-scraper towering over us and wondered if Sabina Khan was at home, looking down on me. But even though I professed enjoy-ment at being Anjoli's tour guide, I felt increasingly alienated from these sights, as familiar as they were to me. Abba's revela-tions had completely unmoored me and I really didn't know where home was anymore – it wasn't London and Brick Lane and Abba's confession had totally destroyed any chance of my staying in Kolkata. Dinners at home were tense, with much unspoken, and I was relieved when we said our final goodbyes and left for the airport.

Getting through immigration had me wound up tight after my Home Office experience, but they let me through without any questions. I'd spent the flight wriggling in my seat, replay-ing the interactions I'd had with Abba, tracing back to see his finger in everything that had happened. In my heart I knew he had only been trying to help my career, but the sense of betrayal was overwhelming. His probity, which had been my North Star throughout my life, had turned out to be a mirage. It was like looking at a cloudless sky at midnight and seeing only inky blackness, the stars snuffed out. I was directionless, adrift. I needed to take back control.

'Don't congratulate me yet, it's just an interview,' Anjoli said. 'But you can take me to lunch and help me prepare.'

We arrived home (perhaps the flat above Tandoori Knights was more home than my parents' flat now) and Saibal went to tell Maya about the trip and to give her the silk sari his sister had sent for her ('When has Ma ever worn a sari like that?' said Anjoli incredulously when he proudly pulled the cellophane-wrapped packet out of his suitcase). After unpacking, Anjoli and I walked to the Tuck-In cafe around the corner for lunch.

We ordered two BLTs and coffees. Anjoli looked at me sharply, said, 'So, what's the matter with you?'

'Nothing,' I responded.

'Don't give me that. You've had an "Oh my life is so terrible" expression all the way back from Kolkata. Spill.'

'Just trying to work out a few things.' She listened sympathetically as I told her everything that I had been feeling. I ended with, '... the only regret is that if I *had* kept my mouth shut and not investigated the Asif Khan killing properly, two people would still be alive. My pursuit of Jaideep caused Mitra to be killed, which led to my trying to reveal all to the press, which led to PinRak collapsing, which led to Rakesh setting up his "charity", which led to his death.'

She reached across the table, took my hand and said, 'You can't think like that, Kamil. You might as well say if your dad hadn't met your mum none of this would have happened, blah, blah, blah. It's silly. What happened, happened. Let's learn from it and put it behind us.'

Pretty much what Maliha had told me. All these women so much wiser than me.

'Ironic, isn't it?' she continued, a grin coming across her face. 'I remember your telling me weeks ago how tedious detective work was, how it was always the most obvious person who did it and all that stuff. And this turned out to be so complicated with all the cogs turning inside cogs, yet still you cracked it. You should be proud of yourself. You really are a Sherlock Holmes. Maybe I'll get you a deerstalker hat and a pipe for Christmas.'

'I hardly cracked it, Abba just slipped up and then confessed,' I said, squeezing her hand. A thought occurred to me and I withdrew my hand from hers.

'It *was* intricate, though, wasn't it? Maybe the only way I can put it behind me is to confront Arjun with what he did, on both the immigration business and hiring the vaping guy to kill me. He must also know about the Asif Khan cover-up. If I don't let him get away with it like Jaideep and Rakesh did, perhaps *that* will allow me to get back some of my self-respect.'

'What good will it do?' asked Anjoli, doubtfully. 'Even if we got him to admit it, which he probably won't, there's nothing you can do about it. You can hardly take it to the police, you have no evidence.'

'It might give *me* closure. I'm tired of being everyone's patsy. *And* we should do it in Pinky's presence. I don't know how much *she* knows about what Rakesh did in Kolkata, but it would be good to find out.' This was feeling right. 'Can you get them to come to the restaurant for dinner tonight? Say it's to complete the restaurant sale or something?'

Anjoli got excited. 'What if we told them we will let it come out? All Rakesh's dodgy stuff. It's a juicy story. People should find out what a lying, sleazy shit he was. Actually, that might even help Neha! If we can show the police Rakesh was a criminal, they may expand their investigation to see if any of his associates had anything to do with his death.'

Given my experience, I doubted the Met police would reopen the case but maybe Rakesh's death would give me the chance to bring Jaideep's involvement in the Kolkata murder into the open.

'That's a brilliant idea!' I said, echoing her excitement. 'We can tell them we'll send it to a newspaper or a blog or something. PinRak's collapse is still a hot story and someone will pick it up. Jaideep can't shut it down in the UK. Arjun won't want that.'

'Done! I'll text them now.' She brushed breadcrumbs off her *Kill countryside vermin. Bring back hunting Tories* T-shirt and pulled out her mobile.

Arjun and Pinky had plans for dinner so Anjoli agreed on tea-time – she said it'd be better, as we would have the restaurant to ourselves. And so it was. Saibal, Anjoli and I sat on one side of a booth, with Maya, Pinky and Arjun on the other. Saibal and Maya were not thrilled to be seeing them so soon after our return but Anjoli had prevailed as usual.

Arjun wore a fixed smile, dead eyes looking straight through Saibal who chattered on about how much Kolkata had changed. I watched Arjun and experienced hot, rising anger. First the father and now the son had tried to wreck my life. Well, they may have won some battles, but we would see who won the final war.

Anjoli kicked things off, as Saibal took a break from his travelogue to bring us pakoras from the kitchen.

'How're things at work?' she asked Arjun.

'As you'd expect,' he said, sipping his whisky. 'We spend our days with lawyers and accountants. It's a much bigger mess than we expected.'

Anjoli nodded sympathetically.

'So, Anjoli, nice to see you. You said you wanted to talk about the restaurant? I am sorry, but Arjun tells me that there is nothing we can do to save it,' said Pinky, mouth full of onion bhaji.

'Yes. But before we do that, Kamil learned a few things about PinRak's collapse in Kolkata. And we thought we should tell you,' said Anjoli using her none-too-subtle 'dive straight into it' interrogation technique.

'About PinRak?' Arjun looked up from his samosa, alert.

'Yes,' I took up the story. 'The picture's not looking good. You see ...'

I laid out the entire story for them, step by step – from Rakesh's involvement in covering up Asif's death, to Mitra's murder to the collapse of PinRak. I minimised what Abba had done – there was no reason for Saibal to know that his oldest friend was corrupt – but other than that, I let them see the whole squalid truth.

There was a deep silence after I finished. Saibal and Maya looked stunned and tears rose in Pinky's eyes. Anjoli tried to take her hand across the table but she flinched away.

'Rakesh did that?' whispered Saibal. 'I don't believe it.'

'It is shocking Saibal-da,' I said. 'But he was behind every-thing that happened to me in Kolkata.'

Pinky's tears were flowing now and Maya put an arm on her shoulder to comfort her. I felt sorry for Pinky – I understood the shock of discovering your family was not what it seemed.

She finally recovered herself, wiped her face and turned to Arjun. 'Is this true?' she said, sharply. 'Don't lie to me.'

He couldn't meet her eyes and stayed silent.

'Did your father do all that *he* said?' She gestured at me. 'The truth!'

'He *had* to do it, Mummy,' Arjun cried. 'He didn't have a choice. When Jaideep Sanyal asks for help, you help. If you fall out with him … well, you saw what happened.' His face became suffused with fury as he turned to me and waved a finger in my face. 'And this happened because of HIM! I would have been CEO of PinRak when Dad retired, would have had everything. And now, because of this … this two-paisa policeman, I have NOTHING!'

His voice rose in pitch.

'And then he turns up at Dad's house! On his birthday! This … this *waiter*. Strutting around as though he was some kind of hero. And then Neha took Dad away from us …' His voice cracked. 'I had to stop him interfering with our life. I *had* to. To take care of him once and for all. To make him pay.'

He subsided as we looked at him in shock.

'What did you do, Arjun?' asked Pinky, softly.

'He tried to have Kamil deported,' said Anjoli. 'So that he would have to go back to Kolkata and could be "taken care of" there.'

'Arjun would never do anything like that!'

Anjoli showed her the picture of the Home Office form.

'Yes,' Arjun said, defiant. 'He doesn't deserve to be here. We got him fired in Kolkata but then he came here to torment us. Dad told me to get him sent back, so I did. I couldn't believe how long it took the Home Office to do something about it, with all the fuss they make about illegal immigrants!'

'And he was getting closer to the fact that you killed your father?' said Anjoli, taking a flyer.

'Anjoli!' said Maya, shocked.

Arjun's face changed from anger to astonishment. As did Pinky's. Saibal looked puzzled.

'What on earth are you talking about?' said Arjun. 'I didn't kill Dad. Neha did! And anyway, I sent that form to the Home Office weeks before Dad died.'

He wasn't lying. I could tell. Anjoli had timed her question well. In his rage, he would have reacted differently if he had been the killer – Arjun, like his mother, was not one to hide his emotions.

'What are you saying, Anjoli?' asked Pinky, visibly disturbed by this.

And from her reaction she wasn't the killer either. But Anjoli wasn't giving up easily.

'When Neha was searching for Rakesh Uncle, you slipped down to the pool, killed him and put Neha's ring in his hand. Admit it.'

Arjun broke into amazed laughter.

'Is that what this nonsense is about Anjoli? You trying to get your friend off? Don't be ridiculous, of course I didn't kill Dad. I loved him. How on earth would I have got Neha's ring? I was with Mummy all the time. Unless you're now going to say we killed him together?'

Anjoli moodily tore a naan into pieces.

'Arjun was not involved with Rakesh's death,' Pinky said firmly. 'He was with me when Neha went to find Rakesh. I swear on my only child's life,' she said, putting her hand on Arjun's head, though he immediately shrugged it off irritably. 'Look, she is your friend, Anjoli, and you don't want her to go to jail, but she did do it. And you should never have put her in Rakesh's office.' Anjoli frowned at her, and Pinky added hurriedly, 'I'm not blaming you.'

'You may not have killed your father, Arjun, but you tried to have *me* killed,' I said, quietly. 'You got your man to shove me under a train.'

'Yes,' said Anjoli, without missing a beat. 'Kamil saw him in Watford station.'

This gave Arjun pause.

'He did no such thing!' exclaimed Pinky. 'Did you Arjun? What man?'

'Biren,' I said.

'Biren?' said Pinky, confused. 'Our driver?'

Their driver! That explained why he was in the UK.

'When the Home Office did nothing about Kamil, to make doubly sure that Kamil was out of the way, he had him pushed under a train. Except I pulled him back just in time,' said Anjoli, her eyes defying Arjun to contradict her.

'I ... didn't,' Arjun mumbled, looking down. It was obvious to everyone that he was lying.

Anjoli continued, 'And when Kamil was attacked at the funeral – that was your driver's handiwork, too.'

Pinky looked at Arjun in stupefaction. 'Biren did have a few bruises and his clothes were all scuffed when he drove us home that day. He said he had been mugged while we were at the funeral.' She turned to me. 'I am surrounded by mad, violent men it seems. Nothing will happen to you, Kamil. I will make sure of that. I don't know what has got into Arjun, must be the shock of his father's death. I am sorry. I will deal with him.' She turned back to Anjoli. 'Anjoli, what do you plan to do with this information?'

'Pinky Aunty, we have to go the press about Rakesh's nefarious activities, tell them about what happened in Kolkata and clear Kamil's name,' said Anjoli. 'We can't let Uncle Rakesh ruin his reputation and career for life. It's just not fair. And if Neha killed him, well, the world must see what a monster he was. It will help her at her trial.'

Arjun and Pinky looked at each other, shock creeping into their eyes.

'I can understand that, Beti,' said Pinky, carefully. 'But do you have any proof? They won't publish without confirmation.'

'I *will* put it on the internet and then it will be out there,' said Anjoli. 'You can sue me if you like, then everything will come out in court. I'll do anything to help Neha.'

As Anjoli gave them her ultimatum, I realised she was wrong. We couldn't publish any of this. If everything came out, then so would Abba's involvement. Much as I despised Abba for what he had done, I couldn't let the papers drag him through the mud. I couldn't do that to Ma.

'Listen,' I said. 'I have another way out.'

They turned towards me.

'We won't say anything to anyone if you buy back Saibal-da's business from the administrator and gift it to him. I'm sure the administrator will give you a good deal if you ask.'

Anjoli looked at me in surprise as Arjun said, 'What?' And Saibal said simultaneously, 'What are you saying, Kamil?'

'Just that,' I said. 'Look, Saibal-da is losing what he and Maya-di spent decades building because of something rotten Rakesh did. None of this was their fault but they stand to be deprived of their business and their home because of it. What will they do? Where will they live? So, make amends for Rakesh. Get them their home and business back. Then we can draw a line under this. I won't say anything to anyone and neither will Anjoli. You know it's the right thing to do for your oldest friends.'

Anjoli started to say something then subsided as Pinky contemplated what I had said, then looked at Arjun and said, 'Let me talk to him.' She hauled herself out of the booth and they walked outside to the street. My eyes followed them as they stood next to a dark blue BMW with the number plate ARJ88N. As I watched, I saw Biren, vape in hand, get out to open the door for them but Arjun waved him away as Pinky spoke to him. I had to restrain myself from rushing out of the restaurant and finishing what I had started at the funeral.

'Are you sure about this, Kamil?' Anjoli burst out. 'If we publish everything you'll be absolved from any wrongdoing. You can go back to Kolkata with your head held high – they might even give you your job back in the police – you might even get a book deal! All the world will see how skilled and incorruptible you are. I mean, what you said was very nice and considerate but . . .'

'I agree with her, Kamil,' said Saibal-da. 'As Anjoli said, it will help Neha at her trial and we need to do what we can to help her. I can't accept this. Rakesh was my friend but if he did all of this, it must see the light of day. Neha is like a daughter to me.'

'I don't know how much it really will help Neha, Anjoli,' I said. 'She is refusing to admit she did it and that's playing against her. She might claim Rakesh was abusing her and—'

'She wouldn't lie,' said Anjoli despondently. 'Rakesh was kind to her.'

'Take this, Anjoli,' I said firmly. 'Saibal-da you have been a better father to me than my own in many ways. I'll be fine and we'll find another way to help Neha.'

'Don't say things like that, Kamil,' muttered Saibal. 'Adil is a principled man.'

Maya looked at me, eyes wet, and said, 'Are you sure, Kamil? This is what you want?'

'Yes, Maya-di,' I said. 'I haven't been as sure about anything for a long time.'

She nodded and said, 'Thank you, son,' as Anjoli took my hand and squeezed it.

Pinky and Arjun came back in. I tried to read their faces to see if my bluff had worked.

'Okay, we have discussed it,' announced Pinky. 'Arjun will see what he can do with the administrator to get Saibal his business back. I can't promise but we will try our best. We must go now, though. I need to talk to this boy alone.'

I breathed a silent sigh of relief. I had won.

'Wait, I want one more thing,' I said. 'And this one's for me.'

'What?' said Pinky.

'Your driver, Biren. I assume he is here on a work visa? You need to end his employment and send him back to India. I will take care of him there. Not only did he try to kill me here, he murdered a man in Kolkata and kidnapped an innocent girl. He has to pay for his crimes.'

Arjun turned pale with fury. 'Who are you to make demands? We are not—'

'Be quiet, Arjun!' Pinky snapped. 'We will send him back this week, Kamil. I will personally send you the details confirming his return.'

Arjun subsided, shooting me another murderous look. I didn't care. I would call Abba and tell him he could start redeeming himself with me by having that vaping scumbag arrested when he landed and thrown into a cell for decades.

'Thank you,' I replied.

'Come, Arjun,' commanded Pinky.

As they left, Maya gasped and covered her face with her hands. 'Eh Maa!' she wept. 'Thank you, son. This means everything to us. Thank you.'

'She has been so worried,' said Saibal, looking at Maya. 'But she was showing a brave face, as always.'

Maya stood and squeezed my face between her hands as I hugged her. Anjoli had an enormous grin across her face. She embraced me too.

'Thank you so much Kamil, you're amazing! Mind you, it would have been perfectly perfect if you had got Neha off by discovering that somehow Arjun had killed Rakesh as well!'

'Well, you gave it your best shot,' I smiled at her using Saibal's pet phrase. 'I did believe Pinky and Arjun, though.'

Saibal's face fell. 'I feel terrible for Neha. But I don't know what else we can do. I have tried everything. Tell me if you have any other ideas, Kamil.'

'You have to accept it was her, Saibal-da,' I said. 'She had lost everything, and her husband was sleeping around. Let's try to speak to her. If she claims he provoked her into a sudden fit of lunacy, it will help her case.'

'I'll convince her. It was my fault,' said Anjoli. 'I should never have introduced them.'

'Now you're doing what you told me not to do,' I said. 'Creating cause and effect where it doesn't exist. It was as much my fault as it was yours. Rakesh got what he deserved; I'm just sorry Arjun has got away with the shit that he did.'

'Don't worry,' Anjoli said. 'Pinky Aunty will make his life a misery. If you get past her pain and anger towards Neha, she is an honest person and would have been horrified by what she heard.'

'I am tired and going to bed, Saibal, this has been too much for me,' said Maya. 'Thank you again, Kamil.'

I had done something good for these people who had taken me in with open arms. A tiny voice in my head asked if I had just been paid off by the Sharmas to stay silent about Rakesh's crimes, but I damped it down. This was definitely not the same as what Abba had done. This was for a good cause.

After we finished dinner at Tandoori Knights, we traipsed upstairs to the flat. Saibal, bleary after several beers, hugged me, announcing over his shoulder as he staggered up the flight of stairs to their bedroom, 'I will make you a partner in the business! Not a waiter anymore. Full partner ... okay, twenty-per-cent partner! I will get you a Vindaloo Visa!'

Anjoli and I were left with the living room to ourselves.

'Well, that was quite a day,' I said, flopping down on the sofa next to her. She had poured two glasses of red wine, and Prince sang from the speaker about the gentle breeze blowing with ease.

'Started the day as a waiter and ended it as a full twenty-per-cent partner in the business,' she laughed. 'Impressive career progression, Mr Rahman.'

'That *was* funny,' I said, joining in with her laughter. 'Full partner! No, only twenty per cent! Won't do me much good, though. I still have to return to India in a few weeks when my visa expires. If they don't chuck me out before. What's a Vindaloo Visa, anyway?'

'A visa for curry chefs – hard to get experienced cooks from the subcontinent so they are being fast-tracked. The British can't live without our curry houses dontcha know,' said Anjoli.

My heart quickened. Was this a way to stay in the UK?

Sympathy softened her face, 'I'm not sure it will apply to an ex-cop though.'

We sat in silence. I looked at the wine throwing darts of colour on her face and had this desperate urge to lean over and hug her. I hesitantly moved my arm and put it across her shoulders. She leaned into me and we sat, silent except for Prince wafting over us. Time stopped. Every sense in my body was hyper-alert. I could feel the weight of her head on my shoulder, her hair tickling my face. Smelt her perfume, faintly mixed with the scent of garlic that she hadn't managed to scrub from her fingers from chopping earlier in the day. Her eyes were closed, and I took in every line of her delicate face, hearing her gentle breathing.

She opened her eyes, saw me staring at her and smiled. 'I'm knackered,' she said, yawning and giving a big stretch. 'I'm off to bed. Good night, effective detective.'

She pecked me on the cheek and padded off, leaving me sipping my wine, alone. But with a butterfly of hope fluttering in my chest.

The Waiter

London. October. Monday.

The electric razor buzzed against my cheek as I gazed at myself in the mirror the next morning. This Vindaloo Visa sounded interesting, I needed to research it. I felt my smooth cheek and was about to switch off the shaver when, with a swift movement I ran it across my top lip and, in a few seconds, the moustache that had adorned it for the last dozen years disappeared in a gentle drizzle of hairdrops into the sink. I smiled at the familiar, yet strange, face in the mirror. I hoped that Anjoli would approve.

'Ah Kamil,' said Saibal when I went to the kitchen. 'Have a coffee. Come, sit. Arre tomake onyo rokom dekhacche? He looks different, no, Maya?'

He and Maya were dressed and at the breakfast table. I stroked my bare lip.

'Oh, you have shaved!' said Maya. 'You look very handsome Kamil.'

'Thank you Maya-di, I felt it was time for a change. Has Anjoli left?' I asked, as I made my coffee.

'She's gone for her interview,' said Maya.

Saibal added, 'Accha Accha. Bhālo dekhacche. Looks nice. I am taking Maya away for the day ... it is her turn to relax. The restaurant can run without us. Mondays are quiet, anyway.'

'That's nice,' I said. 'Where are you going?'

'We are driving to Southend,' he said.

'The seaside? It'll be cold, no?' I asked.

'Doesn't matter, we have our coats and umbrella.'

Maya still looked tired. 'Didn't you sleep well, Maya-di?' I asked. 'It must be a relief?'

'I slept okay, thanks Kamil. Will take time to get over the tension. Thank you again,' she said.

'My pleasure, Maya-di. You have done so much for me. It was the least I could do. I'm just sorry you had to find out about Rakesh like that.'

'Yes,' said Saibal. 'It is hard to find your friend of so many years is not what he seemed. Acchha, "Partner", *you* don't get the day off! Today you can help me with the accounts. I need to collect the invoices from the restaurant and put them in order to give my accountant so he can do my taxes. My computer is there. You know how to do spreadsheet?'

'Sure. Where are the invoices?' I said.

'Start with the ones in the study upstairs. I will get others from the restaurant tomorrow.'

They left and I finished breakfast and cleared away the dishes.

I had one task left before I took on my accounting duties. I picked up my phone and called Abba and, after a stilted start to the conversation, told him about my plan to have Biren arrested on arrival in Kolkata.

'So at least one person will face justice for this whole sorry mess. Will you do this, Abba? If not for me then for your own conscience?'

'Yes,' he said, almost inaudible. 'Yes, at least this much I will do. Leave it to me.'

I hung up without thanking him.

Satisfied with this outcome, I wandered to the study, where I found a cardboard cash-and-carry box containing a mound of receipts, bills, statements and spent cheque books with the stubs filled in erratically, sometimes with no dates, sometimes no figures and sometimes no descriptions. Aaargh, there were hundreds! I would have to cross check them against Saibal's statements.

I picked up a few receipts to get an idea of what I was working with. The cash and carry, the halal meat guy, the frozen fish supplier, written chits of salaries paid to the staff in cash, utility bills. I opened the ancient laptop, which took forever to load Excel. I created a spreadsheet and started entering the information. I wasn't sure if it was the format Saibal wanted, but any organisation was better than what existed.

'Right,' I said out loud. 'Here goes the entire day.' I worked methodically, leafing through bits of paper, which seemed to be in zero order.

3 January VG's Cash and Carry. £339.75 Mastercard.
4 March British Gas. £140.80

Saibal had told me the utility bills were direct debit – apparently not! I inserted another column.

3 October Akbar's Wholesale Halal £460 Barclaycard Visa

I worked away, filing the paper copies into a bunch of used envelopes I'd found in the wastepaper basket. It was boring work but oddly therapeutic. My brain was exhausted and it was a relief to not think about anything taxing. The past few weeks had been intense. The murder investigation; the thought of losing my current job and home if Saibal had lost his business; Maliha's fresh life; my father's revelations. With each entry into the spreadsheet, the load seemed to lighten. For the first time in a long while, I was in control. My mind drifted back to the night before, my arm around Anjoli, the scent of her shampoo, her breathing. I found I was missing her with a joyous desperation.

After an hour and a half, I needed a stretch and was peckish. I found Anjoli's Spotify account on my phone – what was the band she had liked all those years ago? Oh yes, The Killers. I found the song 'Mr. Brightside' and put it on. After a minute or two – no, that's not for me – I switched to Kanye and blissfully entered a world of cop lights, flashlights and spotlights while I continued my mindless task.

I stopped at one headed 'Gehna Jewellers, Dubai' dated a month earlier. Ah, Maya's Dubai jewellery for the party. Do I put this in the spreadsheet too? Or is this personal?

I put it aside and carried on inputting invoices, my fingers tapping out the staccato rhythms of the song on the keyboard. Then stopped. Something had caught my eye. I picked up the jewellery invoice again.

Gehna Jewellers, Dubai

Butterfly pendant in 18K yellow gold with chain: AED 900
Alphabet Bracelet, 'M': AED 200
Blue sapphire ring: AED 2000

I looked again.

Blue sapphire ring: AED 2000

Fuck.
What did this mean?

I thought for a moment, then, in a trance, entered Saibal and Maya's room. I opened the drawers in her dressing table and rifled around until I found a box with bits of jewellery in it. Nothing fitted either description I'd read on the receipt. As I looked about the room, I could feel my heart pounding.

Wait. Wait. What was happening? What was I doing?

My gaze fell upon the narrow chest of drawers in the corner. I opened the first drawer. Full of Maya's underwear. I cringed as I groped around. Second drawer. Saibal's underwear and socks. I emptied it onto the bed and one by one threw each item back in the drawer. No jewellery.

Opposite the bed stood a tall row of four slim cupboards. Inside each was an overfilled hanging rail bowing with the pressure of the clothes stuffed and hung on them. I peered into the cupboards and noticed a green suit-carrier sticking out on the left end. I pulled it out and laid it on the bed. Unzipping it, I noticed it was Saibal's good dark suit, the one he had worn to Rakesh's party and funeral. I checked the pockets. Nothing. I groped in the inside breast pocket and it felt padded. I delved deeper and pulled out a soft drawstring bag with tiny gold script sewn onto it.

Gehna Jewellers

I emptied the bag into my palm and held the jewellery up against the window. There, sparkling in the midday sunshine was the gold and diamond butterfly pendant that Maya had worn to the party, a gold bracelet with an M filled with tiny diamonds and ... no sapphire ring.

I put everything back where I had found it and went to my bedroom, deep in thought.

What *had* Arjun said the night they found the body? The words bubbled up into my consciousness. Finally.

I rushed to Bishops Avenue, keeping the Uber waiting outside the house. When the butler opened the door, I ran past him and took the stairs down to the swimming pool, two at a time. He followed me down, shouting, but I yelled I was with the police.

The cops had torn the place apart. The pool had been emptied, walls stripped, chairs and tables pushed to one side, signs of forensics everywhere. After clocking the carnage, I stood at the pool's edge and took out my mobile. I walked around the entire gym, checking the screen every few paces, the butler expostulating that he would call the police. I retraced my footsteps up the stairs, continuing to check the screen, reached the top, thanked the butler, and got back into the cab.

Back in Brick Lane, I grabbed a pen and pad of Post-it notes from the study, ignoring the pile of receipts and the open laptop. I sat on the bed and wrote out my alternative theory, checking details on my notebook and phone where necessary, step by step, each step on a separate Post-it note. I laid the Post-its on the bed, swapping them around, screwing up and discarding some, re-writing others, and moving them all around until I was satisfied, staring at the squares of yellow laid out in a vertical line against the backdrop of my blue and orange Aztek print bedcover. The colours and patterns darted and swam in front of my eyes, finally falling into place.

Now what? Now what do I do? Fuck. FUCK!

Something else struck me and I called Neha's lawyer, not telling him what I had found. He confirmed my suspicion.

The window-shaped rectangle of light illuminating my dark spiral-patterned carpet looked like a stained-glass window. It was a beautiful day. I needed to get out.

I gathered the Post-its into a neat pile, stuffed them in the back pocket of my jeans and returned to Saibal's study. I looked at the jeweller's invoice again, then folded it and put it into my other back pocket. I stuffed the remaining invoices and bills that were still strewn around back into the cardboard box.

I speed-walked through the crowded streets, away from Brick Lane and towards the river. When I reached the Tower of London, gleaming in the golden sun, lying low like a lion waiting to pounce, I started running. I jogged nonstop for nearly an hour downriver and then looped back inland till I got to the Tower Hamlets Cemetery Park, where I stopped, hands on my knees, panting. I sat next to a grave and tried to figure out what to do next.

I had to tell Saibal and Maya. I couldn't not. But what about Anjoli?

It was just past two. I walked around the graveyard, looking at the headstones without seeing them. I heard a baby crying from a flat next to the park, its exasperated mother shouting at it to be quiet.

All these dead people. Who remembers them? Their lives, their loves. All gone. What's the point? What if I say nothing? Then we can carry on with our lives. Nobody needs to know. Who is it harming?

Neha. That's who. But … can I have this between Anjoli and me? Is there even an Anjoli and me? Nothing happened last night. It was just a moment. But what about Rakesh? Can I cover up another crime? What kind of police officer am I? It's my job to serve justice, not let criminals get away. I'd be as bad as DC Ghosh … or Abba.

I walked through Mile End and Stepney Green till I reached Whitechapel Road. Straight ahead of me glittered the skyscrapers of the City of London yet here I was surrounded by graffitied, shuttered stores. Two worlds that would never touch, within half a mile of each other.

My phone pinged with a WhatsApp.

I got the job!!!! How are you doing? Enjoying being a partner? Out with uni mates all day. Back in the evening … we can celebrate my new gig! Xxx.

My thumbs hovered over a response when the Azan echoed, winding sinuously around me, filling my senses. I realised I was standing in front of the East London Mosque and the faithful were trooping in for prayers. I followed the crowds in and as I entered the men's door, I instantly felt welcomed and at home, even though I had never been here and hadn't set foot in a mosque in years.

The mosque was large, and more modern than the decrepit Nakhoda Masjid I used to go to with my parents, all those years ago. I had nothing to cover my head but took off my shoes, walked past the sign asking me to make Allah's house debt free and obeyed a notice telling me to switch off my mobile as, 'While God might speak to you here, it is unlikely to be on your phone.' I walked down to the ablution area where I performed the oju, washing my feet, arms and face. Cleansed, I came back up and entered the prayer hall, which was filled with men milling around and chatting. Then it was time for the Imam to begin the sermon and everyone quietened down.

'You are like a flowing river. Today you are not who you were yesterday and tomorrow you will differ from today ...' he began. I listened, mesmerised, believing he was speaking directly to me. He used simple language and explained how, while we were in constant flux, there was one thing that was eternal. And how, through love and kindness, we could touch that flow of the everlasting.

After he finished the sermon we moved into our rows. I prayed with the others, not knowing what I was praying for. Perhaps to be given clarity, for something to be revealed. To touch the numinous. The Imam's recitation of the Qur'an pierced through me, awakening memories and feelings that were long dormant, touching areas that had seemed broken. When it was finished, I left without speaking to anyone, my mind clearer, calmer. As I walked home, the lack of direction I had felt since Abba's confession seemed to give way and, however hazily, a path emerged ahead of me. Not a new North Star but perhaps a compass pointing me towards one.

I got home at four to find the members of what now felt like my actual family had returned. Anjoli was putting down her handbag in the kitchen, the back of her T-shirt reading *If you think this looks good, wait till you see the other side.* She saw me, smiled, gave me a quick peck on the cheek then stared.

'Whoah! What happened here?'

'Huh?' I said, distracted.

'Don't "huh" me, Mr Detective! What's with the new look?'

Saibal gave me a friendly nod as Maya, looking more relaxed than she had in a while, asked, 'Cha khabé? Tea?'

I shook my head and stroked my lip. I'd forgotten my impulsive shave. 'Oh, I just thought I'd do something different. Anjoli, can I speak to you for a minute?'

She looked quizzical and followed me up to my bedroom.

'What's up Monsieur Poirot sans moustache? I like it, by the way,' she said cheerily. 'You look good, not like a movie villain anym—'

'I found something while doing the invoices for your dad,' I interrupted, voice flat.

'What?'

I took out the jeweller's invoice and handed it to her.

'Ooh, new jewellery. Is this for me? How exciting! A gold pendant. A bracelet. A sapphire ... Oh.'

The smile vanished from her face and her eyes filled with a sense of dread. She dropped the bill as if it had burst into flames.

Silence.

'What ... what does this mean?' she asked, voice trembling.

'We have to ask them,' I replied, unable to look at her. 'I think I've figured it out but I'm not sure what to do.'

She grabbed the invoice and marched down the stairs.

'Baba? What's this?' She thrust the document at her father.

Saibal looked at it and went pale, then recovered.

'Orre nothing Anjoli. Nothing. I bought your mother jewellery, that is all. Why are you showing me this? Did Kamil give it to you? This has nothing to do with the restaurant.' He looked at

261

me. 'Don't worry, I am not trying to defraud the VAT man if that is what you are worried about. *Partner*,' he said with some emphasis.

'Show me the ring, Ma,' said Anjoli, quietly.

'I ... I ... lost it,' whispered Maya.

'I know,' Saibal interjected. 'Silly woman. Does not matter. Not that expensive. Chalo. Let's go upstairs and change.'

'I went to Bishops Avenue,' I said.

'Ki? Keno? Why?'

'To check something.'

Anjoli looked sick.

'What did you check, Kamil?' she asked.

'See, something had been niggling me for days. Arjun said a few times that he and Neha had "gone up" to call the police and Saibal-da after the murder. Why would they not call from the pool? That would be the logical thing to do. But it *is* what some-one might say if they can't get a signal. So, I checked. And I was right. There's no mobile or Wi-Fi signal anywhere around the swimming pool.'

'So?'

'So, Rakesh *couldn't* have WhatsApp'd anyone from the pool. But your dad and Arjun both got messages from him. It made no sense. I started thinking. What if he wasn't near the pool when he sent the messages? What if he was elsewhere in the house? Or in the garden? But why would he go to the pool with Taania, come up, send the messages and then go down again to be murdered? He wouldn't have gone into the garden in the rain. How can a phone mysteriously send a WhatsApp when ... ?'

'Stop it. Stop it!' cried Anjoli.

I ignored her and continued.

'Maybe the phone wasn't with the body when the messages were sent. And if *that* was the case the entire timeline was wrong. The murderer could have sent the messages after killing

Rakesh. So, the scope of possible suspects was wider than I thought, extending beyond just the family who found the body.'

They stared at me, wordless.

'I went for a long walk and I've worked it out. Tell me if I'm right, Saibal-da. Here's what happened. You knew Rakesh was selling your business. You tried to talk him out of it, but he wouldn't listen. He had made up his mind. Maya-di decided to try to plead with him.'

I carried on, presenting conjectures as facts in the manner of good detectives.

'I saw you together at 1 a.m. then Anjoli came to the kitchen to see me. At 1.15 Rakesh announced he was showing Taania out. You and Maya-di left the living room to talk to him. You see, when Arjun and Neha said you went to fetch Anjoli to go home, I assumed it was much later, when you picked us up from the kitchen. But it couldn't have been. Because Pinky and Arjun told Neha all about the bankruptcy while you were gone, and there were only five minutes between you picking us up and us going back to say goodbye. You had to have been away for longer.

'So, you left the living room at 1.15 a.m., not at 2 a.m. You saw Rakesh taking Taania down to the basement. You waited till she came back up twenty-five minutes later after giving him ... what he wanted. It was you two who Taania sensed in the dining room. Maya-di rushed down to the pool to plead with Rakesh not to sell the restaurant and found him drunk. She couldn't persuade him around.'

'He was so angry we had brought you to the party,' Maya whispered. 'He blamed you for everything, that's why he was so insistent on selling our business. And it was obvious he had been sleeping with Taania. He was cleaning up so no one would notice.'

I stopped short then continued, talking to Maya, looking her straight in the eye.

263

'So maybe the whisky bottle and the phone were on a table nearby as he was cleaning himself up. You lost your temper, Maya-di. You grabbed the bottle by the neck and smashed him on his head. It broke and dropped in the pool. Rakesh fell back, tried to grab your hand and got your ring. He slipped, fell, and smashed his skull on his way into the pool. It killed him. Is that what happened?'

Maya looked at me dumbly, then nodded. 'I don't know what came over me. I begged him not to sell, but he just laughed at me. He said he had looked after Saibal for years and years and now Saibal had to grow up and stand on his own two feet. After everything Saibal has suffered to keep us safe and that man had the nerve to say that? He kept laughing and I saw red and I ...'

I continued, gently. 'You hit him. But you remembered to wipe your prints off the neck of the bottle and toss it in the water. I was an idiot – I should have remembered Neha had held the neck when she opened the bottle for Rakesh. Her prints should have been there. But they weren't. I called her lawyer and checked. The police just assumed she wiped them off. Why would she only wipe the neck and not the entire bottle? You grabbed his phone and ran upstairs ... why take the phone?' I asked.

'I don't know,' said Maya. 'I panicked, I thought they may think it was a robbery. The ring was big for me and it came off in his hand. I didn't even notice ...'

'Well,' I continued, 'you found Saibal-da and told him what happened. He'd been waiting for you in the dining room to see if you'd had any luck persuading Rakesh. The two of you hatched a plan. You guessed the code for his phone – it wasn't hard, I worked it out too. You drafted two WhatsApp messages. Collected Anjoli and me. Said goodbye to Neha and then sent the first message to Arjun, Saibal-da. I remember you had your coat over your arm – that must have been so we wouldn't see the phone, right?'

Saibal wouldn't meet my eye, but nodded slowly as Anjoli looked at him, ashen faced.

I carried on. 'We got into the car, me in the front and Anjoli and Maya-di in the back, because, as you said, Anjoli was drunk and Maya-di had to look after her. Again, I was stupid. It was Maya-di smelling of whisky not you, Saibal-da. When she hit Rakesh and the bottle broke, the whisky must have splashed on her. I just assumed it was you and worried about you driving.

'Saibal-da, when you told me to use the GPS, I thought it was odd, but you needed a witness for what came next. Anjoli was asleep in the back and Maya-di, you sent the WhatsApp to Saibal-da from Rakesh's phone. It arrived. I read it. You were very cool, Saibal-da, asking me to reply. I assume the phone was on silent in Maya-di's hand, so it didn't ping. Alibi well and truly established. As far as the police were concerned, the phone had sent the messages from the house.'

'It was stupid,' said Saibal. 'When Maya told me what she had done, I panicked. I had to save her. I thought if we could make the police think he was still alive when we left then maybe they would think it was an accidental death … I had no idea they would arrest Neha.'

'I understand, Saibal-da, you were in an impossible situation,' I said. 'I've no idea what the next phase of the plan was and how you thought you would get the phone back to the body. But then – a stroke of luck. Neha called. When we rushed back, Maya-di got out of the car and gave the phone to you, before taking Anjoli home. You wiped the fingerprints off the phone and put it back in Rakesh's pocket while you were "examining" him at the pool.

'And everything worked out. Except, as you said, Neha was in the frame. You pleaded with me to get her off because you felt guilty about her being arrested. At least I hope you did.'

Both Saibal and Maya nodded. Maya mumbled, 'When she was arrested, it seemed the world would end. Anjoli, believe me, I wanted to tell the police, but your father persuaded me not to. Saibal, I should never have listened to you.'

'What choice did we have,' he mumbled.

Anjoli went to her mother's side and hugged her, weeping. Maya wiped her tears with her sleeve and whispered, 'It will be all right, baby, don't cry.'

'Who knows, Saibal-da, perhaps you believed you could manipulate me. There's a lot of that going around, useful idiot that I am,' I added. 'And you were lucky. Like a fool I left my fingerprints on Rakesh's mobile or the police would have realised that the phone had been wiped clean of prints. Neha is sent to jail and I got your business back. And everything is now fine. Did I get it right, Maya-di?'

Silence. Anjoli pulled away from her mother and looked at her fiercely, cheeks wet with tears.

'I'm so, so sorry, Ma. I know you didn't mean to do it. And there was I running around playing detective with Kamil while you had this … this horrible thing to deal with. And I never saw what you were going through.'

Maya sighed, rose and stroked Anjoli's face. 'It's okay, sweetie, you did not know. The last two weeks have been the worst of my life.'

'I could not let you go to the police, Maya. It was an accident,' said Saibal, broken.

'It was no accident,' said Maya, exhausted. 'I did it. I killed Rakesh. And now I *will* tell them.'

'Ma!' 'Maya!' cried Anjoli and Saibal simultaneously.

'I'm so tired. Exhausted. I'm glad you have found out, Kamil. I can't sleep, I can't think. Poor Neha. Poor Arjun and Pinky. I did a terrible thing. I must be punished.'

Anjoli wrapped her arms around her mother and they clung to each other. I was unsure who was comforting whom.

'Please don't say that, Ma, it was an accident. He was a monster. Nobody needs to find out. Do they Kamil? Do they?' Anjoli looked pleadingly at me.

'What can I do, Anjoli?' I asked, helplessly. 'This is in part my fault too. It all happened because of the Asif Khan business. Because of me. I've been going crazy all day to find a way out. I'm sorry. I wish I hadn't found that receipt, I really do. Rakesh was a ruthless bastard and deserved what happened. And you're right, it was basically an accident. But … Neha will go to jail if we do nothing. And she doesn't deserve that.' Saibal tried to interrupt, but I carried on.

'What did you say about Rakesh this morning? "It is hard to find your friend of so many years is not what he seemed". That's ironic. Saibal-da, *you* have known Neha for years. She has been here so many times and broken bread with you. You think of her as your daughter. She trusts you. I know you're terrified about Maya-di going to jail. So am I. But I also know that you're a principled man and won't let an innocent woman go in her place.'

'I killed him. It was not an accident,' repeated Maya. 'I was so angry we would lose everything. We had been friends for years and now he wanted to make us suffer.' She spoke as if in a trance. 'I am sorry, Anjoli. It is for the best. Tomorrow I will call the police. I should have told them that very night.' She turned her back to us, before declaring, 'I am too tired, I'm sorry. I'm going to bed now.'

'No, Ma, you can't tell the police! Tell her she can't, Kamil. Tell her.' Anjoli grabbed me and shook me like a rag doll.

'I will not let you do this, Maya,' said Saibal, forcefully. 'It was my fault, not yours. You will not do this. Listen. You are right Kamil, I cannot let Neha go to prison. She is innocent, as you say. But I cannot let Maya go either. I have decided. I will tell the police it was me. That Rakesh and I had an argument because he said he would sell my business and ... and I did it. They will not know any better. It could just as easily have been me.'

Anjoli whispered, 'Baba ...'

Saibal put his arms around both of them. 'I will be okay, my darlings. I will be fine. This was due to me. I should not have taken money from a friend. Kamil, is this all right with you?'

I nodded my head, powerless to do anything else. Saibal's noble gesture caused even more questions to run around my mind. Was it any kind of justice to have *him* take the blame for something he hadn't done? Even if it was to save his family. Was he being virtuous or just perpetrating yet another lie? Who was it benefiting? The law? Pinky and Arjun? Did Rakesh deserve vindication after all that he had done? Maybe it wasn't always right for perpetrators to be punished for their crimes. What if no one had to suffer for Rakesh's death?

Hazily, an idea started to take shape. If it could have been Saibal, maybe it could just as equally have been someone else.

As Saibal took Maya's hand and led her up the stairs, I said, softly, 'Wait!'

They turned.

'Wait a second. Maybe there is a way out.'

A desperate hope came over their faces as they paused, then sat back down, Anjoli standing over me.

My thoughts formed as I spoke. 'What did you say? "It could just as easily have been me." True. And it just as easily could have been Taania. Maybe even someone else. Perhaps we just need to give the police a credible suspect other than Neha.'

'But how will you do that?' said Anjoli. 'They eliminated every-one else.'

'Yes, they did. But they didn't know about the lack of phone signal at the pool. That will widen their list of potential suspects.

Because if Rakesh didn't send the messages, who did? Neha couldn't have – she was in the living room when Arjun got his message. They'll follow the same line of reasoning I did and ...'

' ... and it'll lead them straight to Ma,' Anjoli interjected. 'What good is that going to do, Kamil? We'll be back to where we started.'

'No, we won't. They'll have to release Neha. They will take a harder look at Taania. And she could have done it. She could have killed Rakesh, taken his phone, gone upstairs, sent the messages, put the phone back in his pocket after the WhatsApp to Saibal-da and rushed off in the Uber. It's just about possible.'

'But that could send another innocent girl to jail. I won't do that,' objected Saibal.

He was right. I couldn't risk that either. But how much of a risk was it, really? Perhaps we could chance it.

'She won't go to jail because there is no physical evidence connecting her to the crime,' I said firmly. 'It is completely circumstantial. Any talented defence lawyer would have it thrown out. After all, she *didn't* do it and is back in India. Your Crown Prosecution Service won't send an extradition request to India, based on just a theory.'

'And what if they start looking into Ma and Baba?' asked Anjoli.

'That's a risk we must take. I don't know if they can track the phone when it was in your car, Saibal-da. I'm pretty sure they can't track from where WhatsApp messages were sent.'

'But if Pinky and Arjun say Ma and Baba left the living room just after Rakesh did, then ...'

That pulled me up short. Anjoli was right. The police would find the discrepancy in timings just as I had. And that would put Saibal and Maya in the spotlight.

'Let me think,' I said, as I ran through various possibilities in my mind. Memory was a funny thing. It was likely that Pinky and Arjun wouldn't remember exactly when Anjoli's parents left the room. They'd just know they had left to get Anjoli and me from the kitchen. Could I rely on that? Especially as Arjun and Pinky had spent some considerable time talking to Neha. I needed something more concrete.

Another idea wormed its way into my mind. There *was* one way out, but could I bring myself to do it? Telling a blatant lie went against everything I believed in, everything I had been taught. And I would make myself an accessory to a crime. Would this make me as bad as Abba or the DC? But did I even have a choice? I stilled my conscience. There was a greater good at stake here. Sometimes a lie *was* necessary.

'Okay, Anjoli, here's what happened.' I said, putting a certainty I didn't feel into my words. 'If Pinky or Arjun do say your parents left earlier, then here's what *we* say. Saibal-da and Maya-di did leave after Rakesh to collect us from the kitchen. Anjoli, you persuaded them to sit with us for a last drink and so they sat with us in the kitchen for half an hour or so. We can alibi them.'

'What if the police ask why we didn't tell them that before?' asked Anjoli.

'We just say we were all a little drunk and got the times wrong. I doubt they will even pick up on the inconsistency in the timings, though.'

'But you and Anjoli will be lying to the police, Kamil,' said Saibal-da, a worried look coming over his face.

'I don't care, Baba. It's the right thing to do,' said Anjoli. 'What else, Kamil?'

I paused. 'I don't like lying any more than you do, Saibal-da, but we have no choice,' I said. 'We're all in this together.'

And we were. As I said the words, I was convinced I was doing the right thing. Justice would not be served by Maya going to jail for one reckless act. My duty to save her outweighed my obligation to the law. I continued, 'The police will need hard proof, not just circumstantial evidence. I'll tell them about the prints that should have been on the bottle's neck and how it made little sense for Neha to have just wiped that part of it. The ring was too big for Taania as well, not just Maya-di, so that's helpful. The only hard evidence available is the invoice for the ring and ...'

We all stared at the invoice, still clutched in Anjoli's hand. She looked at us, then deliberately tore it into little pieces, walked to the sink, shoved it down the plughole and ran the water. She turned to look at us, combatively wiping her hands on a tea towel.

'Look,' I said, nodding to her. 'I've no idea if this will work. But it should get Neha off. At best they won't be able to prove who did it, even if they suspect Taania or, God forbid, your mum and dad. The only risk is if they do track the phone, as that might lead them to Maya-di. You need to decide. You can confess to the crime and hope they will be lenient – at worst it is voluntary manslaughter – you had no prior intent to kill but intended to cause him serious bodily harm. I don't know what the sentence for that is in England but I can't believe it will be less than five to ten years. Especially since you didn't come forward after Neha was arrested.'

'No!' exclaimed Anjoli. 'No way Ma is going to jail for ten years for trying to protect us.'

'I will take the blame, Anjoli,' said Saibal. 'Your mother will not go to jail.'

'Well, I'm not losing *you* for ten years either, Baba,' Anjoli replied.

I continued. 'Alternately we can go with the plan I've laid out. Get Neha off, give them another suspect whose guilt can't be proven. And pray they let it go. I'm not advocating this Saibal-da, but I agree with Anjoli. It doesn't feel like any sort of justice for either of you to go to prison for the next ten years.'

Saibal looked at Maya, 'What do you think, Maya?'

'I don't know,' she said, a deep weariness in her voice. 'I did it. I should take my punishment. We brought up Anjoli to take responsibility for her actions – how can I not, now?'

'Because it *was* an accident! You didn't *mean* to murder him!' said Anjoli, fiercely. 'He was a terrible, nasty man and you have suffered enough. We *are* doing this. Tell the police about the phone signal, Kamil. Free Neha. We will look after you, Ma.'

'Are you sure they won't do anything to Taania, Kamil?' asked Maya. 'I could not bear it if anything happened to her.'

'I suppose if they did charge her,' I said, 'then you could come forward and say that you had a mental breakdown, hit Rakesh and couldn't live with the guilt. That might persuade them to be lenient.'

'Yes,' said Saibal. 'We will not make the same mistake we made with Neha. I should have come forward before and am ashamed of my weakness that I didn't. Anjoli, forgive me. Kamil, you talk to the police. Let us see what kismet has in store for us.'

The Waiter

A week later. London. October. Monday.

The knife in my hand looked dull. I polished it with my sleeve and laid it, gleaming, perfectly parallel to the fork on the other side of the white dinner plate. Another hour before the restaurant was due to open for lunch. I looked at the rows of tables with their pristine tablecloths, gleaming silverware and the small white vases, each with a fake pink rose in them. To add class, Saibal said. I would miss this place when I returned to Kolkata in a few weeks to reapply for my Vindaloo Visa. Would anything be resolved by then? I'd also miss the recent friend I had made – the Imam in the mosque. I'd been going regularly over the last week and getting more out of it than I could imagine. *Be kind, for whenever kindness becomes a part of something it beautifies it. Whenever it is taken from something, it leaves it tarnished,* he had recited yesterday. I could only try.

There was a rapping on the restaurant door. I looked up, ready to mouth 'We open at twelve', as I had so many times before, but stopped. Outside the entrance stood Inspector Campbell. My heart jolted. Was this it? Had she come to make the arrest? Had my plan failed? But she was alone. I calmed myself and let her in. 'Mr Rahman,' she gave me a nod. 'Are the Chatterjees here?'

She didn't look like she was here to make an arrest.

'I'll get them. Please, have a seat. Water? Coke?'

'No thank you.'

I went up to the flat. They were watching a quiz on the television in the tiny living room, Anjoli shouting, 'William Shakespeare' at the screen as I entered.

'Restaurant ready for lunch, Kamil? Join us. Oh well done, Anjoli, it *was* Shakespeare. You are so clever!' said Saibal, not looking away from the TV.

'You need to come down. Inspector Campbell is here.'

Saibal's bonhomie disappeared as he snapped the television off.

'Why?' asked Maya, her voice trembling.

'I don't know Maya-di,' I said. 'Come. Let's see what she wants.'

We trooped down to the restaurant to see that Salim Mian had furnished the Inspector with a menu and a glass of water and was standing next to her like an attentive Buddha while she insisted she didn't want to order anything.

'Thik achhé, Salim,' said Saibal. 'I will deal with this. You go to the kitchen and get everything ready for lunch service.'

We sat around the table and looked at Campbell expectantly.

'Sorry for arriving unannounced,' she said. 'I was in the area and thought I'd pop in to give you the news.'

'Yes?' Saibal said.

'Following on from your visit to the station last week, Mr Rahman – thank you for the tip about the phone signal and the fingerprints on the bottle, by the way. That was excellent detective work, we shouldn't have missed it – I've given my team a proper bollocking as you can imagine. Anyway, we have let Mrs Sharma go. The CPS doesn't believe we have enough evidence to prosecute. I know that she's your friend and wanted to let you know.'

Relief flooded our faces. Anjoli grinned in exhilaration as Maya cried silently into her handkerchief. Even Saibal wiped a tear from his eye. I felt an intense, pure white joy. I had finally done something right! Saved an innocent woman from going to prison for years. 'I'm so pleased,' I said. 'So, she couldn't have done it, then? Who is the prime suspect now?'

'I'm afraid I can't tell you that,' said the Inspector. 'The investigation is continuing. You'll find out if we have any news.' She rose from her seat and looked at me speculatively. 'If you have further thoughts about the case, come back to us. We are always looking for skilled detectives from diverse backgrounds.' She turned and left. I took a deep intake of breath. I guess she had finally forgiven me for messing up her crime scene. Well, if diversity in the Met Police could give me a chance to stay in the country long term, I wasn't going to argue.

Anjoli flung her arms around me, gave me a tight hug and a kiss on the cheek, then leapt up. 'I'm going to change, I have to see Neha. Come with me, Kamil. I'm sure she'll want to thank you in person.'

She ran up to the flat as Maya and Saibal looked at me, relief mixed with worry on their faces. I patted Maya's hand. 'Don't worry Maya-di. If they had anything, she wouldn't have been this friendly. Relax. It will be all right.'

It was over. She would have to live with uncertainty for now. It wouldn't be easy, looking over her shoulder, always waiting for the knock on the door. But it was better than being in jail, separated from the family she loved. And, with luck, the case file would be consigned to the annals of unsolved crimes and, over time, Saibal, Maya and Anjoli could go back to their normal lives.

I had made my peace with this killer getting away with her crime and my being complicit in a cover-up. Rakesh deserved to die. His death and PinRak's bankruptcy had brought justice for Asif Khan and Mitra. Maya and Saibal had suffered for what they had done; Maya wasn't a danger to society, so putting her in prison benefited no one. As the Imam had said, through love and kindness we could touch the flow of the eternal. Sometimes the just thing to do may not be legal and the legal solution may not be the just one. I could and *would* live with my collusion in this affair. And getting the restaurant back for my London family was *not* a bribe from Pinky. It was Pinky and Arjun paying restitution for what Rakesh had done. I had finally learned about the real world, as Taania Raazia had recommended.

But … however convinced my rational mind was of this, something inside me fluttered nervously. I knew I would have to live with that trembling on bleak nights when I couldn't sleep. Maliha's words came back to me, 'You have this guilt because you are an honourable man. You have ideals.' I wasn't sure how honourable I was now or what my ideals were anymore.

Maya gave me a weak smile, patted my cheek, got up and walked to the kitchen. Saibal rose as well and said, 'You're a very good boy, Kamil. And a good partner. Go back, I will sponsor you for the visa, then you can shift to London and live with us.' He ruffled my hair and left.

The daily bustle of Bangladeshis, buskers and biryani-seekers continued outside on Brick Lane as I contemplated my future in the quiet, empty restaurant, awaiting the diners that would look at the menu outside then randomly choose us over the competition. To them we were just another restaurant where they hoped to find a memorable meal. They knew nothing of our lives: how the bowtied waiter serving them had lost his starry dreams but gained a new understanding of the realities of life; how the chef stirring the dal in the kitchen had learned that inside her lurked a violence she had never dreamed of; how the jolly owner totting up their bill had an inner cruelty that would sacrifice an innocent girl to save his family; or how the smiling young woman in the *Brick Lane was Cool Before Hipsters* T-shirt who took their credit card had learnt that her parents could do things she would never have dreamed. But then we knew nothing about our customers either, *their* lives, loves and losses – to us they were just mouths and wallets, to be fed and smiled at and never seen again. When they walked out of here, they continued to meander through their own chaotic lives, having so briefly intersected with ours.

I picked up a napkin and, to my surprise, fashioned a perfect helmet. I laughed aloud. I was *finally* a Tandoori Knight in a polyester bowtie. Not quite Sir Lancelot in shining armour, but I knew my place. I placed the napkin delicately on the place setting as the sizzle of frying garlic, ginger and onions wafted through the open kitchen door and broke the silence in the restaurant. I would no longer eat the food my father had determined for me. The ingredients for my new life lay in front of me. I just had to decide how to combine them to make the dish that suited me best. And I had a fresh recipe I wanted to try.

'Kamil, I need you! Let's go!' trilled Anjoli from the kitchen.

'Ami Aaschi!'

Acknowledgements

I have to start by thanking Harvill Secker, Bloody Scotland and Arvon for the incredible honour of awarding me their inaugural BAME crime writer's prize, without which this book would not have existed. The idea of a disgraced Kolkata detective turned East End waiter had been bubbling along inside me for over a decade, but it took my wife Angelina spotting this competition and persuading me to go for it, for me to finally bring Kamil Rahman to life.

And I couldn't have completed this final manuscript without the amazing team of editors at Harvill Secker – Sara Adams, Marigold Atkey, Jade Chandler and Noor Sufi. They delicately and generously gave of their time to improve the book no end. I feel humbled by how much I learned from them during this process. Thanks also to my agent Laetitia Rutherford at Watson Little for her faith in me and her perceptive comments when I needed them most, and Anna Redman Aylward for her marketing expertise.

The details in the book were brought to life by so many friends. Nandini Jaidka introduced me to Kolkata historian Anthony Khatchaturian whose patient clarifications of the methods and procedures of both the Met and the Kolkata Police proved vital to my telling of the story; Partho Chakrabarti laughed at my terrible attempts at Bengali and made the translations I needed into colloquial Kolkata Bengali; Salil Tripathi encouraged me to keep writing; Islam Uddin explained to me the internal workings of mosques; my sister Nandini Chowdhury made crucial suggestions near the end of the process; my esteemed cousin Jayanto Choudhury delved into his vast experience as Director General of the Indian Police Service to guide me on police politics; and of course, my mentor Abir Mukherjee who liberally shared his wisdom to make the book so much better.

Finally, my family – Layla, Eva, Tia and my incredibly patient wife, Angelina. Angelina not only gave me immense support but also read every word I wrote and made countless suggestions that resulted in a far better book. Thank you, Angie, you have been there from the beginning, through the graft of writing to now; for this, and everything else, I am intensely grateful.

Ajay Chowdhury is the winner of the inaugural Harvill Secker and Bloody Scotland crime writing competition. He is a tech entrepreneur and theatre director who grew up in India before moving to London, where he lives with his wife and daughters. His first children's book, *Ayesha and the Firefish,* was published in 2016 and *The Waiter* is his debut crime novel. Follow Ajay on Twitter : @ajaychow or at ajaychowdhury.com.